"My God," he whispered. "You look just the same."

His fingers walked across her shoulder blades, drawing her hesitantly closer as though he feared at any second she might vanish in a puff of smoke. He folded her into his arms, as if he'd never be able to get enough of her.

He held her carefully, almost reverently at first, then closer…harder, and buried his face in her hair. The breath she'd been holding burst from her in a sob. She no longer had to worry about her trembling; it wasn't possible to tell where hers left off and his began.

She had no way of knowing how long they stood there like that. It occurred to her that it was like a refuge, that silence…the closeness, a safe place neither of them wanted to leave.

But they must leave it, of course. And confront what had happened to them and what lay ahead.…

Dear Reader,

The year may be coming to a close, but the excitement never flags here at Silhouette Intimate Moments. We've got four—yes, four—fabulous miniseries for you this month, starting with Carla Cassidy's CHEROKEE CORNERS and *Trace Evidence,* featuring a hero who's a crime scene investigator and now has to investigate the secrets of his own heart. Kathleen Creighton continues STARRS OF THE WEST with *The Top Gun's Return.* Tristan Bauer had been declared dead, but now he was back—and very much alive, as he walked back into true love Jessie Bauer's life. Maggie Price begins LINE OF DUTY with *Sure Bet* and a sham marriage between two undercover officers that suddenly starts feeling extremely real. And don't miss *Nowhere To Hide,* the first in RaeAnne Thayne's trilogy THE SEARCHERS. An on-the-run single mom finds love with the FBI agent next door, but there are still secrets to uncover at book's end.

We've also got two terrific stand-alone titles, starting with Laurey Bright's *Dangerous Waters.* Treasure hunting and a shared legacy provide the catalyst for the attraction of two opposites in an irresistible South Pacific setting. Finally, Jill Limber reveals *Secrets of an Old Flame* in a sexy, suspenseful reunion romance.

Enjoy—and look for more excitement next year, right here in Silhouette Intimate Moments.

Yours.

Leslie J. Wainger
Executive Editor

Please address questions and book requests to:
Silhouette Reader Service
U.S.: 3010 Walden Ave., P.O. Box 1325, Buffalo, NY 14269
Canadian: P.O. Box 609, Fort Erie, Ont. L2A 5X3

The Top Gun's Return
KATHLEEN CREIGHTON

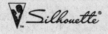
Silhouette®

INTIMATE MOMENTS™

Published by Silhouette Books

America's Publisher of Contemporary Romance

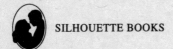 SILHOUETTE BOOKS

ISBN 0-373-27332-0

THE TOP GUN'S RETURN

Visit Silhouette at www.eHarlequin.com

Printed in U.S.A.

Books by Kathleen Creighton

KATHLEEN CREIGHTON

has roots deep in the California soil but has relocated to South Carolina. As a child, she enjoyed listening to old timers' tales, and her fascination with the past only deepened as she grew older. Today, she says she is interested in everything—art, music, gardening, zoology, anthropology and history—but people are at the top of her list. She also has a lifelong passion for writing, and now combines her two loves in romance novels.

To Gail Chasan, my editor and champion
for I'm-not-even-going-to-tell-you-how-many years.
How did I get so lucky?

Prologue

Sammi June stared at the shadows on her ceiling cast by the soccer-ball-shaped night-light beside her bed. Under the covers her knee stung and throbbed where she'd picked the scab off it too soon, and she thought about that while tears tickled their way down the sides of her face and ran into her ears. The tears came from the achy, lonely place inside her, but if she concentrated hard enough she could make herself believe that her skinned knee was to blame for that, too.

Stupid knee. She'd had skinned knees before. It was no big deal. Except, why did it have to happen *now?*

Tomorrow was supposed to be her big day. She was so excited she couldn't fall sleep. It was the most important part, and the teacher had picked *her,* the new kid. *The new kid—wasn't she always? New place, new school, new friends.* She'd wanted so much for them to like her, to be amazed at how smart she was, and how pretty. She even had a dress to wear—a pink one, brand-new, Momma had bought it for her last week at J.C. Penny—and new shoes to go with it, and socks with lace around the tops. And now it was all going to be ruined, because of a stupid skinned knee. It was going to *show,* and look ugly and tacky, and everyone would think she was just a tomboy hick from Georgia.

I wish my daddy was here. If Daddy was here, I wouldn't care if I have a skinned knee. Daddy would find a way to make it be all right.

Sammi June sniffed and wiped her cheeks with her hands, then listened to the darkness as hard as she could. She thought sometimes if she listened hard enough she could make herself hear the sounds she wanted so badly to hear: the front door opening, footsteps on the stairs, Momma's voice, trying to whisper but bubbling brightly with happiness. Daddy's voice whispering back, low and gruff and growly.

After a moment she pushed back the covers and got out of bed and walked over to the window. In the daytime in this new place, there wasn't much to see from the bedroom window except for other people's houses. But at night, if she knelt down and pressed her face close to the glass and looked up…way up…just above the rooftop of the house next door, she could see it. One star, all by itself, so big and bright it didn't seem real. But it was real; Momma said so. She said it was the Evening Star, the one everyone sings to you about when you're real little: "Twinkle twinkle little star, how I wonder what you are…." Momma said if you make a wish on the Evening Star it will come true, and there was a poem for that, too.

Kneeling on the hard floor—on one knee, because the skinned one was sore—Sammi June closed her eyes and whispered the poem:

"Starlight, star bright,
First star I've seen tonight,
I wish I may I wish I might
Have the wish I wish tonight."

Then, staring at the Evening Star until her eyes burned and made new tears, she silently added the wish she'd wished so many times before: *I wish my daddy would come home.*

Chapter 1

May, 1995—Near Athens, Georgia

The day Jessie Bauer's life changed forever began like any other. She worked the day shift as a nurse's aid at the hospital in Athens and came home looking forward to the same three things she always did after a long day on her feet: a glass of Momma's sweet tea, a letter from Tristan and a quiet hour to sit with her feet up while she read it.

"Hey, Momma," Jessie said as she stepped through the open back porch door and put her pocketbook on the kitchen table, "whatcha makin'?" So close to the first day of summer, the year's longest day, the sun was still high in the sky. The house was warm and smelled of burned sugar and overripe fruit.

Her mother lifted damp hair off of her forehead with the back of a hand that held a long-handled wooden spoon. "Oh, I picked up some of those last-of-the-season strawberries Frank had on sale down at the produce stand. They were goin' fast, so I thought I'd better get 'em put up while they still had some good in 'em.'' Red-faced and sweaty, she flashed Jessie a smile.

"Let me get changed," Jessie said. "I'll help you."

"Oh, heavens, I'm about done here—just these last few jars. Then I'm gonna put the kettles to soak and go in and catch Dan Rather. You go on and sit—there's tea in the 'fridge.''

Jessie picked up her pocketbook and slung the strap over her shoulder. "Thanks, I will in a minute. Where's Sammi June? Doing her homework?"

"Finished—at least, that's what she told me. She and J.J. are off ramblin' down by the creek somewhere."

Jessie nodded. "I get a letter today?" She asked it in that way people do when they think they're going to be disappointed.

Not this time, though. Her mother smiled and pointed with the spoon. "You did. It's on the desk in the—"

And Jessie was already gone, her heart going thump-thump in time to the whapping of the swinging door behind her. In the hall, she let the pocketbook fall to the desktop as she picked up the familiar envelope and pressed it against the place where her heart was beating so fast, fighting the little shivers of joy inside her only because she knew if she wasn't careful they'd turn into tears. When she had herself calmed down some she went back into the kitchen and poured herself a glass of tea. She carried the glass and the letter out to the front porch and sank into one of the white-painted rocking chairs that sat there in all kinds of weather.

For a while she rocked and held the letter close in her hands while she thought about how beautiful it was just now, with the day lilies blooming along the lane, and the front lawn dotted with yellow dandelions, and the air warm and smelling sweet from Momma's roses rambling over the porch roof. Finally, having savored the moment about as long as she could stand to, she tore open the envelope and unfolded the single sheet of lined notepaper.

It took only a minute or two—never long enough—to read the words written there. Everyday words about the everyday things that made up Tristan's life on board an aircraft carrier somewhere in the Persian Gulf: what they'd had to eat, the last movie they'd seen, something some buddy or other had done that made him laugh. Then a line or two about how much he missed Jess and Sammi June, but how glad he was to be where he was, doing something so important. The same words that nearly always ended his letters home.

> I know I'm doing what I was meant to do. If I didn't believe that, I wouldn't be able to stand being away from you guys. But I do believe it, with my whole heart and soul, and I want you to, too. I need you to believe in me, honey. I love you and miss you always.

Inside the house she heard the TV turn on. Heard the introductory fanfare to the evening network news. Then Dan Rather's familiar voice.

The screen door creaked open. From inside, her mother's voice called, "Jessie, you need to come in here." Jessie stopped rocking and turned halfway around in the chair, not quite understanding. She saw Momma standing there, holding the door.

"There's been a plane shot down over the no-fly zone," Momma said. "They're saying the pilot's missing. They won't tell who it was until they notify—"

Somehow Jessie was on her feet, and she felt the screen door's wooden frame under her hand. *It's not Tris. He's not dead. I'd know if he were dead. I'd know.* "It can't be Tris," she said. "I'd have heard something. They'd have told me…"

Over the sound of her own voice and the music of a

commercial on television came the crunch of tires on gravel.

As Jessie turned, her world shifted into slow motion. Sounds faded. Floating in the silence, she watched a strange car come along the lane and pull to a gentle stop in front of the house. It was one she'd never seen before, a dark sedan with writing on the doors, but she knew it just the same.

She watched, suspended in time and silence, as the doors opened and two men got out. Men she didn't know. Tall, dignified men wearing dark-blue Navy dress uniforms, their white hats gleaming bright as moons in the evening sun.

Looking back on that day, Jess recalled that she'd stood alone on the wide front porch, watching those two men come toward her across the lawn with its happy polka-dot riot of yellow dandelions. She didn't remember Momma coming to stand with her, putting her hands on her shoulders.

She remembered that she held out her hands when the men took off their hats and began to mount the wooden steps to the porch where she was. She held her hands with the palms out, as if she were going to try to hold them back. As if she were going to push them away. As if by keeping them away, she could keep them from saying to her what they'd come to say. As if keeping them from saying it would make it not be true.

She remembered thinking, *How in the world am I gonna tell Sammi June?*

But after that, she didn't remember much of anything for a very long time.

Eight Years Later—Near Baghdad, Iraq

The bombs had stopped falling. He wondered if it was for keeps this time, but doubted it would be. The bombs had been falling on and off for six days. *On the seventh day they rested?*

Lying in the silent darkness he thought about the bombs. He was sure they were American bombs, and wondered if the next round would finally bring the ancient prison tumbling in on top of him. No telling what this place was disguised as, and no one had any idea he was here, anyway. He thought what irony it would be if it turned out it was the Americans who finally killed him.

"Missed again," came a hoarse whisper from beyond the damp stone walls of his cell.

He grunted a reply. Rising stiffly from his pallet, he made his way to the heavy wooden door and leaned his back against it.

"You think they're done for tonight?" the whisper came again. The whispering was from long habit; talking among prisoners wasn't allowed.

He turned his head and addressed the small barred opening high in the door. Though it was invisible now in the darkness, he knew its position exactly; through it, for the past several weeks, at least, had come everything he depended on to stay alive. As well as everything he most feared. "Maybe. Seems early, though." An unnamed tension gripped his muscles and his nerves quivered as he and the whisperer fell silent, listening to distant noises of chaos: shouts, small explosions and the rattle of gunfire.

"Listen—" It was a faint hiss, like spit in hot coals.

He'd heard the new sound, too. *Footsteps.*

Footsteps spoke a language all their own, one he'd learned well over the years. These were not the usual footsteps, firm with authority and menace, that set his nerves and muscles and sinews to vibrating with conditioned fear responses. These were furtive footsteps. A lot of them. Hurrying footsteps. Running, but not with thumps. Like… scuffles, rhythmic and purposeful.

A shiver crawled down his spine. He pressed it hard against the door, and with the drumming of his pulse in his ears he almost missed the voices. They were only intermittent mutters at first, and whether it was due to that or a self-protective refusal to believe, it was a while before it dawned on him they were speaking in English.

"...*Clear!*"

"*Panther one, clear!*"

"*Move on three...*"

"*Roger that—go, go go!*"

The footsteps were growing louder, now broken by pauses, thumps, brief explosions of gunfire that crashed like thunder against the stone walls. And in the dying echoes of the thunder, the voices came again.

"We got a live one here. Barely."

"Ah, Jeez. Look at this. Poor bastards..."

"What do you want to do with 'em?"

"We got no choice. They'll have to find their own way out. We're here to get one guy."

"We have to find him first. Jeez, there must be a hundred cells in this stinking hell-hole."

There was a pause, and then a controlled shout: "Pearson! Cory Pearson—you in here? If you can hear me—"

"Here! I'm here!" It was the unseen companion's voice, excited, not whispering, now. Cracking with excitement and hope.

"Okay, we hear you," came the reply, calm by contrast. "Keep talking. We're coming to get you."

Huddled in the darkness with filthy stones against his back, he listened to the shouts and the footsteps coming nearer, until they seemed to be right outside his cell. An explosion thumped his eardrums, and he clapped his hands to the sides of his head and opened his mouth in a silent scream of pain. In the seconds that followed he realized he was shaking. His knees and head felt the way they did when he knew he was going to pass out.

Not now, he prayed, gritting his teeth together. *Not... now*.

The darkness around him filled with images, the same

well-loved faces that had kept him sane and clinging to life for so long. Well-remembered voices spoke to him, as they had so many times before. He concentrated on the faces and felt his head clear and his breathing quiet. Drawing on reserves of strength he'd forgotten he had, he drew himself slowly erect, and his chest filled and his shoulders lifted.

"Wait! There's another one!" The unseen companion's voice came again, trembling with emotion. "You can't leave him—"

"Another one—in *here?* What, you mean, another *American?*"

"Yeah, he's—"

"That's impossible. We weren't briefed—"

"Look, I'm not leaving him behind."

Someone swore impatiently. "You sure? Where is he? In here?" The same voice rose to a shout. "Hey, buddy, can you hear me? If you can hear me—"

"Yeah, I hear you." It felt odd to him to be talking so loudly, but he thought his voice sounded okay. Calm. Normal. Not even shaking. Much.

More swearing—startled this time. "I'll be *damned*—uh…okay, buddy, listen, we're gonna get you outa there. I want you to take cover, you understand? I'm gonna blow the door."

"Ready when you are."

He pressed himself into the corner of his cell to one side of the door and covered his head with his arms. The explosion that came then seemed almost an anticlimax, and in its aftermath he turned and drew himself once more erect.

For some reason he'd expected light, but in the rectangle where the door had been there was only the thin gray of starlight and the flickering glow from burning bombsites leaking through the high, narrow windows of the ancient fortress. His rescuers were darker shapes, anonymous and alien in their gear, like something out of science fiction.

"Are you guys SEALS?" he asked. For some reason he knew they would be.

"That's right. Who the hell are you?"

Realizing they'd be able to see him with their night-vision goggles, he gave them the best salute he could. "Lt. Tristan Bauer, United States Navy."

There was a stunned silence. Then one of the shapes said, "You're *Navy?*" just as another said, "That's not possible."

That one, the nonbeliever, pushed past his comrade and into the cell, cradling his weapon across his chest as if he needed the comfort of it. "Lt. Bauer's dead. My brother served with him on the *Teddy Roosevelt.* He was shot down in '95. That's…" His voice wavered. "Jeez, that'd be eight years."

Tris grinned, stretching muscles he hadn't used in a very long time. "Yeah, so, what the hell took you guys so long?"

Early April, New York City, USA

Jessie and her sister, Joy Lynn, were arguing about where to have lunch, as usual.

"*Not* Thai again, *please,*" Jessie said with a shudder as she lengthened her stride in a vain attempt to keep up with her older and considerably shorter sister. Joy Lynn had been a New Yorker for going on ten years, since before her second divorce became final, and had evidently forgotten that GRITS, as in, Girls Raised in the South, never walk if they can help it.

"And don't even *think* about suggesting Indian," she warned as the suggestive tinkle of temple bells floated from a nearby doorway. "Last time you took me to an Indian restaurant I had to go find a hotdog vendor afterward just to put my stomach right. Whatever happened to good old American?" It was a rhetorical question, asked plaintively of the weeping sky, and had less to do with her food preferences than it did the serious second thoughts she was having about visiting her New-York-dwelling sister in the springtime when the air back home in Georgia was warm and sweet and the countryside aflame with azaleas. "What's wrong with KFC?" she whined, hugging her borrowed raincoat close across her chest. "Bojangles with cole slaw an' biscuits?"

Unperturbed, Joy Lynn said, "Don't be such a hick," as she whipped her trilling cell phone out of a raincoat pocket. She glanced at the caller ID, said, "Huh," in a wondering way and put the phone to her ear. "Hey, Momma, what's up?"

"Momma!" Jessie exclaimed. "Why would *she* be callin'?"

Joy Lynn's pace had slowed. She flicked a glance sideways at Jessie and said, "Uh-huh."

Jessie's belly quivered. "She wantin' me?" An alarm had gone off in her head. *Sammi June.*

"Uh-huh," said Joy Lynn again, but not to her, holding up a silencing finger. Then she said, "Okay. Hold on a sec—" She grabbed Jessie by the sleeve of the raincoat and hauled her through a warm doorway that smelled strongly of garlic.

"It's Italian, for God's sake," she hissed at Jessie, who was muttering, "But—but—" and dragging back against the tow. Jessie had nothing against Italian, but butterflies were flopping earnestly in her belly now, and she no longer had any interest whatsoever in eating.

It's Sammi June—oh God, it must be. Why else would Momma be calling me unless something awful's happened to Sammi June?

Numb with foreboding, she let Joy Lynn haul her to a table next to a heavily textured wall that was painted dark green with spiderwebs of white plaster showing through. Her sister tugged a chair out with a thump, pushed Jessie down on it, then wedged herself into the one opposite.

"Okay, she's sittin' down," she said into the phone, breathless and pink in the cheeks. She went silent, listening. Then breathed, "Oh, my Lord."

Something's happened to Sammi June, was the only thought in Jessie's head. She had begun to tremble uncontrollably. Panic washed over her; she couldn't breathe. *No. I can't bear it. I can't. I can't.*

She'd felt like this only one other time in her life. That day came back to her so vividly now…Dan Rather's voice on the television, the screech of the screen door…her mother saying, "Jessie, you need to come in here." The crunch of tires on gravel, the dark-blue sedan, and two tall men coming toward her across a polka-dot lawn. The way the world had gone silent. The way she'd held out her hands to keep those men from coming on up the steps, the same way she was holding out her hands right now, as if she could push away that phone Joy Lynn was trying to give to her. As if by keeping it away she could keep herself from ever having to hear the words Momma was about to say to her. As if by not hearing them she could make them not be true.

"Sammi June—" The words burst from her, exploding like a sneeze past the icy fear, the trembling.

"No, hon', it's not Sammi June." Joy Lynn's voice was gentle, and so was her hand as she took Jessie's and held on to it. Her fingers felt warm, wrapped around Jessie's icy ones. "Sammi June's fine. Everybody's just fine."

Then what…? Dazed, Jess could only give her head an uncomprehending shake.

"Jessie, honey, you need to take this." Joy Lynn pressed the cell phone into Jessie's hand and folded her stiff fingers around it. "Momma's got somethin' to tell you. It's *okay*," she added when Jessie just went on looking at her, dumb and frozen with anguish. Trying her best to smile though there were tears in her eyes, she said, "It's okay, I promise."

Drained and shell-shocked, still trembling, Jessie lifted the phone to her ear. "Momma? What is it? What's wrong?"

"Nothing's wrong, honey." But Momma's voice sounded way too calm, the way it only did when she was about to deliver some painful news. It had sounded like that, Jessie remembered, when she'd told Sammi June and J.J. the old hounddog, General, had been bitten by a copperhead and had to be put to sleep. "But...this is gonna be hard to hear."

Jessie's heart was beating so fast she wondered if there was something seriously wrong with it. She pressed a hand against her chest to hold it still and whispered, "Okay."

"Jessie...honey." There was a single high musical note of laughter or perhaps a sob. "Honey, it's Tristan. They found him. In Baghdad. Oh, sweet child. He's alive."

April, Landstuhl, Germany

Jessica Ann Starr couldn't remember a time when she hadn't loved Tristan Bauer, so it always came as something of a shock to her to realize he'd actually been present in her life for so few of her thirty-six years. Now, sitting in the back seat of a car speeding sedately along a German autobahn, memories of those few, those golden moments...hours...days, seemed to fill her whole existence. Her mind flipped through them like the photographs in the album she'd assembled to share with Joy Lynn and now held in her lap, clutched in nerveless fingers.

She'd been in high school when they'd met, vacationing on a Florida beach with friends, spring break her senior year. Almost exactly eighteen years ago—half her life— though it shamed her to admit she couldn't recall the exact date. He'd seemed to her unattainable as a movie star, impossibly handsome, wonderfully tall—always a plus for a girl who'd hit her current height of five feet ten inches in seventh grade. His thick black hair, brown eyes and olive skin had seemed thrillingly exotic to her, since she was sunshine-blond and wholesome as grits.

There on the beach that morning she'd listened to the lies that came floating out of her own mouth, effortlessly as blowing smoke from a forbidden cigarette, tacking on a couple of years to her age and some mythical college experience to get past his grown man's scruples about dating a high school girl, and hadn't even cared if she went to Hell because of them.

That night he'd kissed her, and she knew it had all been worth the risk. He'd kissed her outside her motel room door, pressing her up against the hard stucco wall so that she'd felt the whole sinewy length of him all up and down her front, and everywhere he'd touched her she'd felt her body tingle and burn as if a million stars were exploding inside her. Or as if millions and millions of cells in her body had waited for that moment to wake up and burst into exuberant life. That was the way it had seemed to her, as if she'd only been partly alive until Tristan, and after that night she'd known she would never again be completely alive without him.

She'd told him the truth about her age before she'd left him to go back home, though, because by that time she'd known she was going to marry him one day. She hadn't known, then, that less than three weeks after her high school graduation she'd be Mrs. Tristan Bauer, wife of a naval aviator, and already well on her way to being someone's mother.

"Ma'am?" The gray-haired, bespectacled naval officer in the front passenger seat broke his respectful silence, turning his head and leaning slightly in order to make eye contact. "We'll be taking you directly to the residence, which is adjacent to the medical center where your husband is receiving treatment. After you've checked in, I can take you to see him there, or you can wait for him in the residence, if you like. Lieutenant Bauer should be cleared to join you shortly. Whichever you prefer.''

His manner was deferential to the point of awe, which Jessie found disconcerting. ''Thank you, Lieutenant Commander—'' She searched her befuddled memory for her casualty assistance officer's name and came up empty. Exhausted by the effort, she was about to fall gratefully back into the cocoon of her own musings when the expectant look on the officer's face registered on her consciousness. He was waiting for her decision. Her forehead tightened as she struggled with it; any logical, reasoning thought was hard work for her today. And this—whether to meet her husband, returned from the dead after eight years, for the first time in the cold antiseptic environment of a hospital room with doctors and nurses all around, or confront him alone in privacy, this man she'd loved and given up for lost long, long ago, now a stranger to her—seemed utterly impossible. Which was better? Or worse?

For better or worse…in sickness and in health.

She tried to smile for Lieutenant Commander—*Rees,* she remembered now. Rees-with-two-*e*s, he'd told her. ''How are these things usually handled?'' She thought of the return of the captives taken during Desert Storm, of television pictures of gaunt men in flight suits engulfed in loved ones' embraces while flags waved and bands played ''Tie a Yellow Ribbon 'Round the Old Oak Tree.'' She'd been active in the wives' support group on the base at the time and had worn a bracelet with a POW's name engraved on it.

The Lieutenant Commander's military bearing melted into a smile of pure irony. ''Ma'am, there isn't any precedent for what happened to your husband. As far as the Navy's concerned, you can have this just about anyway you want it.''

Jessie nodded, too distracted to return the smile. The representative of the Defense Department who'd taken charge of her in New York had said much the same thing: There was no protocol for resurrection. There'd been no yellow ribbons or POW bracelets for Tristan. No support groups or letter-writing campaigns petitioning for his release. For all intents and purposes he'd been abandoned, forgotten, given up for dead, and the country he'd served and sacrificed eight years of his life for now seemed eager—almost desperate—to make amends.

Which was no doubt why Tristan's somewhat unusual request to stay in Germany for part of his treatment and recovery period rather than being sent home to the States as soon as he was deemed fit to travel had immediately been granted. So had his request that his wife be allowed to join him, rather than wait at home for his return. Jessie had been given the choice of waiting in New York for Tristan's phone call or taking the next flight to Germany. She'd chosen the flight, and had been whisked off to the airport by her DOD assistance officer, one jump ahead of the media stampede.

It had been decided that Sammi June would stay and wait with her grandma Betty and the rest of the family back home in Georgia. Jessie wasn't sure who had made that decision, but she knew it was the right one. She'd been told Tristan was still very weak and sick, and she knew he wouldn't want Sammi June to see him like that. Not to mention that *she* was mightily glad not to have Sammi June's emotional baggage to deal with right now. Her own was burden enough.

Morning was only beginning to thin the darkness when Sammi June slipped out of bed. She made little effort to be silent; her roommate slept like the dead and was snoring peacefully, as always, an arm's reach away in the tiny University of Georgia dorm room they'd shared since last September. Sammi June hadn't slept at all, peacefully or otherwise, since Gramma Betty's phone call yesterday afternoon.

Baby girl, your daddy's alive.

Baby girl. Nobody had called her that in years, not since her dad had gone away to fly F-16's over Iraqi deserts, eight years ago. Daddy had still called her his "baby girl," then, even though she'd been ten years old at the time. Would he still call her that now, she wondered, even though she was no baby, hardly even a girl? She was eighteen, an adult in the eyes of the law, old enough to vote and get married without permission and be responsible for her own choices. A grown woman.

Although she didn't feel the least bit like one at the moment.

Uncaring of the morning chill, wearing only the boxer shorts and tank top that served her as pajamas in all seasons, she slumped into the hard-backed chair at her study desk beside the window and fingered apart the blinds. Out there on the still-slumbering campus the other buildings were dark shapes, street and yard lights blurred and haloed by a thin gauze of fog. Flowering trees were beginning to take lacy form among the darker grays of azaleas and new-leafed trees. Stars were few, pale pinpricks in the lavender sky. Search as she might she couldn't locate the Evening Star, the one she'd wished on so many times, all those years ago.

Starlight, star bright,
First star I've seen tonight,
I wish I may, I wish I might…

Anger surged unexpectedly, trembling through her, stinging behind her nose and eyes. *I wish my daddy would come home.* How many times had she wished that when she was little? Wished it so hard sometimes it felt as if all the cells in her brain were vibrating, as if her head might explode. And…nothing.

Instead one day they'd told her her dad was dead, that

he wasn't ever coming home again. She hadn't believed them. She'd begun to wish on the Evening Star again, a different wish this time. *I wish my daddy would be alive.* And still nothing. For eight years.

Nothing. How angry she'd been, deep down inside where nobody could see it, angry with her dad for leaving her, for not being there when she needed him to see her in her class play, to cheer at her soccer games, congratulate her after speech tournament victories, walk her across the field when she was elected Junior Homecoming Princess. To comfort her when she had to get braces, and when she'd missed being selected for the freshman cheerleading squad. How angry she'd been, though she'd never let anybody see it, not even Momma.

And now? Now that she was practically grown-up and didn't really need parents anymore, it seemed all those pathetic little-girl wishes had finally been granted. Her dad was alive. He was coming home. Was God playing a joke on her? She didn't know how she was supposed to feel.

The blinds clanked softly as they slipped back into place, and a tear left its silky track down Sammi June's cheek.

Jessie's fingertips stroked the image in the snapshot album she held in her lap—Sammi June, in her ball gown, head held high and tiara gleaming, radiantly smiling against the backdrop of an indigo sky. So lovely, so grown-up at not quite seventeen, and in her high heels already almost as tall as her escort, her uncle Jimmy Joe. And, Jessie remembered, she'd even managed to look graceful during that walk across the football field, in spite of high heels that kept punching into the damp turf.

A young woman. Would Tris even know his daughter? She'd been a knobby-kneed tomboy in ponytails when he'd seen her last.

The image blurred and wavered inside its protective plastic envelope, and Jessie hurriedly blotted her eyes with the sleeve of her heather-gray blazer. Her hand lingered there, lightly pressing her cheekbone…her temple, smoothing back wisps of hair. There was gray in those wisps now, that hadn't been there eight years ago. She'd changed a lot—lines at the corners of her eyes and around her mouth…her neck. Her breasts weren't as firm, her belly a bit more rounded. *I've changed. Will he know me?*

Lieutenant Commander Rees was waiting politely for her reply.

"I think—" Her voice shook and she drew a breath to steady it. An image rose in her memory of the only other time she'd ever seen Tris in a hospital bed, pale and groggy after the surgery to set the fractured leg that had grounded him during Desert Storm. It was the only time she'd ever seen him vulnerable and helpless. He wouldn't want her to see him like that again. "I think Tristan would rather I waited for him at the residence. He's never been crazy about hospitals."

She struggled to produce a smile for the officer before turning to gaze, unseeing, upon the German countryside.

He's been like that—vulnerable and helpless—for eight years, the man I knew and loved for his strength, his pride, and yes, even his arrogance. What did they do to him? How did he survive, all those years? How could he survive, without being irrevocably changed? Will I know him?

Butterflies danced and shivered inside her, and she thought, *Yes.* That's where the biggest changes will be, in both of us. There, deep inside.

Chapter 2

The guest residence had been privately built by a nonprofit foundation to accommodate the families of military personnel undergoing treatment at the medical facility. It was an imposing structure of stone and slate made hospitable by the boxes filled with tulips, daffodils and hyacinths that adorned every window. As Tristan drank in the sight, the lump that seemed never far away these days came back into his throat. It had been a long time since he had seen daffodils.

The sedan in which he was riding, a modest Mercedes, rolled to a stop beside the building's main entrance. Its driver, a young airman whose name Tristan could not remember, got out and came around to open his door for him.

The man sitting beside him in the back seat touched his arm. Al Sharpe, the air force major assigned as his escort, or ''shadow,'' asked quietly, ''Would you like me to see you inside?''

''Thanks, I'll take it from here.'' Tristan's attention was engaged with employing the cane he'd been given to lever himself out of the car. He wasn't happy about the cane, but the knee he'd injured punching out of his exploding Hornet eight years ago never had healed properly, and the unaccustomed activity of the past few days seemed to have aggravated it. The doctors had told him that, with good physical therapy and possibly some surgery, he'd likely get most of the use of it back. Eventually.

Most of it. Eventually. He wondered what that meant, and whether it applied to other things he'd lost. Eight years with his wife…watching his little girl grow up. The person he'd been. Nobody was ready to assure him so easily and carelessly about his chances of getting those things back.

Upright, he flashed Major Sharpe his out-of-practice smile. "This is one mission I'd like to fly solo, if you don't mind."

"I understand. We'll be back here for you at twenty-one hundred hours, then." He paused to hold Tristan's eyes for a long moment. "Remember what I told you—don't expect too much of yourself. One step at a time. And meanwhile, if you need anything, you just give me a call."

"I will. Thanks. I'll be okay." He nodded at the airman, who saluted briskly, then shut the door and got back in the car.

As he watched the Mercedes drive away it occurred to Tristan that for the first time in nearly eight years he was on his own. Completely alone. Unsupervised. It was a strange feeling. He turned and made his way slowly along the walkway to the door, thinking about the fact that those limping steps were his first without an escort since he'd regained consciousness in an Iraqi desert to find himself surrounded by gun-toting soldiers with hatred in their eyes.

A cold, sick feeling washed over him. He knew the feeling well; he'd lived with it in many forms, the past eight years. *Fear.* Strange, he thought, I'm about to see and touch the one person I dreamed of seeing and touching for all those years…the one whose face and voice in my dreams

I think at times were the only thing keeping me alive. And I'm scared to death.

At the door he paused, turning to let his gaze sweep once more over the parking lot and the new-leafed trees and red-tiled roofs beyond. The sky was overcast, the sun breaking through the clouds in rays, like fingers. Beside the walkway, planters bright with more tulips, daffodils and hyacinths gave off a heady scent. The air was cool and seemed thin and light in his lungs. So different from prison air, which was thick and heavy. Prison air weighed a man down.

I don't know who I am, after breathing that air for so long, he thought. I know I'm not the same man I was when I left her. Nowhere near.

And he let them come, then, the questions he'd tried so hard to hold at bay: *Will she love me still? Will she want this man—this shell—that I've become?*

He closed his eyes and filled his lungs with the scent of flowers, and from long habit, her image came to fill the blank screen of his mind. Jessie's face, so vivid he felt as if he could reach out and touch it, every detail etched in his memory as if in stone. Her lips, curved up at the corners, and her nose, crinkled across the bridge with her smile...

But she'll have changed, too, he reminded himself. They'd warned him to expect that. In eight years, how could she not have changed? And yet—he caught a quick sip of the winey air, as if to give himself courage—she hadn't remarried, they'd told him. Why, when she'd been told he was dead? Did that mean— *What* did it mean? It could mean everything. It could mean nothing.

He realized his heart was pounding so hard it was making his chest hurt. He rubbed the spot ruefully as he reached for the door handle. Whatever it was waiting for him beyond that door, postponing it wasn't going to make it easier to face.

*   *   *

For the life of her, Jessie couldn't make a simple decision. She'd spent what seemed like hours deciding what to wear, not that that was an unheard-of thing for a woman, but it hadn't ever been a particular problem for *her* before. She wore wash-and-wear pants and smocks for work, jeans and sweatshirts or shorts and T-shirts or tank tops at home, depending on the season of the year, and when something more sedate was required, dressy slacks and a blazer, with a sweater or shell, again dictated by the season and the weather. She owned a couple of dresses, basic and eternal in style, which were pretty much reserved for weddings and funerals. What was to decide?

Today, though, she'd stood before the mirror in her room for what seemed like hours, helpless and on the verge of panic. Nothing looked right to her. The blazer she'd worn on the plane seemed too formal, too stiff. The sweater she'd finally chosen was lavender, which used to be Tris's favorite color. Was it still? Would he remember? Was she trying too hard? Had she put on a few pounds? God, she thought, I look *old*.

And her hair. She hadn't had time to shampoo and blow it dry. Should she wear it loose on her shoulders anyway, the way she knew Tris preferred, even though it was definitely looking limp and travel weary? And the gray mixed in with the blond at her temples—oh God, he'd have to be blind not to see that, no matter how she wore it.

She couldn't decide *where* to wait for him. Her room—*their* room—with its hotel-type arrangement of bed, sitting area and desk-table workspace with a separate bathroom, was at least assured of privacy. And the guest house staff had gone out of their way to make it homey, with fresh flowers and a huge basket of fruit on the table. The sweetest thing—there was even a Teddy bear wearing a yellow ribbon around its neck propped on the bed pillows. But, oh, that bed—Lord, it seemed to Jessie it took up most of the space in the room—it dominated…it distracted. She didn't want Tris to think—*she* didn't want to think—her stomach knotted and quivered and she pressed her fist against it to quiet the butterflies. *I won't think about it now.*

In the end, she'd decided on the guest house's common room, just off the lobby reception area and next door to the dining room. It was a gracious, hospitable place, with a gas log fireplace and comfortable furniture arranged for intimate conversation or reading the paper, or settling down with a good book. It was fairly private, being empty at the moment—the house had only a few other occupants besides her, since most of the casualties from the Persian Gulf were being shipped stateside as quickly as possible—but there was no guarantee it would stay that way. So far the news media hadn't caught up with her, but she knew it was only a matter of time before they did. She also knew the guest house staff, as well as Lieutenant Commander Rees, would do everything they could to shield her until she felt ready to face the onslaught. As she would have to, sooner or later. She'd just as well prepare herself.

Prepare myself? Who am I kidding?

Right on cue, she heard the click of the front door opening, the polite trill of a buzzer announcing someone's presence in the lobby. I'm not ready, she thought in panic. *I'm not ready.*

She could hear the receptionist asking if she could be of assistance. The murmur of a masculine response. And—oh God, it was Tristan's voice. For the first time in more than eight years, she was hearing her husband's voice.

Her heart leaped like a fractious Thoroughbred in the starting gates, yet inside her head she felt…*quiet.* Her mind kept touching on unimportant subjects—what she was wearing, what she looked like, her *hair* again, the photo album, Sammi June, arrangements for dinner, the fire on the hearth, even the furniture in the room—like a nervous housewife waiting for guests to arrive. But when she tried to think of Tristan there was only blankness, like an empty page.

Gradually she realized she was trembling, and that her chest was so tight it seemed impossible she could take a breath. She knew her hands were icy and her stomach a roiling mass of butterflies. But *why,* she wondered, when my mind feels so calm? *Whose body is this? How can it be mine when I have so little control over it?*

She couldn't hear his voice now. She strained to catch the sounds of his footsteps but heard only the surflike thunder of her own blood in her ears.

Then he was there, framed in the doorway. Undeniably Tristan, unbearably thin and a little stooped, though she could see he was trying not to be. He was wearing a borrowed jumpsuit. Beyond that she was certain of nothing; her vision blurred and wavered until she saw him through a shimmering fog.

Oh—she wanted to go to him, but that body of hers again refused to obey the orders her brain gave it. No matter how hard she willed them to, her legs wouldn't move. Her feet remained firmly rooted to the floor. She wanted to say something—his name, at least—but when she drew a quivering breath in preparation for speech, nothing came out of her mouth.

"Jess…" It was no more than a breath. A whisper. A sigh.

He was coming toward her, limping. She saw that he had a cane, though he didn't appear to be using it, and when he was within arm's reach of her he let go of it, seeming unaware or uncaring that it toppled to the floor.

Her shoulders rose in a helpless shrug—an apology for not meeting him halfway. And the breath she'd taken—oh, hours ago, it seemed—remained trapped in her chest, prisoner of the certain knowledge that when she released it a sob would go, too.

His hands were on her shoulders, his fingers rubbing in

the softness of her sweater as if he'd never felt its like before. Blurred as her vision was, his face seemed angular and unfamiliar to her, his normally bright, intelligent eyes sunken deep in shadowed sockets. She fought against panic, searching that haggard face for some sign of the Tristan she knew—that arrogant tilt to his mouth, those sun creases at the corners of his eyes? If she could see him clearly—but she dared not blink.

"My God," he whispered, "you look just the same."

His fingers walked across her shoulder blades, drawing her hesitantly closer, as though he feared at any second she might vanish in a puff of smoke. He said nothing more as he folded her into his arms but drew a great breath through his nose, as if filling himself up with the scent, the essence of her. As if he'd never be able to get enough of it.

He held her carefully, almost reverently, at first, then closer…harder, and buried his face in her hair. The breath she'd been holding burst from her in a sob. She no longer had to worry about her trembling; it wasn't possible to tell where hers left off and his began.

She had no way of knowing how long they stood there like that, locked in a silent, almost desperate embrace. It occurred to her that it was like a refuge, that silence…the closeness, a safe place neither of them wanted to leave.

But they must leave it, of course, and confront what had happened to them and what lay ahead. And it came to Jessie in those moments that for the first time in their lives together, she would have to be the one to take the lead.

From the first, maybe because she'd been so young when they'd met, Tristan had been the boss in their relationship, the leader, the strong one. Even when he was away on deployments, he'd made all the important decisions, and more than a few of the small ones, too. But that had changed eight years ago, and there was no going back to the way things had been. *This is who I am now, Tris. I'm not the same Jessie you left behind.*

Fear shivered through her, and she stirred in his arms. They loosened instantly, though he kept her within their circle, his hands still transmitting minute tremors through the fabric of her sweater and deep into her body. That almost imperceptible shaking nearly undid her. She placed her palms on the front of his jumpsuit and tried to laugh. Then gave that up and sniffed loudly, brushing at her eyes. "Told myself I wouldn't do this."

Tristan had told himself the same thing. He'd been raised on the notion that real men don't cry, although eight years in an Iraqi prison had cured him of that notion. He'd heard tougher, stronger men than himself cry like babies, and he wasn't ashamed of the times he'd done so himself. But he wasn't about to let himself cry in front of *her*. He'd learned a lot about self-control in that prison, too, and if it took every ounce he had, he wasn't going to let Jess see him shed a tear.

He had his reasons for feeling that way, most of which he would have a hard time explaining in words. Some of it was plain old masculine pride, probably, normal guy stuff about wanting to stand tall in front of his woman, particularly when he was feeling anything but. Some of it was protective; he didn't want Jess to ever have to try to sleep with the images that filled *his* nightmares. And maybe the biggest part was a combination of those two things. Partly pride, wanting to be for his woman the man he'd once been, the man she expected him to be—a strong man who believed absolutely in himself, and would never give in to weakness. Partly wanting to protect her from knowing about the man he was now—a man who, in the dark and secret places of his mind cringed and cowered in terror, a man who'd cried and screamed and suffered every imaginable kind of humiliation and degradation, and who wasn't sure what he believed in anymore.

His thumb stroked a tear across her cheek, and his eyes followed it hungrily, as if the salty moisture were some rare and wonderful elixir that could cure everything that was wrong with him. "It's incredible," he said, his voice still hushed and disbelieving. "I was prepared—I told myself you wouldn't, but you do—you look exactly the same."

She laughed a shaky denial, while her hand fluttered self-consciously toward her face. It changed direction on the way there and touched his instead. He couldn't control a wince—it had been too many years since he'd felt a gentle touch—and to cover it he caught her hand in his and held it there.

"You look—" she began, and he rushed to interrupt the lie.

"—like bloody hell. I know. I'm sorry, I wish—"

"You *don't.*" She'd expected worse. And yet…she hadn't *really* been prepared—how could she be?—for this gaunt and bony stranger. He'd always been strong and fit, all muscle and not an ounce of excess fat. Now his body felt hard and alien to her. "But you're so *thin,*" she finished, with another shaky laugh.

His face formed a smile, a wry one, beneath her hand. "I guess maybe I have been missing that Georgia cooking. Get me some good ol' Southern fried chicken, some of your momma's biscuits and redeye gravy, and I'll be filled out in no time." Under her palm, the smile quivered and vanished. "You might have to be a little bit patient with me for a while, though, darlin'. They tell me I've picked up an intestinal bug or two, but they're working on that. Once that's cleared up, there'll be no stopping me. Hey, you know, I used to dream about Colonel Sanders? And sweet corn drippin' butter, and bacon and tomato sandwiches with those great big tomatoes—your momma still grow those in her garden?"

Grief and anger at what had been done to him overwhelmed her. Fighting it with all her might, she drew her hand from his grasp, touched his jaw and then the front of his jumpsuit. Frowning with the effort it took to force calm into her voice, she cleared her throat and carefully began, "Did they—"

"How've you been? How's Sammi June?"

It was a hurried interruption, meant to keep her from asking the questions he didn't want to answer. Wasn't ready to answer, she realized, kicking herself, and vowed there and then not to ask again. He'd tell her when he wanted to, when he could, she told herself. *If* he could.

She answered him in the same false, bright tone, which nobody ever did better than a Southern woman. "Oh, we've been doin' fine...just great. Momma's fine..."

"Sammi June?"

"She wanted to come...she's got midterms—"

He looked dazed. "Midterms...my God. She's in *college?* I guess...she would be, wouldn't she? I don't know, I just keep thinking she's still a little girl, you know? I guess...she's pretty much all grown-up, isn't she?"

The quaver of wistfulness and bewilderment in his voice, in his face, once again was almost more than Jessie could bear. "Oh, she sure is that," she said, and her voice, still bright, was thinner now, squeezed past the ache in her throat. "She's taller than I am, if you can believe that. Oh, here, I brought some pictures—" she snatched up the little album she'd left lying on the couch and thrust it at him "—so it won't be such a shock when you see her."

He took the album from her, then simply held it, staring down at it as if he had no idea what it was, as if he'd never seen such a thing before. A shiver rippled through her. There was something in his look, a kind of darkness, that frightened her. As if he'd gone away someplace and left her behind. Someplace terrible.

She realized she was babbling—about Sammi June's classes, the women's soccer team she was on—just to fill up that silence.

Tristan slowly lifted his head, then looked around as if noticing his surroundings for the first time. "Is there someplace we could go?'' Jessie's heart gave a queer little lurch and she was about to tell him about the room upstairs, the one with the enormous bed in the middle of it, when he abruptly bent down and picked up his cane, then used it to point toward the windows. ''For a walk, I mean. Outside. It's a pretty nice day, looks like.'' He looked at her and gave her a smile of apology—that crooked smile she was learning to expect, so different from the old one that showed his beautiful, even teeth and made comma-shaped creases in his cheeks and fans at the corners of his eyes. ''I've been indoors way too much lately.''

A laugh burst from her that was still frighteningly close to a sob. It was partly relief, she knew; relief that he'd come back from that dark place in his mind. And partly a girlish eagerness to please him that made her think of those first giddy days...weeks, when she was eighteen and newly, wildly in love.

''Sure,'' she said, ''I don't see why not. Except—'' She'd almost asked him if he felt up to such a stroll, if he was strong enough. Even weak as he obviously was, she knew he'd hate that, and was glad she'd stopped herself in time. Instead she aimed her doubtful look at the windows. ''Did you see any media people out there? There weren't when I got here, but I figure it's only a matter of time before they find us.''

He gave a snort, and the wry smile flickered on again. ''Yeah, your mom said they were camped out on her lawn.''

''You talked to her?''

''First call I made.'' His gaze brushed her and he spoke in a diffident, offhand way that seemed almost shy—so unlike Tristan. ''It was the only number I was pretty certain would still be the same. I didn't know if you were—if you'd—hey, I mean I'd understand if you did. As far as you knew, I was dead, right? I mean, legally, even if I was just MIA, after eight years—''

His floundering voice stabbed at her. "Tris, I'm not. Married, I mean, I haven't—"

"I know *that*. Your mom told me—well, actually, *they* did. The Navy, I mean. First thing they did was fill me in on the vital statistics, what information they had." He paused, and again touched her face with that shy, uncertain glance as he said almost belligerently, "Not being remarried isn't the same thing as not *having* someone, though, is it?"

"I don't," Jess said gently, and caught the heartbreaking flash of hope that brightened his eyes before he jerked his eyes away. His light, ironic laugh came to her as they moved side by side toward the door that opened onto a patio where guests could sit at outdoor tables when the weather was fine. Beyond that was a wooded area, and a paved bicycle and pedestrian path.

"So, I guess we're still married, then?"

He didn't know what made him ask it, like probing a sore tooth with his tongue. *We're still married, then?* He didn't feel like her husband. He felt like a barbarian invader, bringing pain, ugliness and horror into her soft and lovely, *civilized* life. Everything about her—her hair, her sweater, her skin—was so beautiful, so soft. She smelled so *clean.* He didn't feel clean, and sometimes wondered if he ever would again. Until he did, he knew he'd never be able to touch her without thinking that he was soiling her, somehow.

We're still married, then? What he really wanted to know was, *Do you still love me?* But that was something he couldn't bring himself to ask.

Bleakly, he drew a breath and forced a smile. "Your momma seems just the same," he said as he crossed the brick-paved patio, using the cane in what he hoped was a dashing sort of way rather than leaning on it like an invalid. He considered the pain in his knee only an annoyance— he'd grown accustomed to much worse—but the doctors had told him to keep his weight off of the knee as much as possible. And since his dreams of ever flying again lay pretty much in their hands, he was willing to do what they told him.

Jess gave a light laugh as she came beside him, fitting her stride to his uneven gait. "Did she cry?"

"I…think she might have, yeah, but you know how she is. She'd about die before she'd let you see her shed a tear."

She did a quick scan for reporters, then moved across the strip of grass that separated the guest house from the path. "Yeah, Momma doesn't change much," she said, lifting her face to the sweet spring breeze.

The breeze lifted the hair from her shoulders gently, like the fanning of a butterfly's wings, and the slanting sunlight shone golden through the fine strands. It seemed to Tristan the loveliest sight he'd ever seen.

"Things around her keep changing, but she stays the same. She's like, I don't know…our family's anchor, or something. Our compass. You know—true north?"

He did know. He wanted to tell her how she and Sammi June had been that for him, all that and more—his anchor, his compass, the beacon light on the shore, his sword, his shield, his armor. But that seemed too big a burden of expectation to lay on one person.

"I guess there've been a lot of changes, though," he said.

She threw him a smile. "Yeah, there have. Mostly good ones. Lots of babies. There's a whole new crop of nieces and nephews for you to meet. Jimmy Joe and Mirabella— you remember Mirabella's little girl, Amy Jo? Jimmy Joe delivered her in the cab of his rig on a snowbound interstate in Texas on Christmas Day? Anyway, they have a little boy, now, too, and by the way, J.J.'s a senior in high school, if you can believe that. Then my brother Troy and his wife Charly, they have two little girls. And…let's see.

Oh—oh my God, you'll never guess. You know my little brother, C.J.?''

"You mean, Calvin? The one that dropped out of high school, and everybody'd pretty much given up on?" How good it felt to talk like this, of ordinary, everyday things. Home…family.

"Excepting Momma, of course—Momma never gives up on any of her kids." Laughter bubbled up, and he drank the happiness in that sound like water from a healing fountain. "Yup, that's the one. Well, would you believe he's a lawyer now?"

"A lawyer? Good Lord."

"I know, isn't it wild? He just passed the bar this last March. And guess what else? He's married. No babies yet, but he and his wife—her name's Caitlyn, she's from Iowa, and he met her when she hijacked his rig, and then she got shot and was blind for a while—oh, God, it's a long story— but anyway, they've adopted a little girl. Her name is Emma—she's a doll. And…let's see, who else?"

"What about your other brother—what was his name— Roy?" Tris prompted. "Did he ever get married?"

Jessie sighed. "Not yet. That makes him the last holdout in the marriage department. He's down in Florida, some-place. On the gulf. Captains a charter fishing boat."

"Sounds like a tough life," Tristan said dryly.

"Doesn't it, though. Okay, so who does that leave? Oh, yeah, my oldest sister, Tracy, of course—she's still married to Al, the cop, and they still live in Augusta and still have four kids. And then there's Joy Lynn—''

She broke off while he took her arm and guided her out of the path of a pair of joggers who were overtaking them on the pedestrian side of the pathway. And he thought how easily such a thing came back to him. Sometimes, in fact, it was hard for him to get his mind around how some things, small, everyday things that had been absent from his life for so long, slipped back into it almost as naturally as—well, smiles and laughter, which were two more things he'd been without for a long, long time. If only, he thought, everything could be that easy.

"Joy—how is she? She and her second husband—what was his name?—ever have any kids?"

Jess threw him a look, too quickly. He became conscious once again of the soft fabric of her sweater, warming beneath his fingers, and the tensed muscle of her arm under that. He let go of it and felt her body relax.

"Fred." She bit off the word. "She divorced him—with good reason, by the way. And she swears she's never getting married again. Given her lousy taste in men, it's probably just as well. Anyway, she lives in New York, now. She's working on a novel, but she has a job at a magazine publisher's to pay the bills." She gave Tristan another sidelong look. "I was up there visiting her when I got the call. That's why I wasn't home—"

"I know," he said softly. "Your mom told me." After a long moment he added, "She said you're a nurse now."

"Yeah," she said, watching her feet, "I got my degree four years ago. I work in the NICU—the Neonatal Intensive Care—"

"I remember. You always wanted to do that, after Sammi June. That's great."

They walked on in silence, moving slowly, overcome all at once by the enormity of what had happened to their lives, the catastrophic changes of the past few days. The sun went down, and the air turned cooler. Tristan, who had sometimes doubted he'd ever be completely warm again, couldn't repress a shiver.

Jessie glanced at him but didn't ask if he wanted to turn back. Probably trying not to smother him, he thought, hating how weak he felt. He wondered if he'd ever have any stamina again.

After a while she said, "Granny Calhoun passed away."

He nodded his acceptance of that inevitability; the old

lady, his mother-in-law's mother, had been at least ninety and frail as a twig last time he'd seen her, though still sharp as a tack mentally.

They paced another dozen quiet steps, and he was thinking he was going to have to turn around pretty soon, unless he wanted to humiliate himself by having to call somebody to come and get him and carry him back. Then he looked over and saw that she was crying. Soundlessly, with tears making glistening trails down her cheeks. Only when she felt his gaze did she lift her hand and try to stanch their flow with the sleeve of her sweater.

"Jess," he said, his voice raspy with emotions long and deeply buried.

When she didn't reply he uncertainly touched her elbow. That was all it took to bring her to him, sobbing.

He stood and held her as close as he dared, staring over her head with eyes dry and face aching, hard little muscles clenching and unclenching in his jaws. Joggers and bicyclists hurried past, uncurious, their whirring wheels and labored pants making breathing rhythms in the dusk. A plump woman in a bright-blue coat, hurrying in the wake of an overweight poodle straining at its leash, gave them a glance, then politely averted her eyes.

Chapter 3

Why am I crying? Jessie wondered. Why now, of all times?

Not for Granny Calhoun, although there hadn't been a day in the years since her grandmother had passed on that Jessie didn't miss her. Granny had gone the way most everybody would like to, suddenly and peacefully at an advanced age, in her own home surrounded by her loved ones. Thinking about her brought Jessie only a warm and gentle sadness.

But this… Oh Lord, this grief had come up in her like a geyser, hot, violent, wrenching. This pain was searing…shocking, the pain of a loss so unjust, so unspeakable, it felt as though her entire body was turning itself inside out trying to reject it. These tears were unstoppable; like the grief and the pain, they'd been held back too long, buried beneath the serene, accepting surface of her everyday existence. They were Tristan's tears, she realized. The ones she'd never shed for him, not then, when she'd lost him, nor in all the years since.

Why hadn't she cried for him? Because she'd had to be strong, she'd told herself. For Sammi June, for Momma and the rest of her family and friends who were so worried about her. For Tristan's family and especially his military friends and colleagues, who'd expected her to keep a stiff upper lip, be brave. And for herself. Especially for herself.

"There was a memorial service," she said, pulling back from him to mop at her streaming nose with her sleeve. She didn't mean Granny Calhoun, but she was sure, somehow, he'd know that. "They gave me a flag…." She closed her eyes, once more helpless to stop the tears flooding down her cheeks.

She felt her husband's arms fold around her. She felt his bony, rock-hard chest deflate with a sigh. "I'm sorry," he whispered, as if he didn't know what else to say. He kept saying it, standing there in the growing chill of evening. "I'm sorry…I'm sorry."

"I'm glad I got that out of my system, aren't you?" Jessie said. But her laugh sounded phony, even to her own ears.

When Tristan didn't answer right away, she gathered her courage and looked up at him. But his face was a shadow against the pale sky, and his profile seemed stark and closed.

They were walking back toward the residence, more slowly now than when they'd left it, close together but not touching. It seemed to her that Tristan was leaning more heavily on his cane, and even without touching him she was aware of the tremors that seized him from time to time. She felt a squeezing sensation around her heart.

"I don't know where that came from," she said, rushed and breathless with guilt, "I really don't. I didn't mean—"

"*Don't*—" His voice sounded almost angry. Softening it took an effort even she could see. "God—don't apologize. For anything. Ever.'' He drew a breath, then said stiffly, ''I know this must be difficult for you.''

The understatement left her at a loss for a reply. She looked up at him, lips parted but speechless. He looked back at her, and after a long moment she saw his face relax with his smile. The new, wry smile that was half irony, half apology. ''Sorry, that was—''

She touched two fingers to his lips, stopping him there. ''Don't apologize,'' she said, mimicking him in a voice that quavered. ''About anything. Ever.'' And he laughed and lightly touched her fingertips to his lips before wrapping them in his hand. ''I didn't…know how I was going to handle this,'' she went on, haltingly. ''I haven't known what to do. What to say.''

''There's too much to say,'' he agreed, nodding as they walked on. ''Makes it hard to know how to start. It's like what the doctors have been telling me, I guess. Be patient. Take it slow. One step at a time.''

''Well,'' Jessie said with a breathy laugh, ''we've made it through the first step. That's the hard part, right? From here on it should get easier.''

He gave her hand a squeeze before he released it to open the guest house door for her. She waited for him to say what they both knew to be true, which was that the hardest parts were almost certainly still to come. He didn't say it, but even in the warm and welcoming lobby, she felt him shiver.

''You don't have to eat if you don't want to,'' Jess said.

Tristan looked up at her with a guilty start. It occurred to him that he'd been staring down at his plate for a good bit longer than was polite. Not that there was anything wrong with the food. She'd made a point of ordering some of his favorites—fried chicken with mashed potatoes and gravy and fresh green beans, peach cobbler with thick cream for dessert—and the house staff had gone out of their

way to oblige, even serving them dinner privately in their
room. It was just that it still came as a shock to him to see
so much food in one place, all at one time. More food than
he could possibly eat, even after several days of such
bounty.

"It looks…fantastic," he said, meaning it. It seemed as
if he was always hungry; sometimes he even dreamed about
food. Right now he felt light-headed from hunger; he just
wished his stomach didn't always feel so queasy.

He picked up a piece of chicken—the drumstick; she'd
even remembered he liked them best—and bit into it. The
juice exploded in his mouth, and the rich, greasy flavors
nearly made him lose the tenuous hold he'd been keeping
on his self-control.

"Tris? Are you okay?"

He heard alarm in her voice and managed to smile for
her as he nodded, swallowed, then said softly, "Culture
shock. Things hit me every once in a while."

He wiped his mouth with the napkin he'd been given
without realizing at first what he was doing. Then he caught
himself and looked down at it, almost in wonder. "This,
for example. You have no idea how strange this feels…"
His voice trailed off while he watched his fingertips rubbing
and stroking the crisp, clean white linen.

After a moment he laughed, quietly and painfully.
"When I got to the carrier, they gave me some things…a
little bag of toiletries—you know, a toothbrush and tooth-
paste…a razor…some other stuff. It felt…sort of, I don't
know, overwhelming, to have so much stuff. I didn't want
to let go of it. I carried that damn bag around with me for
three days." He stopped and stared hard at his plateful of
food. Those admissions, like the tears he'd shed in prison,
embarrassed him.

"So," she said, when he'd been silent too long, "what's
going to happen next?"

He looked up and saw that she was wearing her bright,

brave smile, not the one he loved, the one that made her nose wrinkle and her eyes dance and a little fan of lines spray out from their corners. Right now her eyes, that amazing amber brown with thick sable lashes that made so striking a contrast with her blond hair, were wide-open and luminous. They looked fragile as blown glass, as if they'd shatter if she blinked.

His own eyes felt hot, and he looked quickly down at his plate again and concentrated on the task of picking up his fork and loading it with mashed potatoes and gravy. Looking at her was like trying to look at a bright light after being in darkness. It had been like that the first time he'd ever laid eyes on her, he remembered, that day on the beach in Florida. With her golden hair and tawny eyes, she'd seemed to him like a broken-off piece of the sun.

"What happens next?" His hand went reflexively to the little album of photographs lying on the table beside his plate; like that bag of toiletries, he couldn't bring himself to let it out of his reach.

It had occurred to him that Jess would probably like to go through it with him, sitting beside him and telling him the story behind each picture. He'd barely glanced at it, but that had been enough to tell him he wouldn't be able to handle doing that—not now, not yet. He was going to have to do this by slow degrees and in a very private place. It was going to take time to absorb this new reality into who he was now. Time and some emotions he'd rather not have anyone see and wasn't strong enough, yet, to control. He shifted the album slightly, nudging it furtively back under his forearm as he took another bite of mashed potatoes.

"For the next few days I expect there's going to be some more tests. I know the head doctors aren't done with me yet, and then they'd like to get these intestinal bugs under control before they turn me loose." He glanced up and tried to smile. "Sorry—I know that's not a nice topic of conversation for the dinner table."

"What'd I tell you about apologizing?" She smiled back at him, a gentle smile that made him ache to hold her. Touch her.

If I touch her now, he thought, it would be like that napkin. Strange. Alien. If I hold her, it'll be like holding on to that bag of toiletries they gave me. Like a crazy person, holding on because I'm too screwed up, too afraid to let go. I can't do that to her. I can't.

He grinned and said, "Sorry," and saw her relax a little as she accepted his pitiful attempt at humor for the gift it was meant to be. He ate more chicken while she played with hers and the silence thickened. Helplessly he thought, *We're like strangers. And then: We* are *strangers.*

Casting for something with which to break that silence, he cleared his throat and said, "I talked to my dad—" at precisely the same moment she got fed up with it, too, and decided to ask, "Did you call your…dad?"

He laughed and said, "Great minds…"

And she laughed and said, "Yeah."

He began again, nodding as he chewed. "He was my second phone call. We had a good talk." He looked up and flashed her his out-of-practice smile. "Well—actually, he did most of the talking. I guess I was pretty much in a state of shock." His gaze fell, and he was staring at nothing, his mind a bleak landscape of shifting shadows. "Still am, if you want to know the truth. I don't think it's sunk in yet. Nothing seems real. I keep thinking I'm going to wake up at some point and I'll be back in that prison—"

"I imagine that's normal," her voice interrupted, hurrying, trying to hold steady. It scattered the shadows, at least for the moment. They'd be back, he knew. They always came back. "It'll get better, Tris. You just have to give it time. You need to get well, get your strength back. Once we get home and things settle down…" Her voice trailed off.

He looked up and saw her eyes on him, pleading silently

in her pale face, and suddenly felt defeated, overwhelmed. She wanted too much from him. Wanted so much for him to be okay. To be the man she remembered. The Tristan he'd been before.

"You're wondering why I asked to stay over here, aren't you?" he said abruptly. "When they probably would have shipped me home as soon as they had me cleaned up and deloused and knew I was fit to travel." He pushed back his plate. He wanted to reach for her hand, but found the album instead, and curled his fingers around it. "It's not what you're thinking—"

"You don't know what I'm thinking," she said with unexpected heat. It was a flash fire, only a glimpse of the Jess he remembered, but it caught him by surprise and made a nice spreading warmth inside him—like taking a slug of what looked like iced tea and finding out it was whiskey. He smiled, and for the first time since he could remember, felt like the smile came from someplace deeper than his tonsils.

"Anyway, *I* got to thinking, after I'd talked to Dad. He mentioned that where we are now isn't that far from where he grew up, and I thought—"

"I know you always wanted to see Germany." He heard a definite break in her voice. "We talked about it, remember? We always said we'd go, someday, when Sammi June was grown up and gone...." Her eyes had that suspicious glow again, and there were splashes of color in her cheeks. He felt the warm place in his chest grow larger.

"I do remember," he said, staring hard at her, his voice gruff and raspy. "And I guess maybe I have a different take on 'someday' now than I used to. I asked to stay a few extra days in Germany so I could check out the places where my mom and dad grew up. And I wanted you to go with me. Because it was something we talked about. Doing together. If you want to."

"I'd love to." Her voice had a furry quality to it that

made him feel as though the temperature in the room had risen ten degrees. "Are the doctors okay with it? How soon can we go?"

"Oh, the doctors seem to think it's a great idea." He grinned, but it was the new, painful one back again. "They'd like for me to get adjusted to 'normal life'—whatever that means—as soon as possible, but I think they're a little leery of turning me loose on society until they're sure I'm not going to self-destruct at some point on down the road."

He saw her throat tighten, but she nodded and her voice was matter-of-fact as she murmured, "Post-traumatic stress…"

"This way," he continued dryly, "they can let me out on a leash, so to speak, then reel me back in so they can run tests to see how I'm coping." He finished with a shrug and another half smile. "Something like that, anyway. Hey, I don't mind, as long as they let me go. As long as *you* want to go."

"Lord's sake, you *know* I do," she said, and hearing that Southern accent of hers made something tickle inside him, like bubbles in champagne. It came as a surprise to him to realize it was pleasure. "How far is it? When can we go? Tomorrow?"

"Not tomorrow." All at once the heat in him cooled and the bubbles fizzled, swamped by a new wave of fatigue. He wondered if he was ever going to stop feeling tired all the time. He said with a smile of apology, "It's probably gonna be a couple days before I'm up to it, darlin'. Tomorrow they've got me scheduled for some more tests…more debriefing. Which reminds me—" he clutched the edge of the table and clumsily pushed back his chair "—my shadow's supposed to be picking me up at twenty—uh, make that nine o'clock, and if that clock radio over there is right, it's near that now. I'd better be getting downstairs."

"You have to go back?" She was on her feet, too, with her head held high. She kept her voice light, and because he knew she didn't want him to, he tried not to see the disappointment in her eyes. "I just assumed you were staying here tonight."

It was the moment he'd been dreading, and from the tense and defensive way she was holding herself, he wondered if she'd been dreading it, too.

"Jess," he said gently, "I can't. You wouldn't want me to."

She nodded once, quickly—and yes, half-relieved. "It's okay. I understand."

She didn't, though, he knew that. Overwhelmed once more with tiredness and a sense of failure, he tried to explain. "I don't...sleep well. I'm not used to sleeping in a bed—"

"Oh, hell, I *knew* it." Her voice was suddenly bright and quivering with melodrama. "My stars, it's this damn bed, isn't it?" She threw her arms wide to encompass the bed, which he'd already noticed took up a good bit of the room, and he knew she was trying to ease the awkwardness between them by making light of it. "It'd scare anybody off. Not to mention, it's just downright tacky."

"It is a lot to live up to," Tris agreed, coming up behind her. "I don't think my prison cell was as big as that bed." He lifted his hands, but didn't allow himself to touch her. Her scent, one he was familiar with but couldn't place, drifted to his nostrils, and he closed his eyes and drank it in, swaying a little with exhaustion and longing. So sweet...so *clean*.

God, the irony of it was terrible. He'd dreamed of her for so long...how she'd look...how she'd smell. How she'd feel. In his mind he'd explored her body, every inch of it. He knew...he remembered...every detail: the sprinkles of freckles on her shoulders and even across the tops of her breasts where her bikini didn't reach; the way her nipples looked when she was aroused; the tiny red mole, no bigger than the head of a pin, just where the two halves of her rib cage came together; the scar low on her belly from the Caesarean she'd had when Sammi June was born. How he'd loved to kiss her there…then lower…oh yes, lower. Now here she was, inches away…a breath away. *His wife.* And he could hardly bear to touch her.

"I have nightmares," he said, his voice ragged with his anguish. "I'm afraid I might—I don't want to hurt you." He knew how lame it must sound.

She turned back to him, moving in that abrupt, jerky way—and just like that, he was flashing back again to a Florida beach and the first time he'd ever set eyes on her, her body coltish, self-conscious and awkward, and at the same time so *sexy.* Sexy as hell.

"It's *okay,*" she said, breathless and rushed, laying her hand along his jaw. As before, he curled his fingers around hers and drew them away from his face, carefully as he knew how. He wasn't used to being gently touched. "You're here. You're alive. That's all that matters." She paused, and he nodded. A smile trembled on her lips. "So. You'll be back tomorrow? After you're finished with the tests and the debriefing?"

He nodded, then started violently when the phone rang. She went to pick it up, and he waited for his heartbeat to slow down before he said, "That's probably Al now."

The big red-gold letters on the digital clock beside the bed said nine o'clock on the money, and he thought what a luxury it was to always know the exact time. He was accustomed to determining the passage of days by the waning of darkness and light, and weeks by counting scratches he'd made on the walls of his cell. One of the first things he'd do when he got back to the world, he decided, was buy himself a watch.

That reminded him of something he'd forgotten to ask Jess.

She put the phone down and turned to him, eyes too bright. "That was your ride. He's waitin' for you downstairs."

He nodded and reached for the cane he'd left propped against the bed. "Jess, there's something—"

"He said to take your time." She was hugging herself, and her smile looked strained. He wished he felt strong enough to put his arms around her and make her feel safe and protected, the way he used to. But he knew he wasn't.

"Come down with me," he said. "You can meet my shadow. Al's a good guy."

She nodded, and waited while he shifted the cane to his left hand and opened the door and held it for her.

"There's one thing you can do for me," he said, and she looked at him again in the eager way he remembered from when they were first dating. "Tomorrow, if you want…while I'm busy at the hospital, you…uh, maybe you could go shopping for me? Pick me up some clothes?" His smile slipped sideways. "Just occurred to me, I don't have any civvies."

"Sure, I'll do that. I'd love to." So eager to please him it made his throat ache. "Where— I mean…"

"I don't know what there is around here. Al can probably tell you. Or—did they assign you somebody?"

"They did—Lieutenant Commander Rees, my casualty assistance officer. He'd probably even take me. Oh—" her eyes darkened as they swept across his body "I don't know what size—"

"Just get me my old size," he said softly as he closed the door behind them. "I'll grow into 'em."

"Promise?"

He took a deep breath. "That's a promise," he said fervently. Then he put his arm around her shoulders and brought her to his side. Suspense hummed in his muscles until he felt her body relax against him, and there was an aching familiarity about her softness as she slipped her arm around his waist.

* * *

Back in her room half an hour later, Jessie closed the door and leaned against it. She felt drained and lonely. It had taken all the emotional stamina she'd had left to make brave small talk for Major Sharpe, and then to smile and let her husband slip away from her side and walk away. Funny—as apprehensive as she'd been about this reunion, and as awkward and difficult as it had turned out to be, watching him leave again had been the worst. She'd wanted to cling to him and cry like a child. Instead she'd kept her smile plastered in place and returned his little farewell wave—it had seemed so uncharacteristically tentative, for Tris—and then turned and walked back inside and up the stairs on legs that were suddenly trembly. Now, with no one to see her, she clamped her hand over her mouth and let the tears come.

Gulping sobs, she felt her way to the huge bed and sank onto it. Shaking, bereft, she reached blindly for something to hold on to—a pillow—and found herself hugging a large plump Teddy bear instead.

She stared at it in surprise, and then a gust of laughter replaced her sobs. Intermittently laughing and sobbing, she gazed at the fat brown bear while she mopped at her tears with the sleeve of her sweater. Whose idea had it been to leave her such a thing? she wondered, poking and tugging distractedly at its cheery yellow bow.

Heavens, she'd never been the Teddy bear type, even when she was little. Joy, now—*she* was the one for bears. Joy Lynn, Ms. Sophisticated New York Career Person, had bears all over her apartment. She had them on her bed and her sofa and her dressertop. She had one sitting on the back of her *toilet,* for heaven's sake.

Jessie had been…well, somewhere between the baseball mitt and the Nancy Drew type, which was a hard place for a Southern girl raised in the seventies to be. In fact, come to think of it, she'd had a hard time fitting into any recognizable niche, growing up in Oglethorpe County, Georgia.

Until Tristan Bauer had come along. Right then, for the first time in her life, she'd known exactly who she was and where she belonged.

She lay back on the bed, hugging the bear to her chest. With her eyes closed she could see him walking away from her, not the way he'd looked tonight, thin and worn, steps uneven, but on a night half her lifetime ago, striding down the second-floor walkway of a Florida beachfront motel, tall and strong and straight, head set with that proud and arrogant tilt, radiating self-assurance in almost visible waves.

And she, leaning against the wall outside her door because she feared her legs weren't going to hold her up if she left it, and her lips still throbbing from his kiss and her insides turning upside down, had called out to him. "You don't have to go, you know."

At the top of the stairs he'd paused to look back at her, one hand on the railing, smile tender, eyes dark with regret.

"You can stay if you want to," Jessie had said to him in a husky, grown-up voice that hardly trembled at all. Lauren Bacall, sexy and sleepy-eyed. But inside her head she was crying in panic, *If you leave me now, I'll just have to die.*

He sauntered back toward her while her heart tried to beat its way out of her chest, and when he was close enough to touch her he stopped. Smiling wryly, teeth white against his dusky skin, he murmured, "Darlin', much as I wish I could, I don't have any protection, and I'm pretty sure you don't, either." He lifted a hand and lightly brushed her cheek with the backs of his fingers. Then he turned away once more.

And she'd known—she'd absolutely *known*—that if he

went ahead and walked away from her then, it was going to be forever, that she was about to lose her one and only chance for true love and lifelong happiness. The man was gorgeous, and this was Florida, spring break. There had to be hundreds—no, thousands!—of girls out there on those beaches more beautiful, more sophisticated, more *prepared* than she was. If she let him slip away tonight she was gonna lose him—simple as that.

Trembling, she'd heard herself say, "I'm on the pill." In the comparative innocence of that long-ago time, pregnancy had been the only concern on both their minds.

He turned back to her once more, looked down into her eyes and smiled. Then he tucked his finger under her chin, lifted it and kissed her, pressing her back against the wall until she felt the whole hard length of him against her. He kissed her in ways she'd never known before, then took her room key from her nerveless fingers and unlocked her door. Somehow or other they found their way inside.

The door had barely closed behind them before he was taking off her clothes—not that it was a hard thing to do, a tug on the tie of her new beach coverup, another on the string of her new matching bikini—and kissing her all the while, until her mouth felt hot and swollen and her breathing was only desperate sips, caught between whimpers. He kissed her throat until the pressure made her pulse pound like a bass drum, then moved his mouth downward, kissing his way across the tops of her naked breasts. Hot as she was, her nipples went puckered and hard as if she had a chill, until he began to warm them, pulling one deep into his mouth and sucking and stroking it with his tongue while his hand covered and chafed the other, and she thought she couldn't possibly stand so much...so much *feeling*. Then his mouth moved to the other breast while his hand came to warm the one his mouth had abandoned, and she moaned and drove her fingers into his hair and clutched him harder against her, pleading for…she didn't know what.

His hands stroked down her sides, hooked under the strings of her bikini bottoms and yanked them down, and the heat bubbled up in her like a geyser. Her legs buckled, and he caught her hips and held her while his mouth pressed kisses across her belly, and then lower. And…oh, no—*lower.* His tongue slipped into her, and she uttered a sharp, shocked cry. She gripped his shoulders and sagged against the wall, legs spasming as his arms held her captive and his tongue moved rhythmically inside her.

Her mind left her. Later she would marvel and wonder at what had happened to her, stunned to think that she, Jessica Ann Starr, had allowed a man to do to her what he'd done. Stunned to discover her body was capable of such sensations. But *then,* utterly mindless, she'd gasped as her body jerked out of her control and he'd surged upward to wrap her in his arms and hold her while she sobbed and quaked through her first-ever climax.

Before reason could return and find her perched on the brink of utter humiliation, she was lying in a tumble of sheets, and Tristan's hard, hot body was covering hers and he was kissing her again—her belly, her breasts, her mouth—and the bubbling, searing heat was spreading once more beneath her skin. His hand stroked her thighs, coaxed them apart and cupped the moist, pulsing place between. A finger gently probed while he kissed her mouth deeply…and then he held her intimately in the warmth of his hand, raised his head and looked into her eyes.

"You're a virgin, aren't you?" he said.

Breathless and belligerent, she'd replied, "What if I am?"

He'd laughed softly and kissed her again. Sometime later, breathless and trembling now himself, he'd lifted his head again to ask in a broken whisper, "Are you really on the pill?"

She'd told him the truth, but by then it was too late, and neither of them cared.

Seven months later, while Tristan was on an aircraft carrier in the Indian Ocean, Jessie had been rushed to the base hospital for an emergency Caesarean. The baby, a girl, had weighed a little over three pounds, and since Tristan hadn't been there to say otherwise, Jessie named her Samantha June.

That's who the bear's for, Jessie realized as the pounding heat ebbed from her body. Whoever was responsible for warming her quarters with flowers and a fruit basket would have known Tristan had a teenage daughter. The Teddy bear had obviously been meant for Sammi June. And they'd forgotten to call her.

She sat up, hands smoothing the bear's fur and straightening the yellow ribbon around its neck. She felt terrible, ashamed; she was a miserable excuse for a mother. She'd meant to phone Sammi June while Tris was here. Of course, she hadn't known he was going to be with her for such a short time, but the truth was, she'd forgotten. She'd been so focused on herself and on Tris. She'd been selfish, thinking like a lovesick girl instead of somebody's mother.

Placing the Teddy bear back in its nest amongst the pillows, Jessie wiped her face with the sleeves of her sweater and reached for the phone.

Chapter 4

Sammi June set the computer on Hibernate, shut it down, stretched, then shoved back her chair and bent over to slip on her running shoes. She tied the laces and grabbed up her fanny pack as she stood, shaking the cramps out of her legs. She was halfway out the door, buckling on the fanny pack as she went, when the phone rang. She said a bad word and thought about ignoring it; she was starving, and on Sundays the cafeteria's hot food line closed early. And frankly, after working on that stupid psych paper all day, she was not in the mood for yogurt.

But then a little shiver ran through her, and before she could stop it came the thought: *What if it's my dad?*

She went back into the room, closed the door carefully behind her and picked up the cordless handset from its nest in the pile of comforter and discarded clothing on her bed. She punched the button and said, "Samantha June's Funeral and Pizza Parlor, how may I help you?"

"Hey," said her mother's voice.

"Hey," said Sammi June. Her knees gave out unexpectedly and she sat down on the bed. "So, where are you?" Her hand, the one holding the phone, had started to shake, so she lay back in the jumble, pillowing her head on one arm.

"I'm in Landstuhl. Right now I'm in my room in the guest house. Hon', I'm sorry I didn't call earlier—"

"'S'okay, I've been working on this stupid paper all day, anyway. I was just going out to get something to eat." And she rushed on without pausing for breath, "So, is Dad with you?"

She heard her mom take a breath. "Not right now, no. He was, but he left about half an hour ago. He had to go back to the hospital. Hon', I'm so sorry—"

"The hospital! What's wrong? Gramma said he was okay."

"No, no—it's nothing—there's nothing wrong, he just has to stay in the hospital so they can monitor him for a little while longer, that's all."

"But you've seen him." Sammi June pressed the phone hard against her ear.

"Yeah…" Her mom's voice sounded very gentle, the way it did sometimes when she was totally exhausted after a gut-wrenching day in the NICU where she worked. Then she added in a brighter tone, "Hey, we had dinner together—fried chicken and peach cobbler," and Sammi June could almost see her mom trying to straighten up and put on a happy face for her. Which really bugged her. *I'm not a child,* she thought. *Jeez, Mom, like I need for you to sugarcoat everything for me.*

"So," she said, putting it right out there, "how is he?"

"He's okay. He's…pretty good, considering," her mother said, too carefully. Sammi June wanted to yell at her.

"Well, what does he look like?" She felt like she was suffocating. Even after she realized she was holding her breath, she couldn't seem to let it go. "I mean, you know.

Does he look…'' *Like my dad? Like the dad I remember? Like, of course he doesn't, stupid. Duh, he's been in a prison camp for eight years.* Finally she settled for, ''Has he changed a lot?'' And then, eyes closed, she waited, pleading silently. *Don't lie to me, Momma. I'll never forgive you if you lie to me. Don't treat me like a child.*

After what seemed like forever, she heard her mother take another careful breath. ''Well, he's…thin.''

''He always was,'' said Sammi June, struggling to breathe.

''No—'' there was a little rush of laughter ''—*really* thin.''

''You mean like…concentration-camp thin?''

''Oh—Lord. Well…'' Her mother was laughing still, but in a way that made Sammi June wonder if she was crying at the same time. She felt a sob pushing against her own throat, but was determined to keep it there. ''No, not that bad. Just…way *too* thin, is all. And his hair's got a lot of gray in it, especially at the temples. It looks kind of good, actually. You know—''

''Distinguished,'' said Sammi June, and cleared her throat. ''Does he have any—you know…scars? I mean, did they—'' But she couldn't bring herself to ask.

''I don't know,'' her mother said quietly. ''He…doesn't like to talk about…what happened to him. He has a knee injury—he'll probably have to have surgery for that, eventually. Right now he's using a cane, but he says that's just temporary. Honey, we have to give him time, that's all. We have to be patient.''

''I know…that's okay, I was just wondering. So—what happens now? Are you gonna see him tomorrow?''

''In the evening, yes, I think so.'' There was another little laugh. ''Tomorrow I'm going shopping, actually. I have to buy him something to wear. He hasn't got any civilian clothes at all.''

''No way.'' Sammi June pushed herself upright. ''Okay,

this is cool. This is your big chance, Mom. Europe's way ahead of us. Promise you'll get him some really stylin' stuff, okay?''

Her mom laughed. ''I'm gonna try. Listen, you better go on and get something to eat, now, okay? I just wanted to let you know what's going on. Everything's okay. We'll call you tomorrow when he's here, I promise.''

''Sure, that's fine.'' Sammi June hugged herself and the phone and wished she could stop shivering. ''Uh, Momma? Is there…do you think there's any chance he might still call tonight?''

There was a little pause before her mother said gently, ''I don't know, honey, he was pretty tired when he left. Late as it is here, I think you should just go on and get yourself something to eat. We'll call tomorrow, for sure. Okay?''

''Yeah. Okay. Sure.''

''Okay then. Bye-bye, honey. Love you.''

''Love you, too, Momma. Bye.''

For a long time after she pressed the disconnect button, Sammi June sat on the bed, holding the phone cradled to her chest and rocking herself. She no longer felt the least little bit like eating.

And in her room in the guest house in Landstuhl, Germany, Jessie set the phone back on its cradle and picked up the Teddy bear. After gazing at it for a moment, she wrapped her arms around it and cradled it against her heart.

Does he have any scars?

She didn't know how to tell Sammi June that the worst of her daddy's scars were most likely deep down inside him, where nobody could see them.

At eleven o'clock next morning, Lieutenant Commander Rees arrived in a European model Ford to take Jessie shopping. He took her to a larger town near the air base where, he said, most of the families of base personnel did their shopping. Before turning her loose in the shops, however, he took her to lunch at a small bistro that served mostly Italian food, including pizza. Normally Jessie was very fond of pizza, but it was going to be a while before she stopped associating the smell of Italian food with the heartstopping terror of that phone call from her mother, telling her that her husband had come back from the dead after eight years.

She ordered a small antipasto and a diet soda, and since the weather was unusually sunny and warm for April, they chose one of the small tables outdoors on the sidewalk.

Lieutenant Commander Rees didn't mess around. He stabbed a fork into his baked ziti, then asked Jessie straight-out how things were going with her and Tristan.

Jessie, being a true Southern woman, was all set to smile brightly and assure him that everything was *Fine, just fine,* but for some reason, didn't. Maybe it was something to do with the lieutenant commander's air of authority and self-assurance, which all military officers seemed to have, in her experience, and the fact that Jessie had barely known her own father growing up and was wanting to confide in somebody strong and wise, but all at once she found herself blurting out the truth.

"I don't know," she said. Her throat closed and she stared bleakly at her salad. "I don't know how it's going." She took a breath and belatedly fought for control. "I'm a nurse, I feel like I ought to have a better handle on this than I do. Hey, I'm used to taking care of tiny little babies. What do I know about how to deal with…with—"

"I'm not gonna lie to you," the lieutenant commander said in his brisk military way, matter-of-factly munching a bite of ziti. "Lieutenant Bauer's got a rough road ahead of him, and so do you. It's not gonna be easy." Jessie nodded miserably, and after a moment he wiped his mouth with his napkin and went on. "The fact is, some POWs have an easier time adjusting than others. And sometimes their marriages don't survive the strain. Now, Mrs. Bauer, your husband is a man with a good, strong character to begin with—if he wasn't, he'd never have survived what he did as long as he did. If I were a betting man I'd have to put my money on him to make it back all the way. But that doesn't mean it's gonna be a cakewalk. He's gonna need you to be strong. And, he's gonna have to reach down inside himself and find some strength maybe *he* doesn't know he has.''

She took a breath and tried to smile. ''He always was strong. His parents were—well, his dad still is, I guess—strong people. If that helps. They're German, you know. His dad grew up not far from here.''

Rees nodded as he chewed. ''I did know that, yes.''

''He wants to go and visit the places where his mom and dad grew up. Do you think—''

''I think it's a good idea,'' Rees said, still nodding.

''Do you? I mean, are you sure he's…I don't know…''

''Okay, let me think how to say this.'' Rees put down his fork and pushed the plate aside, then leaned forward to command her eyes. ''Mrs. Bauer, what it sounds to me like, is that your husband might be looking for that strength I was talking about.''

''Do you think so?''

He nodded. ''I think what he's maybe doing is going to the source, trying to find out what it is that made him strong to begin with. Looking to find the extra stuff that's gonna get him through this.''

''The right stuff.'' Jessie tried her best to smile though her face felt as if it might crack under the strain.

Rees beamed back. ''Exactly.''

When the lieutenant commander took her back to the guest house several hours later, a second car and driver were there waiting for them. Rees helped Jessie unload her shopping bags, then handed her the keys to the Ford.

''You're on your own,'' he said, and laughed at her look of dismay. ''Hey, don't look like that, it's no different from driving in the states—it's not like they drive on the wrong side of the road. Just remember to convert miles to kilometers. It's a fairly straight shot back to the shopping center, in case you think of anything else you need. It'll be good practice for that trip you two are planning. You're gonna be the one driving, you know. In case you've forgotten, Lieutenant Bauer doesn't have a valid driver's license.''

"Oh Lord," Jessie whispered.

Al Sharpe drove Tristan back to the guest house that evening, around the same time as before, after doing a drive-by of the parking area to check for signs of news media invasion. But it appeared the Defense Department's stalling and diversionary press releases were having the desired effect.

It does feel easier this time, Tris thought as he made his way to the door. But still awkward, like the second time out with someone he'd met on a blind date. Like now things might start to get complicated.

And then he saw Jess coming toward him through the lobby, and he felt a bubble of forgotten pleasure burst somewhere inside him and pour warmth all through his chest that felt like a gulp of brandy on a cold day.

"Hey," she said, in that eager way he remembered so well.

"Hey," he said back to her, and she walked into his arms, and for a few aching moments it felt completely right again. She was the wife he remembered, and her body fit his in familiar ways, soft where it needed to be in spite of that long-boned angularity that had always particularly excited him. She was *Jess,* and against all odds, the same.

But then something, the fresh clean sunshiney smell of her hair, maybe, reminded him of where he'd been, and how much he was not the same Tristan *she* remembered, and he felt a coldness come over him and the darkness that was never far away creep back around his heart.

After too brief a time he put her away from him, and catching one of her hands, he brought it to his lips in mute apology. He held on to it while they walked through the guest house public rooms and out the back door, exchanging "How are you?"'s and "How was your day?"'s, hoping that would be enough to make up for his stiffness. He was so conscious of the feel of her hand, its shape and texture, warmth and moisture, every minute flaw and roughness in her skin, the fragile strength of bones and supple strength of muscles, that he could barely keep his mind on what she was saying to him.

They walked outdoors again, dodging bicyclists and joggers and dog walkers in the cool April evening while she told him about the shopping she'd done for him, and what Sammi June had said when she'd heard about that. When he started to tell her how bad he felt for not having called his daughter yet, Jess brushed his apology aside.

"Sammi June understands," she said, lifting her head with a little shake so her hair ruffled, then sort of resettled just behind her shoulders. "She's not a child. In fact, she's pretty well grown-up for eighteen—kind of like her momma was," she added with a sideways look and a tentative smile.

Tristan gave a dry snort of laughter. "I think that's what worries me—that I'm not gonna know what to say to her. I don't think I know how to be the father of a grown-up woman."

She threw him another look and said quietly, "It's not any easier for her, you know. As a grown-up woman, she doesn't know how to have a daddy, either." She walked on beside him for several more steps, head down. "But," she said, then paused and took a deep breath before finishing in a brave rush, "you *are,* and she *does,* and…well, dammit, the two of you are just gonna have to work it out between you…somehow.''

I shouldn't have said that, Jessie thought, when he didn't answer but just walked on, with his head slightly tilted as if he were listening to something only he could hear. *Definitely not as patient and understanding as I ought to have been.*

She was about to apologize when Tris's hand tightened around hers and he pulled her off the path. With newly sprouting grass underfoot and big old trees looming like protective uncles beside them, he turned and drew her around to face him. ''You're right,'' he said, his voice husky. ''I'm behaving like a damn coward. I'll call her tonight. As soon as we get back to the room. I promise.'' He brought her hand to his lips—something he'd been doing a lot, she noticed. But…never more than that. He still hadn't kissed her. ''Okay?''

Her throat tightened as she nodded. She tried, but couldn't stop herself from saying, ''She's changed, Tris. From what you remember. Of course she has. We all have. I have. Even though you say I haven't, that's just not true.'' Her voice broke just a little. ''There's nothing we can do about that. It just…is.''

''I know that.'' He studied her intently, and with her heart pounding so it was a moment or two before she realized his thumb was rubbing back and forth over her fingers—specifically, the third finger. He'd been holding her left hand, and the place he kept rubbing was the place where she'd once worn a wedding ring.

She turned her hand so she could see it, remembering clearly the day she'd taken off her wedding ring and put it away in her jewelry box. Remembering how she'd ached inside, and how for a long time she stared dry-eyed at the little blue velvet box and willed the tears to come, hoping they'd give her some kind of relief. ''It's at home,'' she said, aching the same way now. ''I put it away. I was in

New York when I found out you were alive. I flew straight here—I didn't have a chance—''

She halted then, because he was making a soft shushing sound. He'd enfolded her hand in both of his and was still holding it close to his lips. Above their hands, his eyes were closed, and she could see little knots of tension in his forehead and across his cheekbones. His face seemed tight and dark and closed, and she thought how different it was from the face she remembered…all warmth and charm, with an easygoing grin and laughing eyes.

Jolted, she shifted her gaze away from his face and found herself staring at his hands instead. But there was nothing familiar about them, either. They were a stranger's hands— bony and big-knuckled, striped with ropy tendons and irregular scars. Unbidden, the memories from the night before came rushing into her mind and collided with the image before her eyes, and suddenly she was imagining—no, *feeling*—those hard, alien hands touching her in the most intimate ways. Forgotten yearnings flooded her body with heat and she shuddered in spite of it, the way coming to a roaring fire when she was chilled clear through could sometimes make her shiver.

''That's okay. I think I'd like to be the one to put it back on you, anyway.'' He cleared his throat. ''Maybe I ought to buy you a new one. Something better.''

''The old one's just fine,'' Jessie said, giving her hand an indignant tug. Tristan laughed as he reclaimed it and they started back toward the guest house, their clasped hands swinging gently between them.

''Oh—we have a car,'' Jessie said as they were weaving their way through the clutter of tables on the patio, Tris maneuvering awkwardly with his cane. She told him about the Ford, and what Lieutenant Commander Rees had said about her being the one who'd be doing the driving.

''Oh Lord,'' he said, and Jessie burst out laughing.

''That's what I said.'' He was holding the door for her,

and she arched her eyebrows teasingly as she passed him. "You gonna be able to handle that?"

Her driving style always had just about driven Tris crazy, which was why he'd always done the driving whenever they'd gone anywhere together. Driving herself had been one of the things she'd had to get used to doing every time her husband was sent away—and cheerfully given up again when he came home. It was just one of the realities of being a military wife, of course, learning to be completely self-sufficient during her husband's deployments, then cheerfully handing the reins back over to him when he came home. Something they all learned to deal with.

Only, she thought, I doubt very many wives ever had to adjust to a husband's return after a deployment of eight years.

"I guess that remains to be seen," Tristan said. "Has your driving improved any since I've been gone?"

"There's not a thing the matter with my driving, and never was," Jessie said indignantly, punching him smartly on the arm.

"Ow!" He feigned outrage, then grinned at her, a ghost of his old self. And she grinned back, irrationally, idiotically delighted with that small, bantering exchange.

They had dinner in the privacy of Jessie's room again, pork chops and applesauce and corn bread stuffing this time, with cherry pie for dessert. More of Tristan's favorites, and he tried his best to do them justice, he really did, even though his appetite was still a long way from what it should have been.

"You trying to fatten me up?" he said in the teasing tone that had made her smile, rolling a cherry around on his tongue and marveling at the tart-sweet miracle of it.

"You bet I am," she replied smugly, then paused to give the forkful of pie that had been on its way to her mouth a long, sad look. "Only, I think the wrong one of us is gonna end up puttin' on weight.'' She put the fork down on the plate with a sigh.

"You look great to me,'' Tristan said, and saw her cheeks warm with a quick flush of pink. He went on looking at her, unable to take his eyes from her, remembering the times he'd watched that same flush creep across her chest, her breasts…her belly…and her whole body lush and blooming in the aftermath of lovemaking like a sun-drenched rose. Remembering what it had felt like to hold her, his body entwined with hers and her warmth soaking into his very bones.

He saw her looking back at him, cheeks glowing like Georgia peaches—remembering how she'd hated it when he'd said that to her…about the peaches. Long ago. And he thought, *This is now—not long ago. She's here and she's real, not a memory, not imagination.* My wife. *I could be lying with her now, making love to her in that big bed, enjoying her warmth and her softness…*

Then came the thought, *No, Tristan, you couldn't. Because she may be real, but you're sure as hell not.*

The truth was, though the thoughts, the memories, the desires were all there, they were only in his head. From the neck down he was just a tangle of muscle, bone and sinew, without warmth or feeling. Once upon a time he'd learned to survive by separating his mind from his body, and both of those from his emotions, and he'd been that way for so long, he didn't know how to start putting himself back together again.

He swallowed the bite of cherry pie and said, "We should call Sammi June,'' forcing the bittersweetness past the tightness of his throat. "Think she'd be in about now?''

Jess put down her fork with a clatter, snatched up her napkin and dabbed at her lips with it as she twisted around to look at the clock on the nightstand. "Um…lemme see, it's Monday…if she doesn't have a class she could be in her room studying. We can give it a try.''

He watched her make the call, standing beside her as she sat on the edge of the bed with her little pocket address book in one hand and the phone tucked between her jaw and shoulder. He watched her supple fingers punch in numbers, preparing himself, distancing himself from the remembered tug of a little girl's arms around his neck…the feel of a small grubby hand creeping into his. He listened to Jess's voice, speaking to someone in a thickening Southern accent, asking if Sammi June was there. He listened, preparing…arming himself with the images in the photo album Jess had given him, of a lovely young woman in a ball gown, smiling confidently, her tiara worn at a rakish tilt atop casually upswept blond hair.

"Hang on just a minute, hon'," Jess was saying, "there's somebody here wants to talk to you." With an abrupt, almost angry thrust, she handed the phone to Tris.

He took it calmly; his new crooked smile was fixed firmly to his lips as. he put the receiver to his ear and said, "Hello…Sammi June?"

"Daddy?" A high, breaking voice. A little girl's voice.

Something burst, stinging, inside his head. He croaked, "Hey, baby girl…" Suddenly he was sitting on the edge of the bed with his elbows braced on his knees, head bowed, one hand shading his eyes. Dimly, thankfully, he heard Jess get up and go into the bathroom, as tears dropped from the end of his nose.

Chapter 5

Toddling along in the autobahn's slow lane at 100 kilometers per hour, Jessie flicked sideways glances alternately between the freshly plowed fields of the German landscape and Tris's silent profile. Reassured by the fact that he hadn't made any comments on her driving so far, she edged the Ford's speed up to 110 and settled back in the driver's seat.

"There, now—it's not so awful, is it?" she said lightly, flexing tense fingers on the steering wheel. She said it in a teasing way, but the truth was, she'd been a little annoyed by all the fuss over her driving, with herself more than with Tristan. It was true her driving had always given him fits, but that had been a long time ago. She'd been more than competent behind the wheel of a car for a good many years now, and there wasn't any reason in the world why she should start having doubts about her driving skills just because Tris happened to be sitting beside her. Okay, she'd never driven in a foreign country before, but as Lieutenant Commander Rees said, it wasn't as though this was England where they drove on the wrong side of the road. Interstate or autobahn, they both looked the same, and the signs were pretty much universal, so what was the big deal?

Why do I keep going back to where I was when I first met him? That was eighteen years ago. I'm not—I can't be that person now. It's not who I am.

"You're doin' okay." Tristan glanced at her and a grin flickered. "Long as you don't get us run over."

"I'm doin' 110!"

"Kilometers, darlin'—that's sixty-six miles an hour. That'd get you a ticket for obstructing traffic in Atlanta."

Jessie snorted. "Oh, well—Atlanta drivers are crazy, you can't go by them." She said it in a scoffing tone, but it was hard to hide a smile and a little shiver—of what, hopefulness? Encouragement? Optimism? It had been two days since the phone call to Sammi June, and although Tris still wouldn't stay the night with her, he seemed a little more like himself every day.

But he still hasn't kissed me.

Her heart gave a queer little bump at the thought. She glanced over at him, frowning, but he'd gone back to gazing out the window, silently watching the fields and billboards and the occasional town flash by.

The weather was holding fine and cool, and the sky was a clear and lovely blue between billows of puffy white clouds. It felt good to be out on the open highway, going somewhere together, just the two of them…almost like old times. *Freedom,* she thought, after the days of being confined to the guest house and the adjoining towns. And her throat tightened as she wondered what it must be like for Tristan, whose days since being rescued from an Iraqi prison had so far been spent almost entirely within the confines of a military hospital, in an unrelenting schedule of tests, therapies and debriefings.

She said softly, "It must seem so strange to you. After…"

He jerked his gaze away from the window, giving her his familiar half smile. "I was thinking how normal it feels."

"Normal! How is that possible?"

He shrugged. "I don't know, there was a period right at first when I was sort of in shock, I guess, when it didn't seem real. It was like it was a dream, and any minute I was going to wake up and I'd be back there…. I think I was afraid to believe it. But then…your brain makes some kind of adjustment or something, and where you are, no matter how crazy or terrible or impossible it is, *that* becomes your norm. Your brain adapts to whatever your reality is." He paused. "That's what people do, I guess. They adapt." His face darkened and he added, "Some better than others, obviously."

She held her breath, waiting for more, but he'd lapsed once again into silence, watching the world flash by the car windows.

You don't have to tell me about adapting, she thought as the lightness and optimism inside her suddenly congealed into a cold, gray lump of anger, and tears peppered her eyes. I know what it means to have the man you love, your husband and the father of your child, go away and then come back…go away and then come back. Go away and then *not* come back. I've had to go from being a dependent wife and stay-at-home mom to being a single parent and breadwinner. From a woman who deferred to my husband in every little thing to one who now, on a daily basis, holds the lives of the tiniest, sickest babies in my hands. Don't tell *me* what it is to adapt!

"Hey, now you're cookin'," Tristan said.

Blinking back the tears, Jessie glanced at the speedometer and saw that the needle was hovering around 140. Muttering a word her momma wouldn't have approved of, she eased up on the gas pedal while beside her Tris chuckled softly.

They left the autobahn behind sooner than she'd expected and quickly wound down through woods and hillsides dotted with grazing sheep and into a deep river valley bordered on both sides by vineyards. Now the road followed the river's twisting, looping path, criss-crossing it on medieval-looking bridges, passing through towns of picture-book yellow and white half-timbered houses on narrow, brick-paved streets. The houses all had roofs of slate tiles laid like fish scales, and some were decorated with carved wood or patterns in contrasting brick and stone. Here and there, climbing up walls or creeping across arches, Jess saw the pale-green tendrils of new grapevines.

She wished now that she didn't have to be the one driving. She wanted to be free to look and look and look. Instead, she had to content herself with glimpses snatched from bridge crossings and high points in the road, of the river and its traffic of stately white riverboats and great cargo barges. Vineyards covered both sides of the valley, from gently rolling plains to mountainsides so steep they seemed inaccessible except to mountain goats and eagles. And here and there, high on one of those mountains, above the slate rooftops of a town—and she would have missed them entirely if Tristan hadn't pointed them out for her—the ruins of medieval castles.

In one of those towns, one even smaller than all the rest, huddled on a spit of land that barely missed being an island where the river looped back upon itself, he instructed her to stop. She pulled into a parking area next to what appeared to have been a train station but was now a grassy park that meandered along the riverbank among new-leafed trees.

"Are you sure this is it?" Jessie asked, peering through the windows, searching signs attached to the quaint-looking hotels and restaurants that fronted on the river for the village's name. She'd been too busy reading warnings of rapidly decreasing speed limits to have noticed on the way into town.

"Has to be," said Tristan. He didn't bother to consult the road map that was spread across his lap; they already knew the town they'd come to find wasn't on it. No surprise—it was so small, he'd told her, it didn't have a single store, much less a post office. "That was Traben-Trarbach back there, and Dad said Wolf was on a piece of land where the river makes a loop. This must be it. Come on—let's see if we can find somebody to ask."

She turned off the engine and opened the car door. The coolness of the breeze surprised her—the bright April sunshine and intense blue sky were misleading—and she reached into the back seat for her coat. As she belted it around her—the same borrowed raincoat that had felt so inadequate in New York City—she watched Tristan maneuver himself and his cane out of the car, then shrug into his own jacket. He was wearing some of the clothes she'd bought for him—black cargo pants, a heather-toned turtleneck pullover bulky enough to camouflage his painful thinness. The jacket was sleek black leather. With the silver peppering his dark hair and a bit of a shadow on his jaws, he looked lean and dark and dangerous, and, Jessie thought, quite European. Sammi June would approve.

For herself, looking at him gave her a queer little kick under her ribs, and her pulse quickened. He looks so different, she thought, for maybe the thousandth time. He'd always been so *open,* so carefree, the quintessential American flyboy, wholesome and uncomplicated as apples. Now he looked…mysterious. Forbidding…exciting. Damned attractive, but…so very different.

She snagged her pocketbook from the back seat and hooked it over her shoulder and locked the car. She was pocketing the keys when she caught a glimpse of something that drove every disquieting thought from her mind—for a moment, anyway.

"Tris," she cried, "look—is that—are those..."

Tristan had already started toward the row of hotels and restaurants across the street. He turned to see what she was pointing at, then changed direction and came around the car to join her. "Those? What, you've never seen swans before?"

Too awed to answer, Jessie was edging closer to the riverbank, where, in the shallows just offshore, two huge white birds were nibbling and nuzzling among the reeds. She could see others now, too, on the river, gliding in graceful formation.

"Not like this, I haven't," she whispered as Tristan came up beside her. "I thought they were just in theme parks and zoos." She glanced at him and saw that he was grinning at her, amused at her naiveté, so mature himself, so superior—the old Tris. And the old Jessie might have felt embarrassed, young and a bit silly, but the Jessie she was now gave him a jab with her elbow and said, "And don't you try to tell me *you* have, either, mister. Aren't they the most beautiful thing you've ever seen?"

It was a moment before he answered, in a strangely thickened voice, "Not the *most* beautiful, no..."

She glanced at him and met his gaze for barely an instant before he turned. The naked hunger in his eyes shocked her.

Shaken, now, and jangling inside, she followed him across the parking lot. At that hour—late morning—in the middle of the week, there were no other people about, and since it was obviously too early in the season for tourists, Jessie wondered whether any of the business establishments that catered to them would even be open. Tris, however, appeared to have no such doubts. He chose the closest one, a small *Gasthaus* of yellow and white stucco decorated with carved half timbers, and a sign in front that was artistically hand-painted with heavily laden grapevines and crossed wineglasses. He stomped confidently up the steps to the front door and turned the handle.

The heavy wooden door opened onto dimness and silence. That is, until a voice, friendly but cracked and hoarse—a smoker's voice—called out to them in German.

Jessie's heart sank, but once again Tris wasn't the least bit deterred. "Ah," he said, catching Jessie's hand as he veered toward the voice, "yes, hello."

The owner of the voice, a middle-aged man with very little hair and great pouches under his eyes, came out from behind a high counter, stubbing out what appeared to be a hand-rolled cigarette on the way. Obviously accustomed to tourists of all nationalities, the man switched to slow and careful English.

"Yes. Please. Come in. May I help you?"

Jessie was surprised when Tris, instead of asking the directions they'd come for, took a stool at the counter and ordered them both glasses of wine.

"It's a courtesy," he murmured in an aside to her while their host was busy opening a bottle and filling their glasses—unusual little glasses with etched leaves on the bowl and stubby, twisty green stems. "Besides, this is what the place is known for. According to Dad, it's *all* it's known for. Can't very well visit without sampling the local product, can we?"

Jessie had never been that fond of wine, but she discovered she actually liked this one, a white wine somewhat on the sweet side. Since she was thirsty and it had been several hours since breakfast, she drained her glass rather quickly. Their host, who turned out to be a naturally gregarious fellow and obviously hungry for company, promptly refilled it before he went back to chatting amiably with Tris.

He told them his name was Sigfrid, and when Tris returned the favor along with a brisk handshake, beamed and said, "Ah—Bauer. You must be German, then, yes?"

When Tris explained that his father had grown up in that

very town, and asked if Sigfrid might have known him, the *Gasthaus* keeper reluctantly shook his head and explained that he himself was from Traben-Trarbach, all of ten kilometers down the road, and had only taken over the *Gasthaus* from his wife's family twenty years or so ago. He readily gave them directions to the town's only cemetery, though, and urged them to visit the *Kloster* while they were there.

"Kloster?" Jessie whispered when Sigfrid had slipped away with their Euros to make change. "Is that what I think it is?"

Tristan nodded. "The cloister—Dad told me about it. That's the local ruin. It's on the hilltop above town—Sigfrid says you can see the whole loop of the river from up there. Apparently they have outdoor concerts during summer tourist season and at harvest festival time, so you can drive most of the way, and it's an easy hike after that. Why, would you like to see it?"

Jessie twirled off her stool and was surprised to discover that she had quite a pleasant little buzz going from the wine. How many times, she wondered, had Sigfrid refilled her glass when she wasn't looking? "It's up to you," she said solemnly. Tris's only reply was a chuckle, which, along with the wine she'd drunk made something warm and shivery pool in her insides.

They said their farewells to Sigfrid, who followed them out the door to the accompaniment of what was apparently the German version of the Southerner's "Y'all come back, now, y'hear?"

Jessie was making her careful way down the steps ahead of Tristan when she noticed a series of wooden markers affixed to the stucco wall of the building. Each had the initials H.W. burned into it, followed by a four-digit number she thought must be a year. The topmost marker, several feet above her head, bore the number 1784. A foot or two below that was one marked 1993.

"What does 'H.W.' stand for?" she asked Sigfrid.

"Hochwasser," he answered unhelpfully, and it was Tristan who provided the translation.

"That's 'high water'—the mark where the water came to in that particular flood year."

Jessie stared at him. "You're kidding. You mean—" She looked at Sigfrid, who shrugged and muttered something, evidently the German equivalent of *"C'est la vie."*

"The river floods," Tristan said with the same shrug. "It's a narrow valley, and when conditions are right…hey, it's not that big a deal here. They expect it, and cope with it. Like Canadians and snow." He pointed to a marker halfway up the row. "This one, 1954—that must be the one Dad remembers. They lived—" he paused, then gestured toward a pair of windows high in the gable of the *Gasthaus,* two floors above the door "—right there."

Jessie gasped. "Right *here?* Your dad lived in this house?"

He gave another shrug. "Might have. I don't know which one, exactly, but he told me after the war his mother worked as a cook in one of the *Gasthauses* fronting the river, and they lived in a room upstairs." His dark smile flickered. "So at least they never went hungry. In the wintertime he walked to school in Traben-Trarbach. Summers he worked in the vineyards—gave whatever money he made to his mother. He left for Canada the year after the flood. He was eighteen then."

They waved a final goodbye to Sigfrid and went back to the car. There were others out enjoying the brisk sunshine now—a middle-aged woman walking a dog, a young mother with two small children bundled in sweaters and knit caps against the chilly wind. Jessie waved to them and got tentative—and surprised—little waves in return.

At Al Sharpe's suggestion, Jessie had asked the guest house kitchen to pack a small cooler with sandwiches and fruit for Tristan, who was almost constantly hungry and tended, Al had confided to her with a grin, to get testy when forced to wait for his meals. Still feeling the effects of the wine she'd drunk, Jessie wasn't at all hungry and nibbled on a plum while Tris downed a chunk of thick German wurst wrapped in a stubby bun and slathered with hot German mustard. Afterward she tossed bits of the bun to the swans, while Tris leaned on his cane and watched her with unreadable eyes and a crooked smile.

Back in the car, following Sigfrid's directions they turned uphill, passing through a tiny triangular town "square" where a statue of a wolf loomed menacingly from a bed of yellow daffodils. The narrow, brick-paved street wound past slender stone churches with tall slate steeples, and between yellow and white half-timbered houses with carved shutters. Here and there Jessie saw an elderly man or woman out in front of a house tending a postage-stamp-size garden. She waved at them all. In her mellow state she thought the town was enchanting—like a toy village. It reminded her of Disney movies—*Pinocchio,* maybe.

They found the cemetery easily. It was a rectangular plot enclosed by a thick green hedge located just at the edge of the town, before the vineyards began. Within this secluded lot, separated by immaculate gravel pathways, each gravesite was framed by a low curbing of concrete or stone, and inside each frame was a tiny garden, lovingly tended, with a carved headstone at one end. Armed only with a date, Tristan and Jessie wandered the gravel pathways until they found the gravestone they were looking for. It bore a simple cross, the name Hannah Bauer, and the dates: 1906-1975.

"There," Tris said. "That's my grandmother. Dad's mother."

"She wasn't very old," Jessie murmured. She found the child-size gardens enchanting. Kneeling to touch the fat purple stalk of a hyacinth bloom, she looked up at Tristan, silhouetted against the sky. "Who tends them?"

"The graves? Members of the families, mostly, I'd guess."

"But you don't have any family left here."

"I seem to remember Dad telling me he sends money to the church. They have somebody who takes care of it." His voice sounded faraway. He propped his cane against the headstone and took a throw-away camera out of his jacket pocket, snapped a picture, then dropped the camera back in his pocket. He picked up the cane, plainly ready to move on.

Jessie scrambled to her feet, brushing bits of gravel from the knees of her best gray wool slacks. "Where's your grandfather's grave? Is he buried here too?"

He shook his head. "He was killed in the war. I don't think Dad even knows where he's buried."

"You could probably find out. The government must know. Wouldn't they have some kind of record?" In her enthusiasm she didn't notice how distant he'd become.

"Unless they were destroyed. You have to remember, this country lost the war. Things were pretty chaotic toward the end and for a long time afterward. Anything to do with government or the military was in ruins."

Jessie nodded somberly, but it was a glorious spring day with cotton clouds drifting in a cobalt sky, the scent of new grass and hyacinths perfuming the air. Her head was pleasantly fogged with wine; the horrors of war—all wars—seemed far away.

They got back in the car and, once again following Sigfrid's directions, easily found the road that led to the ruins of the *Kloster,* which they could see now, rising out of a wooded knoll above the gently sloping vineyards. For most of the way the wide, paved road ran arrow straight between fields of well-groomed vines that were just beginning to send new tendrils curling along their wire supports. Past the vineyards, pavement gave way to dirt and gravel that had been washed and rutted by winter rains, and then that, too, ended at a heavy rope barrier looped between two low posts. Beyond the barrier a grassy track angled upward along the hillside and disappeared into the woods.

Jessie stopped the car with its bumper nudging the rope barricade and peered through the windshield. "Oops—far as we go," she said, but Tristan had his door open and was already maneuvering himself out of the car. She hastily shut off the motor and scrambled after him. "You want to *walk* up there?"

He paused to look at her. "You want to see it, don't you?"

"Well, sure I do, but—"

"Then it looks like we're gonna have to walk."

"But what about—I mean, are you sure you're up to it?"

"Jessie." His voice was gentle and very soft. "I'm fine."

"But, your knee—"

No longer gentle, he snapped, "Dammit, I said I'm *fine.*"

But there were no clouds in her sky this morning. She hooked her arm around his and gave it a quick hug, flashed him a grin and in a voice that was pure Georgia, said, "Darlin', am I motherin' you?"

Thoroughly ashamed, Tristan let out his breath in a whispering chuckle, and with it went a little of the tension that had been building in him since the cemetery. Something about seeing his grandmother's name carved in cold gray stone, with pansies and hyacinths clustered all around... He didn't begin to understand the tension, and what's more, he didn't intend to try.

"Yeah, you are," he said, and gave her his poor excuse for a smile.

The fact that it seemed to be enough for her humbled him. She smiled back at him, her nose crinkling across the bridge in that way he loved, and he felt her body snuggle close to him, her breast nudging full and soft against his arm. His heart thumped and his belly warmed, and he eased himself out of her embrace as gently as he could and took her hand instead.

She's more than a little bit buzzed, he thought. *And happy.* After the fear and tension of the past few days, her happiness—the sparkle in her amber eyes, the glow in her cheeks—made his throat ache. She reminded him of warm, sunshiny things. She was full-blown roses and ripe peaches and hot sand beaches. And he…he was still darkness. He was rain clouds and 2:00 a.m. nightmares and cold empty rooms. Please God, he prayed, don't let me do anything to spoil this for her. Not today.

The ruins of the cloister, blunt gray fingers of stone thrusting into view above the emerald-draped shoulder of the hill, reminded her, she said, of a fairy-tale castle. A hedgehog playing dead in the grass beside the path thrilled her—she'd never seen one before, and it was just like the one in Disney's *Alice in Wonderland.* She cried out in surprise and delight, like a little kid finding packages on Christmas morning, over the spires of pink foxgloves rising out of the slate shale hillside on the edge of a vineyard. And when they reached the top of the hill and she saw the blue ribbon of the river far below them, curving and looping between mountain slopes covered in a pale-green quilt of vineyards, fairy-tale villages nestled along its banks, she leaned against a thick stone wall and gave a soft and, he thought, rather wistful sigh.

"It's so beautiful," she murmured, as the wind picked up the sides of her hair and made them flutter like the wings of a butterfly. The chilly air had turned the tip of her nose pink and made her eyes glisten…but looking at her made his own eyes sting and burn, and after a moment he had to look away. "I don't know how your father could stand to leave it."

"There wasn't much of a future for him here," Tristan

said, more harshly than he meant to. "Unless he wanted to work in the vineyards."

She threw him a quick, abashed look that jolted him with a reminder of his vow not to blight her happiness. "Oh—right. I suppose not. Your dad worked for Boeing, didn't he? He was a mechanic—for airplanes."

Wanting to make amends, Tristan levered himself onto the low stone wall she was leaning against and propped his cane beside him. "Dad always did love airplanes. The only thing he ever really wanted to do was fly, and when he got to Canada that was the first thing he did—joined the Canadian Air Force. He was going to be a bush pilot after that, but then he met my mother. She had other ideas—far as she was concerned, flying the Canadian bush was way too dangerous for the father of her child." He'd told her the story before, of course, many times—about how his dad had gotten the job with Boeing, and his parents had moved to Seattle, where Tristan was born. He told it to her again now, and she listened with held breath and avid eyes, as if she were hearing it for the first time.

"Dad told me," he said, gazing at the thickly wooded hillside below the ruin, "that when he was a kid, right after the war, he and some of his buddies found the wreckage of a plane in these woods—he thinks it was an American fighter plane, but he couldn't swear to that. He said they used to go there to play. And look for souvenirs, I guess. Dad said from that moment on he dreamed of flying fighters someday."

"Did he ever regret it?" Jessie asked. And there was a thickness in her voice that told him he'd already failed somehow to keep his secret vow to her. He glanced at her, and though her head was turned away from him and he couldn't see her face, he knew his cloud had covered her sun. "Not being a pilot, I mean."

"He says not," he said. "He always said Mom was

right, and that he probably wouldn't have lived to be my father if she hadn't made him quit when she did."

"And then, he had you to fulfill his dream for him, didn't he." She tried to say it lightly, but that was a mistake. With no gentleness to soften them, the words sounded sharp and edgy. As if to deny them, or—who knows?—maybe trying to recapture the joy she could feel slipping away from her, like reaching for a butterfly that was floating off into the sky beyond her reach, she pushed away from the wall he was sitting on and went dancing across the rubble-strewn grass.

"Hey, you have a camera, you should take a picture of this—the ruins, the view. Sammi June would love it. It's incredible...." And she was scrambling up a tumbled spill of stone to where a lonely section of wall still stood, framing an arched window opening. "Look here, you can see everything—the town, the river—and there's a boat, one of those big white ones. Tris—let me have the camera—quick, before it goes around the bend."

He got up slowly, not wanting to remind her that towering stone walls had grim associations for him, but not wanting to dim the brightness of her mood more than he already had, either. Though the fatigue he couldn't seem to shake was catching up with him and his knee had begun to ache, he couldn't help but smile as he watched her pick her way over the stones, searching for hand- and footholds until she'd managed to climb into the window opening. Sitting there in grinning triumph, she waved at him, then held out her hand and wiggled her fingers, demanding that he hand her his throw-away camera. He felt a curious *lifting,* as if, he thought, there was a new and different Tristan inside him somewhere trying to break out.

He took the camera out of his coat pocket and snapped a picture of her, framed in the window opening with the sun shining through her hair. She said, "Oh, *Tris,*" and laughed in an embarrassed way, and he remembered that she never had understood how beautiful she was.

He went over to the wall and reached up to give her the camera. She took it from his hand, and at the same time tried to stand up on the wide, uneven window ledge. He managed to get the word "Careful—" out of his mouth before her foot slipped on a mossy stone and instead of standing up she gave a startled squawk and came sliding down the wall practically on top of him.

He didn't have time to brace himself, but even if he had, Jess was not exactly a tiny woman, and his strength wasn't even close to what it once had been. She hit him full in the chest. His arms went around her and they went down together—fortunately missing any significant stones—and he was flat on his back in the soft spring grass and she was lying on top of him, from her chest all the way down to the tips of her toes.

There was a moment of shocked silence, and then she gasped, "Oh…oh my God. Tris, I'm sorry. I'm so sorry. Are you all right? Did I hurt you?"

Brown eyes, so well remembered, now dark pools of dismay, gazed down into his. Flushed cheeks dusted with a sheen of gold hovered above him, so close he could feel their warmth on his own face. Even through several layers of clothing he could feel her heart thumping—or was that his?

He felt the lifting sensation again, more powerful this time. And then something inside him seemed to burst and heat flooded his body like a fever.

"I'm fairly sure I'll survive," he drawled, and she had barely begun to laugh when he lifted up his head and kissed her.

Chapter 6

It had been so many years. His body had forgotten the sensations of desire…of lust. He was like a wild thing set free, dazed at first, into frozen stillness…then all at once leaping blindly toward his freedom. The warm tumescence of her lips shocked him; his breath stilled as he lightly skimmed them as if in awe of a miracle.

He felt her breathing catch, and the smallest pulling back…a tiny hesitation. He felt his fingers sink into the sun-warmed pool of her hair, and the pressure of her mouth on his increase. Her lips softened…and opened, like a gift.

He felt thought and reason leave him and go soaring beyond his reach, and it was like watching an eagle rise toward the sun. All he knew was brightness and warmth…then blinding light and burning heat. Shuddering, like a man consumed by fever, he wasn't even aware of where and how his hands touched her. Like a starving man, he filled his mouth and arms and his very soul with her, and despaired because it couldn't possibly be enough.

He didn't know what brought him back. Her soft moan,

perhaps, flowing like a whispered promise from her mouth
into his. He became aware of small things—the crisp cool
feel of her raincoat in his hands...the winey taste of her
mouth and the smell of crushed grass. He realized that she
was no longer lying on top of him, that he'd rolled her
over, half under him, and that one of his legs was wedged
between hers, tightly pressed against her soft feminine
places. She moaned again, and he withdrew from her
slowly, clawing his way toward reason like a drowning man
swimming toward the light.

Lying back in the grass, he covered his eyes with his
forearm and whispered, "God...Jess. I'm sorry. I didn't
mean... I don't know what—"

"You better *not* be apologizing," she said, choked and
breathless. Her fist poked him in the chest. "It was about
damn *time* you kissed me."

He lifted his arm just far enough so he could see her.
She'd raised herself on one elbow in order to look down
at him, and though her words were brave, even defiant,
even with the light sky behind her it was impossible to miss
the evidence of his mishandling...the fear and uncertainty
in her eyes...the glistening, crushed look of her mouth.

He lifted his hand and touched her lower lip with his
thumb, stroking the glaze his own mouth had left there
across the soft, swollen pillow. His jaws cramped and his
mouth watered, and newly awakened desire coiled in his
belly like a captive beast raging against fragile tethers. He
took a deep breath and sat up, drawing in his feet and
resting his arms on his knees as he pivoted away from her.
Words fought their way through the chaos in his mind.

"That's not...the way," he said, his voice constricted
and hoarse. "That's sure as hell not the way I wanted to
kiss you. God help me, Jess, I—" he waved a helpless
hand, intensely conscious of her, crouched there in
wounded silence behind him "—I tried to warn you. I don't
have the judgment...the control...the strength—I don't

know what to call it. I just know I don't know myself...the way I am. I can't...trust myself. Neither should you.''

"You'd never hurt me." Her voice sounded shocked... appalled. He could feel her shaking. "You'd never do that. *Never.*"

He swiveled back to her, and after a long moment's silence, lifted a hand and laid it gently along her jaw. His thumb again stroked back and forth, just once and ever so lightly—a feather's touch—across her lips. "I just did," he said softly, and saw a tear quiver on the edge of her eyelid. Her throat moved convulsively against his hand. Cold with exhaustion, he went on gently. "I won't ever do that to you again, I can promise you that."

"But what—" she licked her lips and tried again "—what if I want you to?"

He gazed at her for a long silent moment before he took his hand away, shaking his head. "You don't know," he mumbled indistinctly as he turned.

Rebuffed, outraged and vulnerable, Jessie thought, *I don't know?* And you think *you* do? She wanted to shout at him, Look, Mr. Rip Van Winkle, you've been dead for eight years, and *you're* calling all the shots? What *is* this?

What was that? He'd never kissed her like that before— *never.* Not even in the first dizzy days of courtship when his slightest touch could turn her into a mindless bundle of simmering heat and thumping desire. It had scared her, sure it had. First, because it had made her feel things she'd never felt before. But—to be honest—mostly because she'd known instantly that the man kissing her wasn't the man she'd known, the husband she'd loved, the lover she remembered. It had been the most powerful, mind-blowing kiss she'd ever received in her life...*from a stranger.* What the hell was she supposed to do with that? How was she supposed to feel?

"We'd better be getting back," Tris said. He was standing over her, one hand extended to help her up.

Angry, confused and bewildered, she gave him her hand and let him pull her to her feet, then stared, hot-eyed, at his back as he bent down to retrieve the camera. He dropped it into his pocket and reached for his cane, and her heart turned over when she saw his face. How gaunt and drawn he looked...there were hollows in his cheeks and deep shadows around his eyes.

Remorse and misery flooded her; she sniffed desperately and pivoted away from him before he could see her face. She felt his eyes on her but he didn't say anything, and they walked side by side down the trail to the car in shimmering, electric silence.

When they reached the car, Jessie asked Tristan in a choked voice if he wanted another sandwich. He shook his head and instead held out his hand.

"Give me the keys."

"What?" Her head was still fuzzy—with suppressed tears, not wine—and it was a moment before she understood. Then her mouth dropped open and she stared at him. "The *car* keys? *No.* No way. Tris, you're not driving."

"Yes, I am." His tone was stern, his jaw implacable; very much the old Tristan.

"But—you don't have a license. And you haven't—"

"Driving isn't something you forget," he said grimly. "I'm in better shape to drive than you are. You've had too much to drink. Come on—hand 'em over."

She gave an outraged gasp. "Too much to— I have *not.* What, a couple glasses of wine? Besides, I already drove—"

"Half a bottle. And you never could handle wine, remember?" His voice had gentled; his eyes caught and held hers with an unrelenting gaze that somehow both demanded and implored.

She drew a shuddering breath and said tightly, "What about your license? And your knee?"

"My knee's fine—it's my left one, anyway. The license

won't be a problem unless somebody stops us, and I've no intention of that happening. Come on, Jess.'' He grinned crookedly. ''I'm gonna have to drive again sometime. Might as well be now.''

It's that grin, she told herself as she reluctantly handed him the keys to the Ford. *I never could resist him smilin' at me; old behavior patterns are just damn hard to break. Anyway, I probably* have *had too much to drink. It's better this way.*

But she didn't feel the slightest bit buzzed, pleasantly or otherwise, as she settled into the passenger seat and buckled her seat belt. She felt battered and emotionally frail.

Her misgivings began to fade, though, as they made their way slowly back along the river. Since they were backtracking and very little was required from her in the way of directions, she was free to watch Tristan—though surreptitiously under the pretense of sight-seeing so as not to annoy him—as he familiarized himself with the car and the process of driving. All signs of tiredness had magically disappeared; he sat straight and alert in the driver's seat, and his hands lingered over the controls with an almost caressing touch. He handled the steering wheel with the gentle assurance of an experienced mother bathing a new baby, while his eyes held a joyful light she hadn't seen in them since his release. How must it feel, she wondered as tears sprang to her own eyes, to be in control of your personal self again, after so many years?

They stopped to eat in one of the larger river towns, in a restaurant that no doubt catered to tourists during the summer and autumn harvest season. They ate on an enclosed deck overlooking the river where they were the only diners at that hour, far too late for lunch, yet early for dinner. Jessie ordered Wiener schnitzel, which was the only thing on the menu she was sure she recognized. Tristan chose something that turned out to be pork chops—huge, thick and smothered in sauerkraut and browned potatoes.

He ate every bite, and part of Jessie's dinner besides, while he told her what he knew of his father's boyhood in the vineyards and on the river.

He looks so normal, she thought. Right then he seemed almost himself, even flirting with the plump middle-aged waitress until she blushed like a rose. And was it wishful thinking, or had he even gained a little weight? Were the hollows in his cheeks a little less deep? Were his eyes a little less haunted? Dared she hope it might be so easy?

Like an alarm going off somewhere in a distant room, she heard the faraway voice of Lieutenant Commander Rees. *I'm not gonna lie to you…he's got a rough road ahead of him and so do you. It's not gonna be easy.* The last of the afternoon's winey glow faded away, and though she tried hard to suppress it, a shiver ran through her.

Traffic was light on the autobahn, and although Jessie's heart did a little skip when Tristan moved into the fast lane first thing, she told herself it was only what she'd have expected him to do, especially after the cracks he'd made about her speed—or lack of it. She tried not to look at the speedometer, but she couldn't help it. And her heart began to beat faster as the needle crept relentlessly around the dial.

"Tris…" she breathed when it reached 130…then 140.

"Relax," he drawled, "no speed limit here, remember?"

"I know, but—" Her body tensed involuntarily as the speedometer needle edged up to 150. *"Tris—"* This time it came out sharp and scared as another car loomed ahead, growing larger at an alarming rate. She held her breath while he calmly tipped the blinker and moved into the next lane, and went around the other car as if it were standing still. "Tristan," she ground out on the exhalation, *"Dammit, slow down."*

His only answer was a confident chuckle, and she threw him a furious glare. And then the anger left her like the air from a popped balloon, and she knew all at once that what she really was, was afraid. And that it wasn't the car's speed that was scaring her…not anymore. It was something she saw in Tris's face, in the profile that had been so familiar to her but was now subtly changed by a nose that had been broken at least once. The profile that used to make her heart skip a beat and her pulse quicken, as she rode beside him in the sweet, sultry darkness of a Georgia summer night, country music thumping on the stereo…. The profile that was still strong and arrogant, even aristocratic in spite of the nose, teeth bared in a smile, a comma bracketing his mouth and an irresistible fan of wrinkles at the corner of his eye. But now there was something dark about the smile, and the eyes held a glitter of excitement…and danger.

The speedometer needle wobbled unsteadily—she couldn't see the number through the mist of her fear. But she could feel the vibrating of the car's engine in her bones. "Tris—" she cried out, trembling. She didn't know what was happening to him. To her shame, she had begun to cry.

When she thought she wouldn't be able to stand the terrible tension another second, she saw speed limit warning signs flash past through the shimmering haze of her tears. Tristan muttered something under his breath and the car's engine vibrations eased. The speedometer needle swiveled slowly back to 120. And as it fell, Jessie's fury returned.

Helpless to stop it, unable to express it, she ranted silently to herself: *What was that? What did he just do? What am I supposed to do with that?*

Because at the same time she felt so angry, she also felt guilty for it. How could she be angry at somebody who was back from the dead, for God's sake? This was a man who'd spent the past eight years in an Iraqi prison, Lord only knew what they'd done to him there, and she was supposed to be patient with him, wasn't she? Give him time, they'd told her.

But, a tiny voice whispered in the back of her mind, what if Tris isn't going to give *himself* time?

I don't think I can do this. It played over and over inside her head as she sat in furious, trembling silence and Tristan drove the rest of the way back to the guest house sedately within posted speed limits. *I don't think I can do this.*

It was a lone voice at first, but gradually she came to realize that what was going on in her head wasn't a monologue or a mantra any longer, but rather an argument. And what the dissenting voice—was it Momma's? Tristan's? Her own? Who knows?—anyway, what it was saying was, *Sure you can. Suck it up, girl. If he could survive eight years in prison, you sure as hell can handle his return.*

Okay, but we have to talk about this, she argued back desperately. I have to get him to talk to me about what happened to him. I just have to. And soon. This can't wait much longer. Tonight. We'll talk tonight.

But when they turned into the guest house parking lot, she realized that any confrontation with Tristan was going to have to wait a little while longer. The previously almost empty lot was suddenly full of vehicles, many of them vans and panel trucks bearing satellite dishes and multiple antennae on their rooftops. The world news media had caught up with them.

"Oh no," she murmured.

"Looks like the honeymoon's over." Tristan's smile barely stretched the hollows in his cheeks as he maneuvered the car into a vacant spot on the edge of the lot, well outside the huddled circle of media vehicles and equipment. "They were bound to find us sooner or later. The military's done a helluva job to hold 'em off this long." He turned off the motor and looked over at Jessie. "Ready to face the music?"

The skin under his eyes looked bruised. Seeing that, she felt something swell inside her and a shivering sensation crawl under the skin along her back, neck and chest. She knew what it was, she'd felt it before: maternal outrage. If she'd been a momma wolf her hackles would have been rising. Or, in her case, maybe a more apt comparison would be one of Granny Calhoun's hens fluffing up her feathers so as to look twice her actual size, ready to defend her nest against all comers.

"Tris, you're exhausted," she said as he opened his door, "maybe we can sneak in the back way."

He shook his head, already easing his bad knee over the sill. "I'm not gonna go skulking around like a coward."

Outside the car he paused to steady himself with a hand on the door frame, then leaned over to pick up his cane from the back seat. When he straightened again his skin looked gray, but Jessie saw him, with a visible effort, pull himself up to a military stance, and a muscle tighten in his jaw. "Gonna have to face them sometime. Might as well do it and get it over with."

Duty calls, she thought, rekindling an old resentment. And at the same time a familiar sense of pride. Taking his arm as they crossed the parking lot, she could feel tremors of exhaustion and weakness racking his body, and yet she knew he'd die before he'd ever admit it. And looking at his rock-hard features, nobody would ever guess he was holding himself together by sheer strength of will. But that's how he did it, she thought. That's how he's been surviving. *Sheer willpower.*

Not even willpower, though, could keep him from faltering when the mass of reporters spotted them and descended like a human tidal wave. She felt his body flinch as if from a physical blow. Glancing up at him, she saw that his face had turned a sickly bluish white—a familiar phenomenon from her experience as a nurse and one she knew was usually a prelude to somebody hitting the floor.

And with that thought, there it was again, that swelling, feather-fluffing, hackles-raising momma-bear fury, and without even thinking about it, she had taken an iron grip on Tristan's arm, and with her free arm thrown out like an icebreaker, was ploughing him through the river of pushing, shoving reporters, thrusting microphones and whirring, clicking cameras.

Having achieved the guest house steps, she turned to face the crowd, and as she did she was shoving Tristan behind her, shielding him from them with her own body. Somehow, he'd gathered the strength to lift his hand to ask for quiet. The din subsided, but before Tristan could begin to speak, Jessie heard her own voice—firm, forceful and calm—the one she used to reassure frightened parents in the NICU.

"I know how anxious y'all are to hear from my husband. I just want to ask you to please be patient and respect our privacy a little while longer. Lieutenant Bauer has had a long day. I know he'll be a lot better able to answer your questions after he's had some rest. Now, if you would…please…" Her voice faltered, and she felt Tris's hands on her shoulders—lending her his strength, she wondered, or drawing from hers?

She heard his deep, quiet voice, and a thrill rushed through her. "I just want to thank you all, and let you know I'll try to answer your questions in due time. I believe the base's public affairs officer is planning a press conference before I leave for the states, if you—"

"Lieutenant Bauer, just one question," someone shouted. "How does it feel to be back from the dead?"

Again she felt his hands tighten on her shoulders. "It feels…great." She knew from his voice that he had to be grinning, and that it could only be one of those great big honest-to-God old-fashioned Tristan grins she loved so much. Her eyes filled with tears.

A reporter shouted, "Mrs. Bauer, would you mind if we asked *you* a few questions?"

She hadn't expected that. Not sure what she should do,

she tilted her head back and glanced up at Tristan. He gave
her a nod and his skewed half smile, but the tiredness in
his eyes seemed bottomless. She put her hand over his
where it rested on her shoulder and gave it a squeeze.
"Why don't you go on?" she murmured for his ears only.
"I don't mind stayin' a minute."

He hesitated, then murmured back, "If you're sure…"

"I'll be fine. Go on—*go*." She turned back to the crowd
of reporters with a determined smile. A moment later she
felt him leave her, and there was a tingling coldness on her
shoulders where his hands had been.

"Mrs. Bauer—when did you find out your husband was
alive?"

"Mrs. Bauer, Mrs. Bauer—what's it been like to have
your husband come back from the dead?"

"How is he feeling, Mrs. Bauer?"

"When do you plan to—"

"First of all," Jessie began in a loud voice, holding up
her hands, "y'all have to understand, this has been hap-
penin' awfully fast. I don't think it's really hit me yet."
There was a ripple of sympathetic laughter. Somewhere
behind her she heard the guest house door open and close.
She paused, and the crowd grew hushed, listening as she
went quietly on. "All I know is, my husband is alive, he's
here with me, and very soon now he's gonna be back home
where he belongs. It might have taken a while longer than
I'd have liked for it to, but the good Lord has answered an
awful lot of prayers."

In the genteel stillness of the guest house lobby, Tristan
paused to listen to the rise and fall of Jessie's voice…the
occasional rustle of reporters' laughter. *Jess's voice.* It was
hers, yes…the one he remembered but different, somehow.
Quietly confident, matter-of-fact. It came to him suddenly,
what it reminded him of: the voices he heard every day at
the hospital, voices of strength and comfort and encour-

agement. The cheerful, no-nonsense, reassuring voices of the nurses.

Instead of heading for the elevator, he turned as if drawn by a magnet to one of the multipaned windows that overlooked the front walk. From there, hidden from view by the curtains, he watched his wife face the crowd of reporters alone. And maybe it was seeing her from a distance like that, and hearing her voice that was so much the same and yet so different, but something in his perception suddenly shifted—like one of those optical illusions where one moment you're looking at a face right side up, and the next second it's upside down. *She has changed. She's not the same Jessie I left behind.*

He hadn't really thought she would be…had he? He'd prepared himself, or thought he had, for her to have gotten older…even to have found someone else. Then he'd found her looking just the way he'd pictured her in his mind, still slim, sunshine blond and beautiful, still a little bit awkward and eager to please him. Just the way he remembered her. Now he knew he'd been kidding himself. Of course she'd changed—in eight years, how could she not? But she hadn't gotten older; what she'd done was *matured.* And she hadn't found someone else. She'd found herself.

Watching the tall, self-assured woman—a stranger to him—out there on the guest house steps, he felt a stabbing sense of loss. His chest filled with the pressure of grief— for the young, accommodating girl he'd left behind and remembered so well…grief, too, for the impossible dream he'd clung to like a life preserver and that had kept him alive for so long.

Then, as he watched the beautiful, confident woman on the steps, her hair haloed by the television crews' spotlights, he felt something new come and take root in the empty place those losses had left inside him, and slowly begin to grow. *Respect. Admiration.* And the pressure in his chest was no longer grief. It was pride.

* * *

When Jessie slipped quietly into her room sometime later, she was hoping Tris might have gone to sleep. Instead she found him sitting in a straight-backed chair beside the table. A tissue spread on the tabletop near his elbow held a neat pile of orange and banana peels. The TV was tuned to a soccer game.

"Everybody gone?" he asked as he turned off the television set, stifling a yawn.

She dropped her pocketbook beside the dresser and nodded. "I think so. For now, anyway. I imagine they'll be back in the mornin'." Still flushed and, if she wanted to be entirely truthful, just a wee bit *exhilarated,* she took a deep breath and lifted her fingers to rake them through her hair. "Whoo—hope I don't have to do *that* again. That was somethin' else."

"I think you'd better get used to it," Tristan said dryly. "I wouldn't worry about it, though—you handled it beautifully." There was something in the way he looked at her…something soft and golden in his eyes…that made her pulse quicken.

She went toward him, wishing she could just walk right up to him and put her arms around him, and that he would put his arms around her and pull her into the vee of his legs and nestle his face against her breasts. Once, long ago, it would have been a natural, easy thing.

"You don't look very comfortable," she said, reaching out a hand to touch his hair, lightly nudging it off his forehead with a finger while her throat ached with longing. "Don't you want to lie down? Put your feet up, rest your knee awhile?"

"Naw…if I do that I'm afraid I'll fall asleep. I need to call Al…have him come get me. Just wanted to make sure the crowd was gone." His voice sounded gravelly. His eyes searched her face as if she were someone he'd just met and he was trying to commit her face to memory.

Her mouth went dry and her tongue thickened. The

words slurred as she said, "Tris, you're so tired. Why don't you stay here tonight?"

"You know I can't do that."

"No, I do not know that." Primed with new confidence and resolve, she grabbed the second chair, turned it around and sat in it, facing him with her knees almost but not quite touching his. "I know you *tell* me you can't, because of some fear you have in your mind that you might do something that's gonna shock me or hurt me or…I don't know, drive me screamin' from the room. Which, if you want to know the truth, I think is just plain ridiculous."

"Jess—"

"No. You listen to me. In the first place, in case you've forgotten, I am a nurse, and while I might work in a NICU now, I've done rotations in psych wards. I've handled episodes of PTSD before. Believe me, there's nothin' you could do that's gonna shock me. But Tris—" she reached for his hands and enfolded them, stiff and resisting, in hers "—what's more important is, I'm your *wife*. You understand me? *I am your wife.* That is for better or worse and sickness and health, in case you don't remember the vows we said to one another. You don't get to protect me from this. This has happened to both of us, dammit. You are not allowed to shut me out."

Something dripped from her nose. She dashed it furiously away, then stared down at the moisture on the back of her hand. She couldn't imagine how it had come to be there. She hadn't known she was crying.

"Jessie…" Now it was his hand lifted to her face, his fingers wiping away tears.

She caught his hand and held it pressed against her cheek. Eyes closed, she said in a fierce, choking voice, "Look, all I'm asking you to do is sleep here, in this bed. I'm not planning on ravishing your bones, if that's what's worryin' you."

"Bones would be the operative word." His voice was bumpy with amusement.

She opened her eyes and glared at him through tears. "Really? I'd hoped it was ravish."

Hunger flared in his eyes and was quickly extinguished, as if someone had slammed a lid over a fire.

If she only knew, he thought, how close to the truth that might be. Since this afternoon he no longer had any doubts that his normal masculine urges, dormant for so long, were alive and stirring again. It was his ability to control those urges he wasn't sure he could trust, and until he was sure, he didn't intend to put himself—or her—to the test.

"If I stay," he said, closing his eyes, "you have to promise me…"

"Yes—what? Anything." Her hands clutched his eagerly, and his lips twitched into a patient smile.

"You have to promise you won't touch me if I, uh, seem to be—if I'm, you know…having a nightmare. Don't try to wake me up, okay? Whatever you do." He was thinking of the nurse he'd given a fat lip to just the night before, striking out blindly at an imagined attacker. He lifted her hands to his lips and looked at her gravely over them. "If I start yelling or thrashing around, I want you to go in the bathroom and lock the door. You hear me? I know you're my wife and I know you're a nurse, and you're just naturally gonna want to help me, but I'm telling you you can't. Okay? I have to know you'll get out of my way and stay there. Promise me." His voice, harsh to begin with, became a croak when he repeated it, gripping her hands too hard. *"Promise me."*

Her eyes swam as she whispered brokenly, "I promise."

He let go of her hands and leaned back in the chair, exhaling like a steam valve letting go. He felt inexpressibly weary. And he hoped he wasn't going to regret giving in to the temptation…to the lure of incredible luxury of a night in a private room, in a soft bed next to his wife's warm body. The hospital staff had gone to great lengths to make his room there comfortable and homey, but it was still a hospital. He hated hospitals—always had.

"Do you want anything to eat?" Her voice sounded shaky. She had risen and was looking anxiously at him, hugging herself.

He shook his head and nodded at the pile of peelings. "I had a little something while I was waiting for you. I think I might just lie down for a while."

Getting to his feet took the last remnants of his strength. The room whirled and tilted as he started toward the bed, and he felt Jessie's strong arm come around his waist and her shoulder fit itself under his arm. "Thanks," he muttered as the bed came up to meet him, a great pillowy softness that threatened to swallow him completely.

"Don't you want to undress? Get inside…" Her voice was fading into the distance.

"No. 'S okay…better this way…" He sighed and let the softness have him.

Jessie had more trouble than she'd thought she would falling asleep. It had been a long time since she'd shared a bed with anyone, and as big as this one was, with Tristan in it, it still seemed crowded. He had always been a cuddler. She remembered that, in the first years of their marriage, she'd had a hard time adjusting to the heat, confinement and distraction of his body entwined with hers. Eventually, though, she had gotten used to it, so much so that their bed during his absences had seemed unbearably empty. Then, during his last absence, she'd gotten used to that, too. Now, though he lay on top of the covers and she underneath them, the heat from his body felt suffocating to her. His quiet breathing seemed loud in her ears.

Eventually she fell into a restless, sweaty doze, painted with erotic dreams. In her dream, hands were touching her…a stranger's hands, rawboned and hard. They were

stroking and caressing her body all over, and in her dream
she moaned softly. She writhed and opened herself to the
hands, inviting every imaginable intimacy. Heat suffused
her skin and thumped inside her chest. She moaned again,
lifting into the caressing hands, and felt a cool familiar
tickle of hair on her belly. Her breasts ached and her nipples hardened in response to the sucking pressure that engulfed them. She whimpered when that same pressure
found the throbbing place between her thighs. The heat
became intolerable…the throbbing threatened to tear her
body apart. She cried out…again…and again. And woke
up.

But the crying went on. She sat up, shivering violently.
The light she'd left burning in the bathroom threw stripes
of light and shadow across the bed, but she didn't need that
to tell her the terrible moans she could still hear were coming from Tristan's side of the bed.

Chapter 7

He was lying on his side, huddled in a fetal curl. His face was turned away from her and his arms covered his head as if to shield it from blows. The sounds he made would have been heartrending coming from anyone—a child…a woman…a stranger. Coming from her husband, who had always been so proud, so stoic and strong, they shocked her to the very depths of her soul.

"Oh, Tris," she whispered. Tears were streaming down her face. He was right—her instincts, every nerve impulse in her body, compelled her to reach for him, gather him into her arms and stroke and comfort him, soothe away the terrible nightmare that was tormenting him so. She even put out a hand, holding her breath to confine her sobs.

Promise me…promise me…

As the sobs she'd fought so hard to hold back burst from her, she flung herself out of bed and lurched across the room to the bathroom. Pulling the door closed behind her, she fumbled blindly with the latch, then leaned against the sink and buried her face in her hands. Shudders racked her, and dry sobs that tore at her throat. *Oh, Tristan…love, what did they do to you?*

The shaking and sobs subsided gradually. Jessie nurtured and quieted herself with slow, deep breaths, then turned to the sink and washed her face with cool water. As she blotted it with a towel she was surprised to see that the image gazing back at her from the mirror above the sink looked remarkably calm. Only the eyes betrayed the fear and despair in her heart.

All seemed quiet now, in the room beyond the bathroom door. She listened with her ear to the panels, then cautiously eased the door open a crack. She heard nothing, at first—then, the faint rhythmic rasp of breathing. Opening the door wider, she saw a shape framed in the rectangle of light that stretched across the carpet toward the bed. *Tris.* He was lying on the floor, half on his side with one leg drawn up and one arm pillowing his head. Fear grabbed her throat and froze her where she was, until she saw that he was soundly, peacefully asleep.

When Jessie woke again she was astonished to find it was daylight, and even more astonished that she'd actually gone back to sleep. She'd been certain she wouldn't, lying stiff and tense in the great huge bed, thinking of Tristan on the cold floor, so near yet so far away in the private hell he wouldn't share with her. Which, damn him, he undoubtedly wouldn't because of his enormous sense of honor, and undoubtedly believed by so doing he was protecting her. The thought made her feel helpless and angry.

A cautious check showed her that the rug beside the bed was unoccupied, and she could hear the shower running in the bathroom. The sound, one she hadn't heard in a very long time, brought a nourishing and unexpected joy, and for a moment she allowed herself to bask in it, smiling to herself as she stretched and fidgeted herself into full wakefulness. Then the water sounds ceased and her heart leaped and quickened.

Suspenseful moments passed before the door opened. Tristan took one full step toward her before it evidently came to him that she was awake and watching him. Then he halted, framed by the doorway, his body silhouetted against the light.

"Hi," he said, diffident and casual as a stranger, blotting his face and hair with the ends of the towel draped around his neck, "hope I didn't wake you."

"Oh, no...you didn't. What time is it?" Her voice was a sandy whisper as she scooted herself back and up on the pillows. Half sitting, she combed her fingers through her hair and then wiped her eyes with her hands, using the excuse of sleepiness to dispose of the tears that had sprung into them unexpectedly. *Oh, Tris...what did they do to you?*

She'd known he was thin; even through his clothing she'd felt the startling boniness of his body. But, dammit, she hadn't been prepared for *wasted.* Standing before her now, he reminded her of old photographs she'd seen of concentration camp survivors, the outline of his pelvis plainly visible under standard military issue undershorts, the long bones of his legs broken by the knotted knobs of his knees. His collarbones stood out like branches, and when he moved out of the backlighting from the bathroom doorway she saw that his ribs were crisscrossed with ropy ridges of scar tissue.

"Not that late. Just figured I ought to get in gear—call Al—let him know we made it back last night okay." He tossed the towel over the back of a chair and, with a jerky, self-conscious gesture that reminded her poignantly of how graceful and confident he'd once been, reached for the undershirt he'd left hanging there. He threw her a crooked smile before he pulled the shirt over his head. "Sorry. Didn't mean for you to see that."

"Oh, yeah?" In the process of flinging back the covers and sliding her legs over the side of the bed, Jessie paused to glare at him, covering her true emotions with crankiness. "What did you think you were gonna do, hide out in a monastery while you gained forty pounds?" Frustration and rage—frustration with her husband's all-too-familiar stubbornness, rage at the evil monsters that could treat another human being with such cruelty—made her tremble. She gripped the edge of the mattress and rocked herself while she fought to keep the trembling out of her voice. "What did you think I was gonna do, cover my eyes and run screamin' from the sight of you?"

"Guess *not.*" His grin, emerging from the neck of his undershirt, tried briefly to cajole her before he turned away to pull on his pants.

"Dammit, Tris—so you're scrawny as an ol' hound dog—do you think I *care?*" She stood up, teetered, caught herself and went unsteadily toward him. "All I care about—"

"—is havin' me back. Yeah, I know." With his back to her, his voice sounded muffled and tight. He yanked the zipper of his black cargo pants and jerked around to face her. "And there's nothing I want more than to *be* back, Jess, but I want to be back *whole,* you understand? I don't want to come back to you less than I *was*—" his voice cracked, and he clenched his fists and let them drop to his sides "—dammit." Then he finished in a gritty whisper, "I do have a *little* bit of pride."

"A *little* bit?" She wanted to take hold of him and shake him till his teeth rattled. "You listen to me, Tristan Bauer, there is no room for pride between a husband and wife. Like I told you last night—'For better or worse,' remember? Don't you dare…" Her voice died. All at once she was intensely aware of the fact—of the *way*—that he was looking at her.

Her T-shirt type nightgown covered her from her neck

to her knees and was shapeless as a sack, but from the hunger in his eyes she might just as well have been standing before him stark naked. She *felt* naked; a cool breeze wafted under her gown and over her skin, shivering it with goose bumps. Her nipples poked against the soft knit fabric. Nerve impulses sang through her body. She remembered her dreams, and fever bloomed in her cheeks.

"Jess, don't fight with me…please."

Fight with him? Numbly, silently, she searched his face, the dark, unfamiliar hollows, the haunted, hungry eyes. Lord knew, that was the *last* thing she wanted.

"I don't wanna fight with you," she mumbled. "All I wanna do is *feed* you. Is that so awful?"

He lifted his hands toward her, and her heartbeat thumped an eager welcome. But instead of putting his arms around her, he folded them across his chest and tucked his hands between his ropy biceps and his rib cage as though for safekeeping. He shook his head and looked away into the far corner of the room, squinting as if the sight of her was painful to his eyes.

"Jessie…honey. I just want to get myself back. Okay? To get my *life* back. Until I can figure out how to do that, I'm not gonna be any use to you or anybody else."

"I understand that," Jessie said, although she didn't. "I do. I just want to help, is all. That's all I'm tryin' to do. If we can just get you well…if we could get you *home*—" As she spoke the word her voice broke. A wave of homesickness caught her by surprise and she ended in a whisper, "Tris—can't we go home?"

He turned away from her to pick up the pullover he'd worn the day before. "We will. I promise you we will do that. I just have one more thing I want to do here first. Okay? I want to go to Düsseldorf—see if I can find where my mother lived." He frowned distractedly at the sweater before pulling it over his head.

Ignored, left standing there shivering in her nightshirt,

Jessie felt isolated and irrelevant. Folding her arms across her breasts to shield her sensitized and betraying nipples, she watched his head burrow through the pullover's turtleneck, the dark, still-damp spikes of his hair emerging tousled, like a small boy's. She remembered how she'd loved to feel the tickle of his hair on her skin, especially like this, fresh from the shower. *Like in the dream...* Her lips felt swollen as she murmured, ''You want to go today?''

''Thought we would, yeah.'' Once again it was a smile that broke free from the sweater's confines, trying hard to be jaunty, though exhaustion and weakness lurked in the purple hollows around his eyes. ''First, though, I've got to see about getting some food—I'm runnin' on empty.'' His smile slipped, the way it did so often now. ''I'd say I was starving, but I don't use that word so lightly nowadays.''

She went to the phone, glad for the diversion of something helpful to do. ''I'll call the desk. They've been so nice about bringing us dinner—maybe they'll do breakfast....''

Tristan nodded, briskly combing back his hair with his fingers. ''That'd be great. While you're getting yourself together, I'll see if I can get hold of Al. I'm gonna need him to bring me some clean clothes...my shaving gear, for starters. Then, I think we're probably gonna need his help if we're gonna get away from here without the wolf pack hot on our trail.''

''Are we taking the car?'' Jess asked, carefully not looking at him. Carefully keeping her voice neutral.

''We don't have to if you'd rather not, honey,'' he said, chuckling. And she knew that was as much of an apology as she was ever going to get.

They took the train to Düsseldorf. Jessie was secretly delighted, for reasons that had nothing to do with Tristan's behavior the day before. As far as she could remember, except for the subway during trips to New York to visit

Joy Lynn, she'd never been on a train; certainly, she'd never traveled cross-country on one. She enjoyed sitting in sleek, modern comfort, watching the German countryside streak past the windows without having to worry about traffic or speed limits or whether somebody was going to be criticizing her driving or scaring the living daylights out of her with his.

They had to change trains in Wiesbaden and again in Frankfurt, where they boarded an express train which stopped only in the major cities—Bonn, Cologne, then Düsseldorf. Jessie would have liked to disembark in Cologne long enough to see the cathedral, which was literally across the street from the *Hauptbahnhof,* but didn't suggest it. They had no way of knowing how long it might be before the next train to Düsseldorf, but more than that, she knew that for Tristan this wasn't a sight-seeing trip. And so she had to be content with breathtaking glimpses from the railway bridge across the Rhine.

More than once, as the train sped through a countryside just awakening to spring, Jess thought wistfully of how different it might be if this *had* been a sight-seeing trip, the trip she and Tris had planned, once upon a time. It would be the honeymoon they'd never had, he'd told her then. They'd visit the country of his parents' birth, and then, just for themselves, perhaps…Paris. She tried to imagine herself and Tris poring over maps together, pointing out sights to each other along the way, strolling hand in hand along riverbanks and through the narrow brick-paved streets of ancient cities.

Instead, she sat gazing out the windows of the train while Tristan, isolated in that dark world he retreated to so often now, did the same, his shadowed eyes fixed on faraway things she could never see and barely imagine.

At first she tried to make conversation, comments about the passing sights, telling him about things this or that reminded her of, things she'd seen and done during the years he'd been gone. He listened, polite but strained, and she could tell that behind his fixed and crooked smile his own thoughts were nagging impatiently, like an ill-mannered child demanding his mother's attention. When her words began to sound like chatter to her own ears, she gave up and left him to brood in peace.

Maybe it was because she was feeling isolated and bleak, the way she'd felt that day, but she found herself remembering her lunch with Lieutenant Commander Rees.

Mrs. Bauer, it sounds to me like your husband might be looking for that strength... Looking to find the extra stuff that's gonna get him through this.

Maybe, she thought, he'll find whatever it is he's looking for here. And then we can go home.

It was late afternoon when they arrived in Düsseldorf's Old Town. A cold drizzle was falling, glazing the brick-paved streets, muting the colors of the spring flowers in upstairs windowboxes and keeping most shoppers and sightseers indoors. Jessie had noticed, however, during the taxicab ride from the train station, that the modern downtown shopping streets were crowded, and though she had seen jackets and coats few umbrellas were evident; apparently native Düsseldorfers, like New Yorkers, were stoic and accepting of such minor inconveniences as bad weather.

They'd again packed sandwiches to eat on the train, but Tristan was hungry, as usual, so their first stop in Old Town was at one of its many pubs. Jessie would have loved to sit at one of the tables outside on the street—there was no car traffic allowed in Old Town—but because of the weather they had to settle for the cozy Old World charm of brick and dark wood indoors. Seated at a tiny wooden table set on a rough plank floor, they ate German bratwurst and drank glasses of *Altbier,* the strong dark beer that Tristan had told her was mother's milk to Düsseldorfers, and the drink of choice for most visitors to Old Town. Jessie, never all that fond of beer and mindful of her recent wine-drinking episode, sipped her one glassful slowly. She noticed that the waitress kept replacing Tris's glass as soon as he'd emptied it, keeping track with a pencil mark on the edge of the cardboard coaster as was apparently the custom.

"When my mom was a little girl," Tris said, relaxed after the third glass of beer and a huge meal of bratwurst, sauerkraut and dark dry bread, "she told me—and that was before the war, of course, so she'd have been pretty small—she told me her grandfather used to send her to the pub every morning to fetch his mug of beer. One of those big mugs, you know, with the lid? What do they call 'em...steins? She'd carry the stein down to the pub and knock on the door—the kind that are divided in half—and the owner would open the top half and take the stein and fill it up and hand it down to her, and back she'd go."

"She grew up right here, then? In Old Town?" Jessie thought it would be a little like growing up in Disney World.

He nodded. "I don't know where, though. 'Old Town' is actually pretty new. It was mostly destroyed during the war—it's all been rebuilt. The house my mother lived in isn't here anymore." Bleak again, he signaled the waitress for their check.

Outside, they discovered the drizzle had stopped. The sky was clearing from the west, and the lowering sun painted the tiled roofs and arched and decorated facades of Old Town's buildings a warm and lovely gold, like honey. Since Tristan had retreated into his brooding isolation and Jessie was sure he wouldn't notice, anyway, she rubbernecked shamelessly as they strolled though the darkening streets, now and then making unconscious little murmuring sounds of appreciation. A sundial high on a pink-gabled facade...bells of different sizes mounted on another—was that a glockenspiel, she wondered?—a black musician seated on an upturned suitcase, playing a guitar for a circle

of enchanted children…an open-air market with stalls filled
with tulips and hyacinths, and fat asparagus stalks in shades
of cream, yellow, purple and green.

They paused for a while to watch barges and white cruise
ships churn up and down the Rhine. The sun went down
in a golden blaze, promising a fair tomorrow. Lights
winked on and the streets of Old Town filled with music,
laughter and people. All kinds of people: frumpy tourists,
families with small children, lean young people wearing
black leather and spiky purple hair. With his back to the
river, Tristan leaned against a rope barricade and watched
them all in dark and brooding silence.

With so much happy revelry all around her, Jessie tried
her best to think of a way to brighten his mood—something
she couldn't recall ever having had to do much of before.
The Tris she'd known hadn't been prone to the blues. Finally, bravely, knowing what must be on his mind, she gave
a cheerful sigh and ventured, "This must have been a wonderful place to grow up in."

He snorted. "Before the war, maybe. Don't imagine it
was much fun once the bombing started." He took her
elbow and they started back toward the now-crowded
streets, moving slowly, and for the first time all day he was
leaning on his cane again.

The tables outside the pubs and taverns had gone from
empty to standing room only as if by magic. They snagged
the first available table they came to, a temporary slip on
the shores of a slow-moving river of people. Almost immediately a waitress appeared with the customary coasters,
and before Jessie could say otherwise, Tris had ordered
glasses of *Altbier* for both of them. Once again, she sipped
hers carefully and refused a second one, while the number
of marks on the edges of Tris's coaster grew steadily. A
jolly woman wearing a chef's hat and apron came around
selling giant soft pretzels from a basket lined with a red-
checked cloth. Tris bought them each one and slathered

them with mustard—another Düsseldorf specialty, he told her. Though she wasn't a bit hungry, Jessie had to admit it was delicious.

Once again, mellowed by food and *Altbier,* Tris began to relax. After the third glass, Jessie saw him settle back and the tension visibly drain from his body, though the shadows in his face seemed no less bleak. After a while, gazing at the passing crowd and turning his glass 'round and 'round on its coaster, he quietly picked up where he'd left off beside the river.

"My mom had it tough after the war. Really...hard. Their house was destroyed in the bombing." He glanced at Jessie, his hands still busy with the glass. "You remember the scar on her face? Above her eye...down through here?" He drew a line on his own eyebrow to demonstrate, and Jessie nodded, not wanting to interrupt his reminiscence to remind him that she'd never met his mother, that she'd died the year before they'd met. She remembered the scar, though, from photographs, and Tris had told her how she'd gotten it as a child during the war. "That happened when their house was bombed. She had a brother—much younger, about six or seven, I think. Anyway, he was killed."

Jessie made a horrified sound; she'd never known this part. Tristan went on as if he hadn't heard her. "The hard part was after the war. Everything was in ruins...food was scarce. My mother remembered scavenging for scraps... fighting off dogs and rats." He looked down at the glass between his hands, and his voice sounded choked. "I don't think I understood, when she told me. I didn't know..." Jessie saw his throat move with his swallow.

She held herself still, hardly daring to breathe, hoping he'd go on, praying he'd tell her something about what had happened to him. He did go on talking after a moment, with his wry and painful smile, but it wasn't what she'd hoped to hear.

"At least my dad didn't go hungry," he said dryly. "Out in the country things weren't as bad—more food, less destruction."

He drained his glass and signaled the waitress for another, then waited in tense silence, drumming his fingers on the tabletop, until the foam-topped glass had been placed in front of him and the coaster duly marked. Jessie watched as he picked up the glass and drank, wiped foam from his lips with the back of his hand and only then began to talk again, as if, she thought, the engine that drove his speech mechanism wouldn't operate without the beer to fuel it. Unease stirred in her belly. She told herself she shouldn't worry about Tristan's ability to handle a few glasses of beer; being German, he'd always drunk beer, sometimes quite a bit. Never too much, though, and she'd never seen him drunk in her life. But she'd never seen him drink after spending eight years in a Muslim country without a drop of alcohol the whole time, either.

I shouldn't say anything, she thought. *I can't let myself turn into an ol' mother hen. Tris would hate that.*

He was watching the crowd again, but she knew he wasn't seeing any of the people who passed by their table in an endlessly shifting stream. His eyes were thoughtful and far away. His smile was wry, and when he spoke it was in a drawl, and so low she had to lean closer to hear him. "My mom and dad had it tough, growing up. No doubt about that. They sure never let me forget it, believe me. And I had it easy." He threw Jessie a bitter grin, one she'd never seen before. "They never let me forget *that,* either." He drank beer, wiped his mouth with his hand and stared moodily into his glass.

"I was an only child. I don't think they planned it that way, but…that's how it was. They both worked hard… gave me everything. I never had to work going through school. A lot of my friends did, had part time jobs to pay for the things my parents *gave* to me. So, yeah, I had it easy. I did. I know that. But in other ways, they were tough on me, my parents were. You've met my dad—'' he looked up at Jessie and she nodded and smiled her understanding; she'd always been just a little bit afraid of Max Bauer ''—okay, well, Mom was worse. They both got on me constantly, telling me I had to learn to be *tough*. That I was never going to make it in this life if I didn't. They always made it pretty clear to me they didn't think I was going to measure up in that department.'' He looked away, but not before she saw the shine of an old hurt in his eyes. ''And I probably didn't—not by their standards.''

''Surely,'' Jessie said in a choked voice, ''you don't think—''

''I *think*…'' he began, slurring the words. Then broke it off and shook his head, muttering something she couldn't hear as he lifted his arm to signal the waitress.

''Tris…*please*,'' Jessie said before she could stop herself. Her breath caught when he threw her a brief, fierce look, and she saw in his eyes the same wild and defiant light that had burned in there the day before when he'd pushed the rented Ford recklessly toward suicide speed.

But he only asked the waitress for the check. Jessie saw his teeth catch the gleam of the strings of tiny lights that looped above their head as, with a cool, sardonic smile, he watched her count up the pencil marks on the edges of the coasters. He handed the waitress a wad of Euros and told her to keep the change, then shoved back his chair and rose, swaying as he reached for his cane. Heart pounding, Jessie made it to his side in time to steady him.

''I am a bit tired,'' he said, speaking firmly and distinctly as they eased in among the flow of people in the street. His arm lay heavily across Jessie's shoulders although he held himself almost unnaturally erect. ''My dear, do we have a hotel room around here somewhere?''

Major Sharpe had made a reservation for them at a downtown hotel overlooking the Rhine. It wasn't far from

Old Town, but definitely too far for Tristan to walk in his present condition, so they made their way against the tide of visitors still streaming into Old Town's pubs and taverns and restaurants, heading toward the vehicle traffic streets that bordered the restricted pedestrian zone. There, a long line of taxicabs awaited the usual exodus of revelers, most of whom could be counted on to be suffering the effects of too much *Altbier*. Jessie chose the first cab they came to, but when she opened the door she felt Tristan's body recoil and heard a sharp hiss of breath. Too late, she saw that the driver looked distinctly Middle Eastern.

"Tris, honey, it's okay," she whispered, her arm tight around his waist, a smile for the driver's benefit fixed firmly on her lips. "It's *okay*." Still smiling, she bent down to peer into the cab. "Uh…do you by any chance speak English?"

Confronted only with a blank stare, she hopefully added the name of their hotel and was rewarded with a brisk, "Yes, yes—come, come!" as the driver flipped on his meter.

Light-headed with relief, Jessie half shoved Tristan into the back seat of the cab, then climbed in after him. As she settled breathless and quivery beside him, he gave a sigh and leaned his head against the back of the seat, muttering something she couldn't quite hear…except for one word: "bastards."

She threw the driver a worried glance as she leaned closer to Tristan and whispered, "What'd you say?"

His head moved wearily from side to side. "Couldn't…let 'em break me. Couldn't…don't you see?" He opened his eyes suddenly and turned to her, glaring like a wounded eagle. "I had something to *prove*. Understand? Somethin' to prove…"

Throat knotting and tears welling behind her eyes, Jessie could only nod. After a moment he leaned back with a sigh and closed his eyes.

"Bastards...never broke me," he mumbled, laughing softly, his body shaking with it. "Never...broke me. Guess I showed them, huh? Guess...I showed them."

She fumbled for his hand and found it, bony and strange in the darkness. "You sure did, sweetheart," she whispered. She closed her eyes, and tears oozed between her lashes. "You sure did show 'em."

Chapter 8

Tristan slept in a shadowless room without doors or windows. He could hear no sounds, not even his own heartbeat, his own breathing. He was neither cold nor warm, he felt nothing, not even the press of his body against a bed or a floor…not even the brush of clothing against his skin.

Asleep, he thought… *I wonder if this is death?*

But even as the thought formed, he awoke to find himself in a lovely golden place, a safe place, and his body bathed in warmth. Jessie was coming toward him, her stride long and sexy, her smile like the sun. Her smile and heat wrapped around him like a lovely summer day as she slipped into his arms, smelling of grass and flowers, warm sand and sex. Her lips hovered, breathlessly brushing his as she whispered love words into his mouth. He plunged his fingers into her hair and it poured over his hands like the finest silk…floss spun for gods and goddesses from spiderwebs and sunbeams….

"I've been so empty without you," she whispered. "Fill me…please…"

Yes, he murmured inside his mind. *Yes...*

His hands began to trace her body, and it seemed fluid and malleable as wet clay. His hands glided downward over her back, slalomed through the gentle undulations of waist and buttocks and thighs...his fingers slipped into the tight protected crevasses and explored the tender valleys between. Her breasts hardened as she moved against him, and he, hard already and full of his need for her, pressed himself into the cleft between her thighs. Her mouth, lost in his, made tiny whimpering sounds of need, and he drank in her whimpers and her honeyed essence...greedily nourishing his own need.

He felt the velvety brush of her belly as he moved his body to cover hers. Heat blossomed inside him. Pounding heat enveloped him. He sank into her body like a man on fire into a healing fountain.

There was resistance but it had no meaning for him. The sounds coming from her now were little pants and shuddering breaths, and his groan mingled with them as he pushed past the resistance, pushing inexorably deeper into her body. His need of her was unstoppable...his hunger unquenchable. It had taken him over completely, mind and body. Her body enfolded him...her legs were firm and strong around him...her fingers dug deep into the hard ridges of his shoulders...her breath pumped humid warmth against the rocketing pulse at the base of his throat. His body surged, beyond his control.

She uttered a high, sharp cry, and he opened his eyes and looked down through layers of passion fog to find her eyes fever bright and gazing up at him, their pupils huge, black and deep as wells. Genuine awakening came, and then awareness, but it was far too late. His body shuddered and surged one final time as a cry tore through his throat and grated between his spasming jaws. The muscles in his back and belly contracted with a violence he thought would tear him apart, and left him drained, exhausted, and weak as a newborn babe.

Drenched and heartsick, he held himself utterly still while an exhalation sifted slowly through his nostrils and the last remnants of passion-fog lifted from his brain. His arms quivered with the strain of supporting even his sorely depleted body. Eyes closing, he swallowed and mumbled brokenly, "God, Jess…I—"

"Hush up." Her hands were on his face, a cool and nurturing touch. "It's all right."

"But I didn't… That's not the way I wanted—"

"I know…I know. But it's still all right. You just hush, now, you hear?" Her voice was husky. He'd always loved the sound of it while they were making love. In her mouth love words—sex talk—never sounded crude…just warm and sultry, with enough of a tang to stoke the fires in his blood. Like molasses…

He rolled himself away from her and felt the soft pillow come to cradle his whirling head and smooth fabric comfort his cooling skin. He covered his eyes with his arm and mumbled, "Jessie…love, I—"

There was so much he wanted to say to her…so many things he needed her to understand. But sleep was waiting for him, warm and lovely…voluptuous and seductive as the body he'd just left. He surrendered himself to it with a sigh.

"Mom! Hey…" Cross-legged on her bed, Sammi June nudged the book and notepad off her lap and leaned over to peer at the clock radio on the nightstand.

"Hey, hon', how're you?"

"Wow, Mom, what time is it over there? Two…three in the morning?" Fear clutched at her heart, making her gasp. "Oh God—what's wrong? Is Dad—"

"No, no, nothing's wrong. Your daddy's fine—he's asleep right now. We're in Düsseldorf, in a hotel—I told you he wanted to see where his momma grew up? So that's what we've been doin' today. Anyway, I couldn't sleep, so I thought I might as well give you a call. I thought this might be a good time.''

"Yeah, it is, it's fine. I was just studying…nothing too important. Hey, Mom—''

"I tried calling you at school, but your roommate said you'd gone home. Is everything okay?''

"Oh. Yeah…I guess.'' Sammi June made a disgusted sound as she unfolded her legs and got comfortable. "The media just turned the whole school into a zoo. Nobody could get in and out of the dorm, there wasn't anyplace to park…they even followed me to classes, Mom. Anyway, it was politely 'suggested' I should maybe go home for a while until the furor dies down. So I did. And guess what? Now they're all over *here*.''

"Who, the media? You mean, they're *there?* At Momma's?''

"You guessed it. They're camped out in Randall Jackson's field. You should see it. Place looks like a damn refugee camp.''

"I hope you don't let your gramma hear you talk like that,'' her mother said mildly.

Sammi June snorted. "You should hear *her* cuss when she thinks nobody's listening.'' She shifted around so her legs were hanging over the side of the bed. "Hey, Mom?'' Hunched over and hugging herself, she began to rock gently back and forth. Butterflies…emotions…were quivering and jumping inside her. "I started to tell you. I saw you guys on CNN this morning.''

"You did? What—oh. That must have been from yesterday. Yeah, we were coming back from visiting your grampa Max's hometown and there they were, waitin' for us. Your daddy was tired, but there wasn't any way we could have avoided them. So—'' she hesitated, and Sammi June heard her take a quick, catching breath, the way someone does when they're getting ready to lift something heavy

"—you saw him, then? What'd you think? Does he look like you remember?"

Remember? But what if I don't even know what I remember? The quivering inside Sammi June wanted to jump right out of her stomach and into every part of her, and she fought with everything she had to make her voice firm and strong. "He…looks really good. Thin, though, like you said. You looked good, too, Mom," she added as a guilty afterthought. The truth was, she hadn't been able to tear her eyes away from her dad, standing stoop-shouldered and gaunt behind her mother, like an emaciated shadow. "Kinda tired, but…"

"Yeah, it had been kind of a long day." Sammi June heard a whisper of sound she thought must be laughter. "It's been a whole bunch of long days…actually."

"Mom?" She held herself still, listening intently. "Is everything okay? I mean…really."

And she heard that fortifying breath again. "Oh, hon', everything's just *fine*. I'm ready to come home, is all. I think we both are. Which is actually why I wanted to call you. I think they're plannin' on lettin' your daddy go day after tomorrow, so we'll be leavin' here as soon after that as we can."

Sammi June stared at her finger, making random patterns on the bedspread. She wasn't disappointed in her mother's evasion, not really. She'd expected the lie. "Does that mean you're finally coming home?"

"Well…we have to stop off in Washington, D.C., for a couple of days first. They want him to have some more tests and exams at Bethesda before they release him. But what I'd like for you to do is come and meet us there— can you do that?"

Rocking and hugging herself again, Sammi June stared at the floor as reawakened butterflies danced in her stomach. "Can't I just wait for you guys here?" Aware of how whiney that might sound, she hurriedly added, "Everyone's coming here to see Dad. Grampa Max is coming up from Florida, and Gramma told him he could stay here. I don't think it's right I should leave her with all the company, do you?''

''Well, hon','' her mother said, laughing because she knew how much Sammi June did *not* normally enjoy helping out around the house, ''that's sweet of you to want to be there for your gramma, and all, but you're gonna have to make the sacrifice. Your daddy tells me we've been invited to the White House.''

Her mother's voice had a lilting brightness that made Sammi June think of the times when she'd come home from the NICU after an especially bad day, and she'd have stopped off at the store to pick up ice cream or a cold watermelon, and she'd march into the kitchen with a big determined smile on her face and a light in her eyes. Like a woman on a mission, Sammi June always thought. Happiness or bust.

''No kidding, the White House? Honest to God?''

''Honest to God.''

Was she crazy, Sammi June wondered, or did her mother's laughter have an almost desperate sound?

After the usual exchange of ''Take care now'' and ''Love you,'' Jessie disconnected the phone, then sat and held it and stared at nothing, lacking even the energy to return it to its niche on the bathroom wall. She felt limp, dispirited and utterly drained, a condition she'd been in a lot, lately, alternately with an equally unhappy state of tension, uncertainty and fear.

The White House. The president. CNN. The Today Show, Good Morning, America! *Most likely* 60 Minutes *and God knows how many reporters. Sammi June and Max and Momma and all the rest of the family, not to mention friends...the world...life... They're all out there, waiting for us.*

Huddled on the toilet seat, Jessie hugged herself and shivered. The hotel bathroom was a cocoon of soft gray, illuminated by the single red-gold eye of a night-light. The bedroom beyond seemed a quiet den, isolated…protected. Safe. But out *there,* the world waited. The question was, Was Tristan even remotely ready? Would he be strong enough to face it? *Will I?*

Right now she didn't feel remotely ready, either, and she definitely didn't feel strong. In fact, when she stood up and went to hang the phone back on its cradle, she found that her legs were still wobbly. Her pulse shied and danced when she thought of what had just happened…of Tristan…their lovemaking. And from out of nowhere a sob crept up and caught her by surprise. Gripping the edge of the sink, she leaned on her hands and pressed her lips together and closed her eyes tightly to hold back the tears. But they came, anyway, great rivers of them.

Why am I doing this? she thought. *Why? I don't want to do this! I don't mean to…*

What were they all about, the tears—joy? There was some of that, certainly—and relief, too, at discovering that her husband was capable of healthy male appetites and obviously functioning normally, after all he'd been through. But there was sorrow and loneliness, and—oh, who in the world knew? Just emotions letting go, she supposed, too many emotions all mixed up together. And right now maybe it wasn't all that important that she sort them out. Just that she let them go.

The tears dried up as quickly as they'd come, and she washed her face one more time and slipped quietly out of the bathroom. She left the door open for the light, and in that gentle illumination she could see that Tristan was still in bed, at least, sprawled on his stomach and sleeping soundly, like a child. He was snoring softly, too, though he'd never been a snorer before. Probably something to do with his altered nose, she thought. As she stood gazing down at him she felt tears threaten again—not a great gush this time, but an itchy tingle, like a sneeze coming on. She reached out her hand to finger back a dark comma of hair that had fallen across his forehead, and only just remembered and stopped herself in time. *Promise you won't touch me...promise me...*

Drawing in a great breath to ease the ache in her throat, she released it in a shaky, whimpering laugh. Then she tiptoed around to the other side of the bed, and as silently, as carefully as she knew how, slipped between the tumbled sheets. Beside her Tristan slept on, peaceful and untroubled. And after a while sheer exhaustion allowed Jessie to do the same.

Tristan drifted, floating on his back in warm saltwater, rocked by the rhythm of placid waves. The water caressed, nurtured and supported him; unneeded, his mind drifted away to play with frivolous things...clouds...appleblossoms...seagulls. Mindless and completely relaxed, he didn't notice, at first, that the water had become viscous...oily and dark. Or that instead of caressing and nurturing him, now it coated his skin with a smothering thickness, like tar. When he did realize and began to fight it, it was too late. He struggled against the sticky weight that threatened to drag him under, and it seemed to separate into ribbons that wrapped themselves around his arms and legs like tentacles. Gasping and grunting with revulsion, he tore at the ribbons, but the more he ripped them away, the more entangled he became. In full panic, sure he was going to be strangled or drowned, he struck out—and hit something solid.

And his truant mind, returning in the nick of time, informed him there couldn't possibly be anything solid where he was, and therefore it was quite possible he was dreaming. With that enlightenment he ceased thrashing about, and the darkness grew grainy and transparent, and the tentacles

thinned and became ribbons...then softened and blurred
into sheets and blankets. It came to him finally that he was
in a bed—in a hotel room, he remembered now. With his
wife. *With Jessie.*

Freed of the tangle of bedding and with cool air drying
the sweat on his skin, he wanted to bask for a while in the
miracle of that—of waking up in a soft bed, in a world
where no one wanted to hurt him, and his wife—*Jessie!*—
lying warm and sleepy at his side. But his mind was back
on active duty now, and it nagged at him insistently with
the memory that a short while back his hand had struck out
and hit something. *Something solid. And warm. And alive.*

He opened his eyes and heard "Good morning," spoken
in a husky murmur that made him think of the musical hum
of a sultry summer day.

Turning his head, he saw Jess's face in its pillow nest,
wreathed in tousled honey gold. Her eyes peered back at
him, wide and luminous and unblinking, and there was a
distinct red mark on the cheek nearest to him. He sighed
and brushed it—somewhat clumsily—with the back of his
index finger. "I thought so. God, Jess—I'm sorry."

"It's okay. You didn't hit me very hard." A frown of
concern hovered between her eyebrows as she studied him
along one shoulder. "Guess you were havin' a nightmare,
huh? Wrestlin' around and fightin' the covers. Didn't seem
all that bad—really." A smile tugged at one corner of her
mouth. "And I didn't touch you, swear to God."

He groaned. "And I managed to pop you one, anyway."

She sat up, yawning unabashedly as she lifted her arms
in a luxurious stretch. He watched her, enjoying the simple
wonder of her waking-up routine as she combed through
her hair with her fingers...raked it all back, then gathered
it up in both hands...lifted it and briefly held it piled high
on her head. For one sweet moment her neck was bared
for him...graceful curve lightly furred with velvety swirls
of fine golden down, like something newly born, before she

released her hair and it tumbled down in a silken curtain to hide that tender part of her from his view. And he was left with a kick of desire under his rib cage that took his breath away—and for the first time understood why, in some cultures, the nape of a woman's neck was considered her body's most intimate and private place.

He must have made a sound of some kind, because she swiveled toward him, an unspoken question in the lift of her eyebrows, lips barely parted. Her breasts, more voluptuous than he recalled, moved with her body as she turned, swelling and thrusting beneath the drape of the oversize T-shirt that served as her nightgown, and he was suddenly swamped by tactile memories—*recent memories*—of the way those breasts had felt...the way *she'd* felt, filling his hands—of himself pushing into her tender body...her warmth enfolding him. Heartsick, he groaned and folded both arms across his face to hide from her his overwhelming guilt and shame.

"Tris? Honey, what is it? What's wrong?"

He felt her touch, light on his shoulder, and heard the lilt of fear in her voice, but couldn't comfort or reassure her. How could he, when *he* didn't know what was wrong with him? He threw himself away from her and sat on the edge of the bed, where at least, with his back to her, he wouldn't have to see her face. "Last night," he breathed, rocking himself, muscles tense and quivering. "Last night I didn't—"

"Well yes, darlin', as a matter of fact, you did." Her tone was droll, but he wasn't fooled.

"It was the beer," he muttered, his voice tight with self-loathing. "I drank too much. I'm not used to it. I should have known better. Don't know what I was—God, Jess. I'm sorry—"

"So, we made love. Big deal." The bed rocked violently as she left it. "Hey—I'm pretty sure I'll survive the torture."

He snaked out an arm in time to catch hers as she tried to sweep past him on her escape route to the bathroom. She resisted him, tugging angrily against his grasp, and to his surprise and pleasure he felt desire blossoming again in the part of him that had been dormant for so long. He pulled, testing his strength and will against hers, and felt a surge of all-but-forgotten triumph when she began to move slowly and reluctantly toward him. When she was close enough, he let go of her arm and put his hands on her hips. Sliding his hands and the fabric of her T-shirt over that gentle curve and lightly kneading the firm-soft textures underneath, he lifted his eyes to hers. He wasn't surprised to find tears shimmering there.

"Jessie…" He wrapped his arms around her, drew her close and whispered brokenly against her breasts, "I didn't mean— It's not the way I wanted to make love to you. Not the way you deserve to be…"

He felt the breath sigh from her body and her fingers come to sift gently through his hair. "So it wasn't perfect," she said, trying for steadfastness in a voice that was as uneven as his. "Big deal. The main thing is—" and he heard a smile come "—I guess you found out everything still works."

His laughter was painful…and healing. Her words didn't do a thing to ease the guilt he felt for what he'd done to her, or lessen his shame for his lack of self-control. But now, in the most secret part of himself he felt a small but growing ember of triumph. *Yes, by God, everything still works.*

"I'll make it up to you," he said, the embers of his new triumph burning fiercely in his eyes as he looked deep into hers. "That's a promise."

"I'll *say* you will," she said, giving his shoulder a slap. And then she sighed and added reluctantly, "Not right this minute, though. We have to catch a train."

* * *

Not right that minute, nor anytime soon. The next two days were an exhausting blur of meetings and phone calls and tests and reporters and being shuttled from one crowded place to another, beginning when they arrived at the guest house in Landstuhl that evening to find Major Sharpe waiting to take Tris back to the hospital for a last round of tests and debriefings.

Jess spent the night alone, tossing and turning in the great big bed, her body restless and itchy, her mind ricocheting between erotic thoughts and worried ones. *We found out everything still works…* Yeah, okay…physically. She had no fear that eventually Tris's body would heal from the abuse it had endured. It was the rest of him she wasn't so sure about.

The next morning, Lieutenant Commander Rees picked up Jessie and took her to join Tristan and an assortment of doctors and military dignitaries for the long-anticipated press conference. She recognized several of the reporters in the crowd from the impromptu briefing in front of the guest house two days before. They seemed a little surprised when she smiled and greeted them like old friends, apparently not understanding it was just the natural way where she'd been born and raised.

Tristan was wearing a borrowed flight suit for the occasion. It was the first time she'd seen him in one since before his last deployment, and there was a guilty stab of fear mingled with the pride that misted her eyes as she gazed at him, standing erect and composed before a backdrop of a gigantic American flag, alongside all the officers and doctors in their dress uniforms, with their ribbons and buttons and braid gleaming in the camera lights. The truth was, her emotions were a whole stew of things right then. If she'd had to say what they were she'd probably have been able to name the pride, but for the rest…the best she could come up with was a kind of poignant bewilderment. She kept searching his face, still so handsome it made her throat ache to look at him. And there was a new dignity there, now, too, in the silvery shadings at the temples of his dark hair, in the somber hollows of his cheeks, the gentle furrows in his brow…the quiet presence that can only come from having faced the worst the world can throw at a man and survived. But though she kept searching, and even though he was wearing the familiar flight suit, she couldn't seem to find a trace of the fearless young flyboy she remembered, with that cocky and arrogant grin and dark aviator's sunglasses hiding the laughter in his eyes.

The press conference began, as was apparently the customary procedure, with prepared statements from senior military and hospital personnel, outlining Lieutenant Bauer's rescue and recovery, his physical condition and medical treatment. Jessie only half listened to the dry and droning recitals; Lieutenant Commander Rees had already told her all this, in much more detail, and she was preoccupied with her own thoughts, both anxious and eager to hear what Tris would say. He'd told her so little—almost nothing—about what he'd been through. What would he reveal now, with the whole world watching and listening?

Tristan's opening statement was brief but obviously heartfelt. He thanked the brave members of the special forces team responsible for his rescue, the doctors, nurses and med techs who had taken such good care of him during his stay, first on the hospital ship, then at the medical facility in Germany, and everyone else who'd helped to ease his transition back into the world. He expressed his gratitude for his country and family, thoughts of whom had helped sustain him during his captivity—especially those of his wife. His voice broke when he said Jessie's name, and she was instantly struggling to hold back tears. He finished by saying how much he was looking forward to going back home to the U.S.A., being reunited with his daughter and his dad, and getting on with his life.

"How about having dinner at the White House and meeting the president, Lieutenant Bauer?" someone called out.

"Well, yeah, I'm kind of looking forward to that, too," Tris said with a flash of his old grin, and everybody laughed.

Then the questions began. Most of them were directed at Tristan, naturally. The media had had enough of technical data; they wanted the personal story.

"How are you feeling, Lieutenant Bauer?"

Tris gave them his best gung ho grin. "I'm feeling good—getting stronger every day. Just give me some more good home cookin' and I'll be good to go."

"Where were you kept? What were conditions like?"

There was a pause, and then, "I was moved around a lot. Some places were better than others."

"How were you treated?"

Jessie's whole body seemed to be vibrating in anticipation of the answer to that one, but Tris cleared his throat and said, "I'd rather not talk about that, if you don't mind."

"Can you tell us whether or not you were tortured?"

Hovering in the background, Jessie felt riled and jumpy, protective as a mother dog with one pup. The knots in her stomach had tightened with every question; her nerves were singing like high-tension wires. Her gaze and every ounce of her concentration were focused only on Tristan, so she knew just when the strain began to be too much for him. She knew by the set of his shoulders and the angle of his head, the lengthening shadows in his cheeks, the rigidity of his jaw. By the sheen of sweat across his forehead…white knuckles on the hands that gripped the lectern, out of the view of reporters and camera lenses. *Were you tortured, my love? Oh dear God…*

"Sorry—I'm not gonna comment on that."

"Lieutenant Bauer, have you spoken with Cory Pearson since your rescue?"

Tristan gave his head a little shake, apparently not understanding the question. With her thoughts still agonizing over the previous question, it sailed over Jessie's head, too. "I'm sorry—who?"

"Cory Pearson—the AP correspondent who was rescued along with you."

"Oh. No…no, I haven't."

"It's my understanding that in a way he's the one responsible for you being rescued. That the special forces team were, in fact, looking for Mr. Pearson when they entered that prison. Is that true?"

Again Tris cleared his throat before answering. "That's what I'm told, yes."

"Lieutenant Bauer, were you and Mr. Pearson able to communicate with each other?"

"How long were you together? Did you know there was another American in there with you?"

"Did he know who you were?"

Tristan waited patiently until the barrage of questions had died down, then leaned down to the microphone. "Cory and I met when we were both transferred to the location where we were when we were rescued. Before that we'd been kept in different places. They moved us when the bombing started…that'd be about…three weeks before the SEALs showed up. Once I realized he spoke English, we began communicating, yes. We, uh…we talked when the guards weren't around. Mostly in whispers." Jessie could hear the new ironic smile in his voice as he added, "Hey, Cory's the journalist, he'd be a lot better at telling this than I am, why don't you ask him?"

"As a matter of fact, Lieutenant, in his stories filed since his return, Mr. Pearson has described being beaten and starved while he was a prisoner, as well as other forms of physical and psychological torture. Is it safe to assume you suffered similar treatment?"

During the silence that followed the question, Jessie realized that her throat felt raw and sore, as if she'd been screaming and yelling for hours. She took a deep breath and closed her eyes and made herself think about playing on the beach when she was a girl, picking up shells and starfish and dancing barefoot in the lapping surf. It was a coping technique she'd learned to help herself when things went bad in the NICU. Watching a dying baby struggle for its last breaths wasn't an easy thing to do, but neither, she discovered, was watching her husband struggle to escape the horror of his memories.

At last, when she thought she wasn't going to be able to stand the suspense another minute, he ducked his head toward the microphone again. "I'm sorry," he said quietly. "That's something I don't care to get into. That's in the past. I'd like to keep it there—put it behind me and get on with my life. Right now I'm looking ahead to the future I didn't think I was ever gonna have. I'm looking forward to getting back home, seeing my daughter, spending time with my wife…flying again. That's what I want to think about now. The past is over and done with. Let it be. That's all I have to say. Thank you…"

He turned away from the lectern, and Jessie's heart turned over when she saw his face. It was ravaged, haggard…tense and drawn…the face of someone looking into hell.

One of the officers in dress uniform quickly stepped up to the microphone and thanked all the reporters for coming. The press conference—one ordeal, at least—was over.

Chapter 9

Jess didn't say much in the car as they were being driven to the plane. Although Tristan knew there were two good reasons for her reticence—Al Sharpe at the wheel and Lieutenant Commander Rees beside him in the front seat—he still had the feeling the reason for her silence was that once again he'd let her down. Since the news conference he'd felt her disappointment like a physical touch; her unanswered questions were an incessant tapping behind his temples.

But explaining to her why he couldn't give her the answers she wanted seemed utterly beyond him, and eventually he put his head back against the seat and pretended exhaustion. He didn't have to pretend *much,* and the headache he had was real enough. Evidently, he wryly told himself, the aftereffects of a little too much *Altbier.*

It wasn't until they were in the Air Force jet somewhere over the North Atlantic that Jess finally broke a long, droning silence. Out of the blue—so to speak—she said, "It might be better if you talked about it."

Tristan had been dozing, drifting in and out of shadows. Shaking off their wispy remnants, he turned his head to look at her. Her luminous eyes, filled only with compassion and concern, were to him a silent accusation. Pretending to misunderstand, he yawned, grinned and leaned closer to murmur huskily, "I'd a whole lot rather *do* than talk about it, sweetheart. Told you I was gonna make it up to you. Soon as I get the chance."

He could almost feel the heat of her blush, but her gaze didn't waver. She said breathlessly, "That's not what I mean, and you know it. Tris, what happened to you…you can't expect it not to have— I mean, PTSD isn't something to be ashamed—"

He made a sound somewhere between a snort and a sigh and rolled his head away from her. "God, Jess, don't *you* start. I've heard it all from the military shrinks, believe me."

"Then why—"

"What's the *point?*" His voice, though barely above a whisper, was explosive, like an air gun letting go, and he paused for several breaths to force himself to ease up. "Look," he said when he felt calm enough, "who do you think's going to understand? Nobody can understand. Nobody. I can talk about it until the cows come home and it's not gonna make anybody know what it was like. *Ever.* Okay, Cory Pearson's a journalist, he's gonna write about it because that's who he is. It's what he has to do, I guess. But not one word he writes, I don't care how good he is with words, not one word is ever gonna make anyone feel what we felt. So what's the point in talking about it?"

"That's not what it's for—talking about it." Her whisper had a sticky sound. "It's to help *you.*"

"Oh, yeah? Help me do what? Remember?" He fought against the sudden stabbing urge to tell her everything. About the pain, the cold and the hunger, the humiliation, the sense of utter powerlessness, the fear, the isolation, the constant expectation of death. Revulsion overwhelmed him and he couldn't stop a shudder. "Trust me, I don't need any help remembering. What I need is to *forget.*"

"Yes, but you can't—"

"Jess, *don't.* Look…let's get something straight. I'm not gonna dump what's in here—" he tapped his temple "—in *my* head all over you. I won't do that, so don't ask me again." The fine skin around her eyes flinched at his harshness. He couldn't stand to look at her eyes. He drew a quick, hurting breath and after a moment went on brokenly, "Tell me—what kind of a man would I be if I laid all that on you? It's *bad,* Jess. Understand? It's enough one of us has to carry it around. I'm not about to burden you with it, too."

He could see she didn't begin to understand, even before she whispered fiercely, "I'm your *wife,* dammit. It's my job to help you carry your burdens. Please, Tris. *Talk to me.*"

Gazing at her, he felt all at once a tremendous helplessness, a sense that she was slipping away from him, as though a powerful force, like a flood or a tornado wind, had torn her from his grasp and was carrying her farther and farther out of his reach. From across the widening chasm between them, he slowly shook his head. "I can't, Jess. I'm sorry."

"If not to me, then *somebody,* dammit."

Aching with a new grief, he leaned his head back against the seat and closed his eyes.

Pressed against the crowd-control barricade, Sammi June shaded her eyes with her hand and stared across the shimmering tarmac. Behind her she could feel Grampa Max's silent presence, a bulwark against the press of the restless, flag-waving crowd. He wasn't especially tall—only a couple of inches taller than she was—but for an old guy he was solid and strong, and even though she'd never felt close to him and hadn't been thrilled to learn he'd be accompanying her to Washington for the big reunion, she was glad he was with her now.

Sammi June's earliest memories of Grampa Max were of a growly man with fiercely scowling eyebrows who visited now and then and was always pointing a threatening finger at her and barking, "You!" Eventually, and she had no idea how, it came to her that this only was Grampa's way of playing with her, and that it pleased him when she planted her hands on her hips and thrust out her chin and shouted "You!" right back to him. And that if she was brave enough to ignore the scowls and push past that scolding, threatening finger and climb into his lap, he would laugh and hug and cuddle her—although sometimes he'd tickle her roughly instead.

Later she'd learned that Grampa Max wasn't ever going to be the sort of grown-up who tried to "make up" to kids to get them to like him by playing their games or buying them presents or taking them places, but that he was the "go-to" guy when something got broken. Grampa Max could fix anything, and Sammi June used to save all her broken toys in a cardboard box for when he came to visit. Grampa Max could also be counted on to let her sneak sips of his beer when nobody was looking.

After her dad had gone off to the Persian Gulf and hadn't come back, Sammi June saw less and less of Grampa Max. He'd seldom visited Momma and her at Gramma's house, even after he retired and moved to Florida, which was much closer than when he'd had to fly all the way from Seattle. On those rare occasions when he called her on the phone, like on her birthday or Christmas, it was hard to think of things to say to him, and she was always glad to say goodbye and hand the phone over to Mom—although Sammi June had the feeling her mother didn't find it any easier to talk to Grampa Max than she did. It was as if the loss they all shared, rather than bringing them to a common meeting place, had instead made walls between them.

Now, stealing a sideways glance at the grandfather she barely knew, Sammi June thought it was funny—strange funny—that the same things about Grampa Max that had made him seem scary when she was little were what made her glad he was here with her now. A strong, erect, proud man, with that same scowl she remembered, a craggy nose and a jaw that looked as if it had been carved in granite, he looked steadfast and sure and completely in control. No sloppy emotions there for her to have to worry about, that was for sure.

Then she happened to look down. Grampa Max had moved up to stand beside her and was gripping the barricade, leaning forward a little on his hands. She saw a mechanic's hands—big, strong, gnarled and scarred hands that had spent a lifetime building things, mending things... building airplanes, mending broken toys. As Sammi June stared at her grandfather's hands she saw the knuckles whiten. And it came to her like a swift and unexpected blow, the realization of what it must feel like to be a father, to be a proud strong man who builds airplanes and fixes things, and to have your only son die in an airplane, to have your life and the lives of everyone you love broken into a million pieces and know there's nothing in the world you can do to fix it.

Sammi June's throat began to ache, and she shook her head and silently laughed, trying to mock the ache away. *No sloppy emotions, huh?* She glanced up at Grampa Max to see if he'd noticed anything, but he was staring out across the tarmac. His eyes were narrowed and bright as laser beams. Her head jerked as she followed his gaze, and her heart gave a terrible lurch and took off, thundering and racing like a cattle stampede.

A plane was moving toward them, wavering in the heat shimmer, seeming not quite connected to the earth. As

Sammi June watched it come closer, she wondered how it was possible for someone to have their heart beat so hard and still be standing up, straight and still and looking perfectly normal. She wanted to reach for someone and grab on, have someone put their arms around her and hold her up. But there was only Grampa Max, so she did as he did—she gripped the barricade so hard her knuckles turned white and stared at the plane until her eyes burned.

Out on the tarmac, the plane had rolled to a stop. People were bustling around it now, rolling things, pushing things, chocking wheels, rolling out a roll of red carpet, moving some big white stairs up close to the side of the plane. Sammi June's heart bludgeoned her; her mouth felt dry and sticky, and there wasn't any spit when she tried to swallow.

She thought, *This doesn't seem real.* And then, *That's just stupid. Of course it feels real—it's happening to me right now. How can it not feel real when it's actually happening?*

The plane's door was opening. The stairs were pushed into place in front of it and secured. A group of people, some in military uniforms, some in business suits, walked out to the plane down the long red carpet. Two of them went up the stairs and disappeared inside the plane. Time, interminable minutes, passed. Sammi June thought her head was going to explode.

She could see shadowy forms hovering in the doorway. She held her breath. Finally...*finally* people began to emerge from the plane and make their way down the stairs—but so far, no one she recognized, though she stared and stared until her eyes blurred. Now she was shaking so hard she could barely stand.

Grampa Max had left her side. He was leaving her! Moving away from her, pushing through the barricade! Sammi June watched in amazement as he shoved it aside and pushed his way right past it. A military security guard put out his arms to block his way, like someone herding chickens, she thought, and Grampa Max pushed him aside, too, as if he were no bigger than a fly. Sammi June hesitated only for a second before she darted after him. The guard stepped in front of her, immovable as a tank.

"Please—that's my father on that plane," she gasped, and her jaw and chin felt as stony as Grampa Max's as she looked the guard unblinkingly in the eye. He hesitated. Then, to her relief and astonishment, he gave her a short nod and stepped aside.

By that time Grampa Max had made it as far as the strip of carpet and was walking rapidly and determinedly along it toward the group of dignitaries gathered at the foot of the stairs. There were so many bodies clustered around that Sammi June couldn't even see who they were shaking hands with.

And then she halted in her tracks and watched, trembling, as Grampa Max—proud, indomitable, granite-jawed Grampa Max—grabbed hold of a tall, thin man wearing a pilot's flight suit and enfolded him in his arms. Even from where she stood she could see the sunlight glittering on the tears streaming down his cheeks.

A laugh bubbled up inside her chest, but it bumped into a sob on the way out and the two emerged together. Then she was standing in the middle of the tarmac with her hands pressed against her mouth, and all around her were cheering people and band music playing and cameras flashing, and she was desperately trying to hold everything in and scared to death because she was having no success at it whatsoever. And in the middle of all that she felt arms come around her and heard her mom saying her name. It felt good—it had been a long time since her mother's arms around her had felt that good—but at the same time the thought was running through her mind: *Okay, but this is only for a second—I'm not a child—I don't want Dad to see me like this.*

And it struck her then that the feelings a parent has for

a child were a lot less complicated than the ones a child has for its parents. She thought of the tears on Grampa Max's face—pure unselfconscious, unconditional joy. No "How am I supposed to feel?" there, was there? No sir.

Her mother was murmuring huskily in her ear. "Honey, there's somebody else here's been waiting an awful long time to give you a hug."

Sammi June pulled away from her mother's embrace and turned to face the tall, thin man standing next to Grampa Max, who at the moment was loudly blowing his nose into a big white handkerchief. She felt herself grow tall and still. Dry-eyed, now, and calm inside, she looked into the stranger's eyes and said, "Hi, Dad." Vaguely surprised to find herself already out of breath, she caught a quick one before adding, "Welcome home."

She stepped resolutely forward to accept his embrace, and as she felt his arms come around her, found herself inhaling deeply. And she remembered, suddenly, all the times she'd flown joyfully full-tilt into her daddy's arms, when he'd come back from wherever it was he'd been, and whether he'd been gone a day or a week or many months, it hadn't mattered because he was her daddy, and she was glad to have him home. When she was really little, she'd grab him around the knees and then he'd pick her up and carry her. When she got too big to carry, he'd hug her hard and lift her feet off the floor and swing her around. But for her it was always the same: giggling, she'd rub her cheek against his whisker-scratchy face, and then bury her face in his neck and inhale his special daddy smell. Now, although she tried to find it—the daddy smell—she couldn't. Either she couldn't remember it, or it wasn't there.

She felt her dad's breath—his laughter, his voice—gust softly against her temple. "My God. Your mother showed me pictures, but—my God—I can't believe how grown-up you are. How beautiful you are." She felt a tremor go through his body, and his words seemed to catch on something as he whispered, "Guess I can't call you baby girl anymore…"

And even though her father's arms were around her once again, and his same whisker stubble was scratchy against her face, she felt a bewildering, aching sense of loss.

Watching her daughter's face, Jessie pressed clasped hands against her lips and fought to control the dry sobs that rippled through her body. *I won't break down,* she told herself. *I won't. Dammit, I'm not about to let the whole world see me cry.*

She'd only then begun to be aware of the crowd gathered beyond the barricades, many of them wearing the uniforms of the various services. A military band was playing something she couldn't identify because of all the cheering and shouting. American flags were flying everywhere, and farther away behind a high chain-link fence, more people in civilian clothes waved flags and red, white and blue balloons and school children held up signs that said, "Welcome Home, Tristan," and "America Loves You." In another roped-off area, members of the news media pointed microphones and cameras of every size and kind and jostled each other for the best position.

My God, Jessie thought, this is all for Tris. My husband is famous—a celebrity. How will we ever get our lives back? Are things ever going to be normal for us again?

And then she guiltily reminded herself, *But we have him back. That's all that matters.*

Someone—Lieutenant Commander Rees—was touching her elbow, gently guiding her toward the waiting dignitaries. Ahead of her, with one arm still around Sammi June's shoulders, Tristan was making his way down the line, shaking hands, saluting, listening, nodding, saying something to each one, while off to one side Max waited, staring fiercely into the sunlight and occasionally dabbing his nose with his white handkerchief. In a daze Jessie barely remembered shaking hands with the secretary of defense, the secretaries of the various services, numerous generals and admirals, and the vice president of the United States. And then they were being escorted down a long red carpet and into a cavernous hangar that had been decorated with American flags and red, white and blue bunting and balloons.

Tristan, Jessie, Sammi June and Max followed the dignitaries onto a bunting-draped stage. Seated in folding chairs, they watched while the crowd from outside, including the band, poured into the hangar. The media people followed and were herded onto a platform behind another rope barricade. After an interminable period of whispering, shuffling preparation, one of the high-ranking officers—an air force general, Jessie assumed—stepped up to the lectern. As if that were the signal they'd been waiting for, the band struck up *The Star Spangled Banner.*

I'm not gonna cry, Jessie thought, holding her breath as she squinted into the lights. *I'm not gonna cry.* She didn't dare look at Tris, and she couldn't see Sammi June, standing on the other side of her grandfather. Beside her, Max Bauer stood stoic and iron-jawed with his hand over his heart.

When the last notes of the national anthem had died away, another officer—the base commander—spoke a few words of welcome, then introduced the secretary of defense, who also kept his statement mercifully brief. He then introduced Tristan and kept shaking his hand and beaming while cameras flashed and the crowd cheered and roared. After that, another officer, this one an admiral in Navy dress blues, presented Tris with the National Defense Service Medal, the POW Medal, and the Purple Heart.

Please don't let me cry, Jessie begged, as she felt her heart swell and quiver inside her. Beside her, Max swiped unobtrusively at his nose with his big white handkerchief.

Then it was Tristan's turn to speak. He stood quietly at the lectern, not smiling, looking out over the crowd as he waited patiently for the cheering to stop, while Jessie's heart pounded so hard it hurt. Then he ducked his head toward the microphone in that rather awkward way she'd seen him do at the press conference in Landstuhl, and said quietly, ''I've got just one thing to say…'' He paused, then in a louder voice, hoarse with emotion: ''It's great to be back home!'' He thrust both fists into the air and grinned— and it was his old familiar Tristan grin, with his teeth showing and comma-shaped creases around his mouth and fans of smile wrinkles at the corners of his eyes—while the crowd went wild.

Oh, dammit, dammit, Jessie thought. *I didn't want to cry.* Beside her, Max Bauer was nudging her with his elbow. She glanced over at him, sniffing desperately. His eyes gleamed—Tristan's familiar twinkle—as he took a clean white handkerchief out of his jacket pocket and silently handed it to her.

As she mopped at her nose and eyes, Jessie wondered how Tristan's daughter was holding up under the emotional bombardment. Stubborn as she was, Sammi June would just about rather die than cry. It was only later, after the ceremonies were over and done with and the informal reception was in full swing and people were milling all around, that Jessie had a chance to get a good look at her. Sammi June's face appeared calm and composed, as if she'd never shed a tear in her life.

Well, no wonder, Jessie thought, and almost burst out laughing. She was watching her daughter move with a grown-up's poise at Tristan's side while he introduced his family to one dignitary after another. There Sammi June was, sandwiched between her father and grandfather for the first time in her adult life, and Jessie was struck by how much alike they were, the three generations of Bauers. The smile, the jaw, the crinkled eyes—proud, arrogant, stubborn and bullheaded as sin, all of them. Jessie didn't know whether to laugh or be worried to death.

Following the reception in the hangar, Tristan and Jessie, Max and Sammi June were whisked away for a private lunch with the various secretaries and their wives, during which they were briefed on the White House visit scheduled for the next afternoon. During the rest of the meal, cocooned in rich paneling, soft leather and mellow lighting, the defense secretary debated the merits of American versus German motorcycles with Max, while his wife, who was originally from Charleston, South Carolina, flirted quite openly and charmingly with Tris. Jessie tried to listen to the SECNAV's wife talk about her NICU experiences—her most recent grandchild had been born eight weeks premature—but she kept being distracted by the conversation Sammi June was having with the SECNAV. He was quizzing her about her college and career plans.

"Right now I'm a freshman at the University of Georgia," she heard Sammi June say, "mostly because it's close to home. But what I really want to do is learn to fly. I think I'd like to be a pilot."

Jessie's insides turned to ice. She barely heard, through a rushing in her ears, the SECNAV say, "Is that right? Follow in your dad's footsteps, huh?"

"Well, not necessarily military," Sammi June said. "I was thinking more about, you know, commercial aviation?"

"Can't beat the training the military has to offer," said the SECNAV. "Have you considered the Navy? What about Annapolis? I think, under the circumstances, I could probably…"

The SECNAV's wife had asked a question, but Jessie had no earthly idea what it was. She could only smile desperately, because right then all she could hear inside her head was someone frantically screaming, *No, no, no!*

After lunch Lieutenant Commander Rees and Major Sharpe were waiting to drive them to their hotel. After seeing them to the check-in counter, the lieutenant commander said his goodbyes and left. Al, meanwhile, retired to the coffee shop for a bite to eat while he waited for Tristan to "freshen up." Later he'd be taking him to Bethesda for "processing in" for tomorrow's final battery of tests and examinations and debriefings.

A nervous clerk checked them in while a distinguished-looking man wearing a tag that said Manager peered over her shoulder and watched her every move. As the clerk handed them their keys, she cheerily explained that Tristan and Jessie were to occupy a suite, with Max and Sammi June in separate rooms down the hall. "Enjoy your stay," she added, smiling warmly.

Jessie had been mentally adding up the cost of three rooms in a first-class Washington, D.C., hotel and feeling more than queasy about it. She had begun a murmured protest about the suite when the manager interrupted.

"It's on us," he said quietly, reaching across the counter to shake Tristan's hand. "Welcome home, Lieutenant."

Tears sprang into Jessie's eyes. She glanced at Tris, who was smiling and saying, "Thanks, it's good to be home." But the words seemed mechanical, and although his lips formed the smile there wasn't any spark in his eyes. And she thought, *I wonder if he knows he's home. I don't think it's hit him yet.*

But then again, she reminded herself, he's probably just exhausted. After all, they were still on German time, and it had already been a very long day.

After Tristan had gone off with Al to Bethesda, Sammi June, whose body was set to Eastern Daylight Time and a whole lot younger besides, expressed a desire—a little bit surprising to her mother—to see some of the sights around Washington, D.C. She thought it would be especially cool to see the Lincoln Memorial at night. Max offered to accompany her, which was also surprising to her mother—though not nearly so much as when Sammi June readily agreed to the arrangement. As far as Jessie knew, Sammi

June and her grampa Max barely knew one another. They invited Jessie to go with them, but tired as she was, she elected to stay and wait for Tris in their room.

The first thing she did was unpack and take inventory of her clothes, both the ones she'd packed—oh, Lord, it seemed like a hundred years ago—for her original trip to visit Joy Lynn in New York City, and the few new things she'd bought in Germany. She had to conclude, sadly, that even taking full advantage of the hotel's drycleaning and laundry services wasn't going to make what she had with her suitable for meeting the president at the White House. Slacks, sweaters and blazers—that was pretty much it. Tris's wardrobe, though considerably newer, wasn't any better; nearly everything she'd bought for him in Germany had been casual. He'd need a suit, dress shirt and tie, at least.

As it happened Tristan's problem was solved a short time later when Jessie answered a knock on the door of her suite. She opened it to find a hotel bellman standing there holding a garment bag. "This just arrived for Lieutenant Bauer," he announced, and left, refusing a tip.

In the bag was a spanking-new Navy dress uniform. Jessie's throat tightened and her eyes misted as she gazed at it, remembering how devastatingly handsome Tris had looked wearing his dress blues. "No doubt about it," she said aloud to herself, "tomorrow I'm gonna buy myself a new dress."

With that settled, she indulged in a long hot shower, washed her hair and blew it dry, scrubbed her teeth, lotioned every inch of her skin and did her nails. *I'm acting like a bride on her wedding night,* she thought with an inner shiver. Only, she doubted any bride would be topping off all this effort with an oversize T-shirt for a nighty. *Tomorrow while I'm at it,* she thought, *I might just buy myself a new nightgown, too.*

It was late when Tristan came in—probably not by

Washington, D.C., standards, but it would be the wee hours of the morning in Germany. Jessie had fallen asleep in bed, propped up on a pile of pillows, with the TV going and the bedside lamp on, turned down low. She woke up when she heard the door close in the outer room of the suite. Jangly from waking too suddenly from a short, sound sleep, she went to meet him and found him already unzipping his jumpsuit. Even in the dim light she could see that his face was gray with fatigue.

"Hi," she murmured, and walked straight into his arms as if she'd been doing it every night for the past eight years.

"Still up?" After the slightest hesitation, his arms came around her, and she felt his body move with his inhalation, and the tickle of his breath in her hair. "Mmm, your hair smells good," he mumbled, slurring his words.

In her sleepy state it seemed so natural to lift her face for his kiss. His lips felt warm and silky and tasted of beer.

Chapter 10

Because she was half-awake, Jessie ignored it at first. Tristan had always drunk beer. The taste and smell of it on his lips seemed natural to her, almost comforting in its familiarity. And besides, his mouth was warm and vibrant, and after a little murmur of surprise and pleasure, responsive. For a few joyful seconds she allowed herself to sink into the sensations she'd been without for so long.

Then...something in her brain said, *Wait. Beer? But he was at the hospital.*

He must have felt her awareness—the slightest flinch, an instinctive recoil—because when she pulled back to stare at him, his jaw had a set, defensive look to it. "Sorry to be so late," he mumbled, peering narrow-eyed past her at the clock on the nightstand. "Didn't think you'd still be up...stopped downstairs for a beer. Thought it might help me sleep...I'm so damn tired, but my body clock's screwed up...time change, and all."

Jessie thought, *One beer and how many more?* But she only nodded and murmured, "I know, mine, too."

With one arm still draped around her shoulders, he groped his way into the bedroom and sat heavily on the edge of the bed. While he was struggling to free himself from the top half of his jumpsuit, she knelt and pulled off his shoes.

"Stand up," she ordered curtly when he continued to sit, zombielike, and he obeyed like a sleepy child. She tugged the jumpsuit down to his ankles, setting her jaw and clenching her teeth at the sight of his scarred and desperately thin legs. She pulled back the bedclothes and guided his swaying body down onto the waiting sheets. He toppled sideways into the pillows with a sigh, and his eyes were already closing as she pulled his jumpsuit off and drew the covers up to his shoulder.

"I'll make it up to you…" he mumbled on a long, sighing exhalation. "I will…I promise."

"I know…I know…" Swollen and achy with held-back tears, Jessie combed her fingers lightly through the silvery hair on his temples. "You just go to sleep now…that's right…sleep."

His only reply was a gentle snore. Moving stiffly, shivering and goose bumpy under her T-shirt nightgown, Jessie picked up the jumpsuit and hung it carefully over a chair, then went around to her side of the bed and crawled between the sheets, leaving the light on. She was cold, but didn't dare snuggle up to her husband's body for warmth. Instead she lay curled on her side with her back to him and stared at the luxurious and unfamiliar room while she listened to his unfamiliar snores. It was a long time before sleep came.

Tristan awoke with a vague sense of self-disgust. That feeling evaporated rapidly, however, when he realized that once again he'd slept the night through without dreams.

He raised himself on one elbow to gaze down at his sleeping wife. She lay on her side, facing away from him with her cheek pillowed on her hand, and her hair streamed past her ear and across the pillow like a river of molten gold. He thought of her neck and its lovely, vulnerable nape, now a warm and humid hollow that would smell of her hair and her skin and her femaleness. He thought about burying his face there and tasting the velvety textures with his tongue…sucking strongly to make his mark on her skin. His newly reborn ardor rose in him like a fountain, shivering his skin and warming his belly, and he nearly laughed out loud with the thrill of it. *To feel like this again!*

But his mouth tasted foully of the beer he'd drunk the night before, and a glance at the clock on the nightstand told him he'd better get cracking if he wanted a shower before Al came to collect him and haul him back to the hospital—for the last time, he prayed.

Reluctantly he leaned down to brush her cheek with his lips, the thought of how lucky he was to be able to do that tiny thing nearly stopping his breath—and then he saw something that robbed him of it completely. A smudge…a tiny purple mark the size of a thumb print…on her cheekbone. It could have been makeup, or the imprint of her hand made while she was sleeping. But he knew it wasn't. It was a bruise, the one *he'd* made when he'd struck her in his sleep.

He closed his eyes as the passion-heat in his belly turned once more to cold disgust…and a hardening resolve never to let such a thing happen again. He'd had too much to drink that night but it had been the nightmare that had made him hit her. Last night, drunk, he'd slept without dreams. If getting tanked is what it takes, he thought grimly, so be it. The morning-after beer taste in his mouth didn't seem quite so vile as he eased his body out of bed and limped stiffly off to the bathroom.

When he came out, Jessie was sitting on the edge of the bed, brushing her hair. She smiled at him and said, ''G'mornin','' but the smile involved only her mouth. The forced brightness of it, and the veiled hurt in her eyes, were all too familiar to him. Boy, did he remember *that* look. She'd been wearing it, he recalled, when he'd told her he was going to the Persian Gulf, that last time. When he'd tried to explain to her how important it was to him, that this was his last chance at flying combat missions, which was what he'd trained his whole life for, and that it was something he felt he really needed to do.

She'd accepted it, of course—she'd always accepted—but he knew she hadn't understood. Any more than she would understand now if he tried to explain about the darkness and the shadows in his mind, and the filth and the pain and the fear that wouldn't let go of him, that still kept a part of him—maybe the best part, the most important part—locked up in that Iraqi prison. She wouldn't understand that he was never going to be free, that he'd never be home again until he'd found a way to heal the pain, cleanse the filth and banish the fear. And most of all, she'd never understand that she couldn't help him do those things. Nobody could. That was something he had to take care of himself.

"Your dress uniform came," she said. "It's in the closet."

"Oh, yeah?" He didn't look at her as he zipped himself into his jumpsuit. "Great. What time's our meeting with the president?"

"Four o'clock." She got up, walked over to the dresser and laid her hairbrush down. "I thought I might go shopping this morning while you're at the hospital." She said it without turning, carefully not looking at him. "To buy a dress. I don't think I should be wearing slacks to meet the president, d'you? I was thinking maybe Sammi June and I could go."

"Good idea. Don't worry about the money, either. I've got a whole lot of back pay coming—" The phone rang, shrill and jarring in the molasses-thick atmosphere that had

come between them. "Oops—that'll be Al—gotta go."
Shamefully relieved, he ducked his head and swiftly kissed
her cheek. "Buy something pretty," he stupidly said, and
as he left her he was mentally shaking his head.

Meaningless noise. It was the kind of thing he'd say to
a stranger. Which is what she is, he realized, suddenly feeling bleak as he strode through the early-morning stillness
of the hotel corridors, his footsteps soundless on thick
spongy carpeting. A stranger in his wife's body.

"I think I like this one," Jessie said, turning in front of
the three-way mirror. "What do you think?"

Sammi June spared the lavender sheath with its matching
boxy embroidery-trimmed jacket a disdainful glance. "It's
okay."

Jessie's shoulders sagged. "*Okay?* I'm going to meet the
president, I don't need 'okay.'" She paused to consider,
head to one side and lower lip outthrust. "So, what's wrong
with it? It fits, it's your daddy's favorite color." And the
price is right, she thought, fighting once more to quell the
resentment that had flared when Tris had made that little
comment about his back pay. *And isn't that just like a man?
As if I needed his salary in order to buy myself a dress. As
if I hadn't been keeping myself in clothes and everything
else for the past eight years, and very well, thank you!* "It
looks good on me."

"Yeah," said Sammi June, "if you're fifty. Come on,
Mom, you're not even forty, and you've got a great bod.
You should show it off. Look—how 'bout this?" She held
up something black that slithered and floated when she
shook its hanger. "Basic black—can't beat that, right? Plus,
it's bias cut—it'll cling like a glove, and this sweetheart
neckline? Very retro—that's *so* in right now."

"It looks like something your aunt Joy would wear,"
Jessie said with a slight shudder. Joy Lynn was known to
shop for her vintage clothing in thrift stores and on Ebay—

though on her, Jessie had to admit, somehow those old-fashioned styles always looked fantastic.

"Okay, then, how about this one? It's a great color for you, it's got a jacket...long sleeves...your comfort zone, right?"

"Hmm...well..." Jessie fingered the rich deep-plum fabric, then took the hanger and held the jacket in front of herself as she peered at the mirror. "Jacket's nice. Where's the skirt?"

"Right there, Mom. Underneath...see?"

"Good Lord. Sammi June—"

"It's only a couple inches above the knee, Mom. That's *not* too short. Anyway, you've got great legs. Go on—try it on at least. I dare you."

With a sigh and an eye roll, Jessie headed for the dressing room, followed by a smugly triumphant cackle. As she unzipped and stepped out of the lavender sheath, she was thinking about past clothes-shopping trips with Sammi June and how their roles seemed to have flip-flopped suddenly.

A few minutes later mother and daughter met again in front of the three-way mirror.

"Well," said Sammi June after a thoughtful silence, "what do you think? Was I right or was I right?"

"*That* skirt is definitely too short," Jessie said, staring pointedly at her daughter's sleek bare thighs.

"I wasn't asking about me. Face it, Mom. *That* is a stunner. That's not an 'okay.' That is an '*Okay!*'"

No question about it, the color *was* great on her, and the jacket fit like a glove, in a long elegant curving line from shoulder to midthigh. "I don't know. It's kind of low here in front...maybe I should wear a blouse."

"No, no, a great necklace, that's all. And high-heeled sandals with ankle straps. Now me...okay, what this needs is some great boots. Up to about...here. What do you think, Mom?"

What do I think? I think you've grown up way too fast

for me. As she stared at the two images in the mirrors, Jessie saw only one…taller than she was and willow-reed slender, shoulder-length blond hair cut in that spiky, waifish way so popular with the younger set nowadays. And now, wearing not the familiar jeans and T-shirts but a sophisticated chocolate-brown pin-striped suit with a jacket longer than the skirt, that could have come straight out of a fashion magazine. She wasn't looking at the images of a mother and her daughter, she realized, but of two women…two women who were physically very much alike, maybe, but in fact very, very different.

"Sammi June," Jessie said, hating herself for bringing it up and knowing she had to and wouldn't be able to help herself. There was an aching tightness in her throat. "I heard what you told the SECNAV. About wanting to be a pilot."

"Yeah? So?" Sammi June pivoted, studying the effect of her outfit from the rear.

"So…when did you come up with that idea?"

"It's something I've been thinking about for a while, that's all." Sammi June still wasn't looking at her. "Look, it's no big deal."

"If it's 'no big deal,'" Jessie said carefully, "then why didn't you say anything to me about it?"

Sammi June threw her a look, then closed her eyes and gave a put-upon sigh. "Because I knew you'd react this way. Look, Mom, it's not like I'm planning on flying Tomcats and going to war and getting shot down or something. I just want to be a pilot—commercial aviation. What's wrong with that?"

"What's wrong—"

"Just because Dad—"

"This has nothing to do with your dad!"

"Oh, no? Then what? I've got news for you, Mom— women can fly airplanes. They do it all the time. It's no more dangerous than…than…I don't know, just about anything else you can name. Driving a car to work every day is more dangerous than flying an airplane, did you know that?''

"Statistically, maybe," Jessie muttered. Then she waved a hand distractedly and reverted to the Southern woman's tried and true defense. ''Oh…let's don't talk about it right now, we're just gonna get each other upset.'' *I'll think about it tomorrow; tomorrow is another day.* "Are you gonna get that outfit? Because I think I do like this purple thing, and besides, we're runnin' out of time, and we still have to look at shoes…'' *I can't deal with this. Tris is drinking and won't talk to me…and now Sammi June wants to be a pilot. I can't. Not now. It's just too much.*

Trembly and flushed, Jessie fled to the dressing room.

Sammi June was hiding in the White House rose garden. Not literally, of course; the garden was crawling with people, roughly half of whom she estimated were security personnel of one kind or another, the other half, except for Sammi June and her family, being more or less famous. Sammi June had shaken hands with the president and the first lady, and had had about all she could take, for the moment, of being awed, impressed and overwhelmed. Like a small boat in choppy waters, she had chosen to drop anchor in a familiar harbor for a while to ride it out.

This was something she'd learned how to do growing up a military brat, moving around a lot, at least for the first ten years of her life. The technique had served her just as well after she'd settled down in one place only to become "the kid whose daddy got shot down and killed." In either case, she'd always been the one who was different and struggling to fit in, which she'd discovered was easier to do if she could find something that felt familiar to her and focus on it. In this case, roses. A rose was a rose was a rose, she figured, whether it happened to be growing in the

White House garden or climbing over Gramma Betty's front porch.

It was a warm, sunny spring day—already May, Sammi June realized. Finals time was fast approaching! And the roses were in full bud, some even opening. She watched a small black butterfly wallow drunkenly past, then, after glancing over her shoulder to see if anyone was watching, ducked her head to sniff a half-opened blossom. She was disappointed to discover it had no particular scent. Her lips were forming a pout when a voice spoke softly from somewhere close by, making her heart jump and adrenaline squirt through her veins.

"Try this one. It's got a nice smell to it."

Because her pulse was skittering in wild and jerky rhythms, Sammi June made sure to pivot lazily, as if she'd known someone was there all along. With her hands clasped behind her back, she tilted her head in order to study the man who had spoken.

He was tall and thin, probably taller than she was even in her high-heeled boots, which meant he had to be over six feet. He had dark hair, lighter than her dad's, maybe the color of mink. A long, angular face with interesting hollows and creases, a sensitive, smiling mouth and dark-blue deep-set eyes behind rimless glasses. It was a compassionate face...an interesting face, Sammi June thought, which in her opinion was way better than handsome. But since she was annoyed with him for startling her, and with herself for being startled, there was no way she was ever going to let him know she thought so.

He began to stroll toward her casually, as if he just happened to be going in that direction. "Cory Pearson," he said, pausing when he was within handshaking range, though he didn't offer to do so, and instead reached out with his eyes and held on to hers with an intensity that seemed much more presumptuous. And personal. "I was—"

"I know who you are," said Sammi June, giving her head a slight toss and setting her chin a notch higher. "I've seen you on television. You're the reporter who was in Iraq with my dad."

He nodded, and his eyes seemed to darken and retreat deeper into the shadows behind his glasses. "Yes. And you're Sam—"

"Samantha," she inserted in a breathless rush, wondering why.

"Samantha." He acknowledged it with a wry smile. "Tristan talked about you a lot, but I have to tell you, you're not…exactly the way he described you."

"I'm sure," said Sammi June dryly. But she felt an odd little vibration behind her breastbone, and although it was a very warm day, her skin had shivered in a way she found rather pleasant. Even…*exciting.* "The last time he saw me I was, like, ten. I had ponytails. Soccer was my *life.*"

"Wow." He made a soft, ambiguous sound. "I guess you have changed a lot." And his eyes flicked in a particular way that made something inside Sammi June warm and swell and blossom…something uniquely feminine in nature. Though he'd stopped himself from doing it, he'd wanted to look *down,* at *her.* At her *body*…specifically, at the bare stretch of skin between her skirt and her knee-high boots. She was sure of it. And with that assurance came an unfamiliar sense of power…uniquely feminine.

"Not so much," she said in a husky purr, finally conceding him her smile. "I still play soccer. It's just not my life."

He returned her smile, while his eyes continued to study her with that unnerving intensity—unnerving and yet it made her feel as though she were the most fascinating person on the face of the earth. "And…what besides soccer fills up your life these days, Samantha?"

It must have been his eyes, she thought later. Or maybe it was just something—a gift, a knack reporters had for worming secrets out of people. Because Sammi June definitely wasn't the sort to go blabbing her life story to strangers. But somehow, right there in the White House rose garden, she was telling him about her life—all of it—her college classes and her pain-in-the-neck roommate, even the sort of new idea she had about becoming a pilot.

"Ah," he said, nodding. "Because of your dad?"

"Not really…" She lifted a shoulder defensively; that assumption always irritated her. And then, for some reason, she heard herself saying, "Well…I don't know. Maybe. Do you think something like that can be inherited? Like, it's in my genes? I mean, my grampa Max—Dad's father— worked his whole life for Boeing. So Dad grew up around airplanes. I grew up around airplanes…" She shrugged. "Maybe it's just natural?"

"What does your dad think about you flying?"

"Actually…I haven't told him yet." Her brow knit, and she looked away, studying the rosebud she was fondling. "We haven't really talked that much since he's been back. Not that there's been time. Everything's been so…" Her throat tightened.

"This must be hard for you," Cory Pearson said softly. Sammi June threw him a quick, hard look. He was gazing at her with those shadowed, compassionate eyes…and it seemed to her they could see into her very soul. "Having your father come back into your life so suddenly. You grew up without him…spent all those 'little girl and her daddy' years without him. And now that you're all grown-up…" He left it hanging. Sammi June turned her face away from him and stared fixedly at the rosebuds, which were bobbing gracefully in the afternoon breeze, as if in sympathy. She didn't even try to speak.

"Have you told your mom—about flying?" He said it in a lighter, starting-over tone, and Sammi June threw him a grateful glance and a quick, wry smile.

"Sort of. I mean, I didn't exactly *tell* her. We were having lunch yesterday with the secretary of the navy and a bunch of other people, and the SECNAV asked me what I wanted to be when I grow up, so I...told him. And...I guess my mom overheard." She made a face and added ruefully, "She was *not* happy. Like, she thinks I'm going to wind up like my dad, or something, I don't know."

"She's got a lot to deal with right now," the reporter said, and added mildly, "You probably could have picked a better time to spring it on her."

Sammi June sighed. "I know. Like I said, I didn't mean to. I wish I hadn't, but..." She paused to watch the toe of her new boots poke at the grass before she added softly, "I know she has a lot on her mind. I think she's worried...about Dad."

He didn't answer, and after a moment she turned to look at him. For once his eyes weren't studying her. He was staring into the distance at something she couldn't see, and his eyes seemed a hundred years old. Her heartbeat quickened.

"Was it...really bad...in that prison?" she asked, the question halting and breathless, forced bravely past the fear that had kept it locked up tight inside her. Until now. Odd, that it should be a stranger who'd give her the courage to voice it. And then, realizing how dumb a question it was, she hurried quickly past it, hoping he wouldn't notice. "Sometimes I try to imagine, you know? What it must have been like for my dad..."

"You can't." The words were hard and blunt, but when she looked at him, startled, she found that his eyes were kind and his mouth gently smiling. "But that's all right. Nobody should ever have to. Especially—" But he didn't finish it, and instead turned abruptly so that he was facing the same way she was, toward the roses. He reached out his hand and lightly touched the curled petals of a half-open bud, much the same way she was.

"They only had me for four months," he said softly,

"They accused me of being with the CIA…tried to get me to admit it. Every day I expected to die—especially considering what happened to that other correspondent in Pakistan. Four months—" he took a deep breath "—it seemed like four years. And they had your father for eight years. *Eight years.* That's something *I* can't even begin to imagine. What kind of person must it take to survive something like that?" He shook his head, and his face held a look of awe. "Your dad is one very special man, Samantha—that's all I've got to say."

"Mom says he doesn't want to talk about it," Sammi June said slowly, watching his finger stroke the velvety rose petal. "About what happened to him over there. He hasn't said anything, not to her, anyway. He wouldn't at the press conference, either." A warm breeze drifted through the rose bed and languidly touched the bare places on her thighs…the deep vee at her throat…just like that caressing finger, she thought…and was instantly ashamed and dismayed at the behavior of her treacherous mind. To atone, she threw him a look, flipping back her hair, and said in an accusing tone, "*You* talk about it. All the time. You must've been on…I don't know how many TV shows."

He withdrew the hand that had played such havoc with her imagination and tucked it, along with its mate, out of sight between his arms and sides. "I'm not all that comfortable talking about it, either, actually," he said, gazing across the rose bed. "If they ask me, I try to answer, but what I'd rather do is write about it. That's what's helped me more than anything, I think." He paused and after a moment, shook his head. "You dad just has to find his own way of dealing with it. Everybody's different. He has to find what works for him."

"I guess." She, too, turned away from the roses and folded her arms across her chest. In spite of the warm sunshine and friendly breeze, she felt chilled. "But…some people don't, do they? I mean, some people never do make

it work. It's like…last night my grampa—grandfather—
Dad's father, Max, and I went to visit the Vietnam Memorial, and there were all these people there. Some of them
seemed kind of raggedy and…I don't know…*lost.* Like,
you just knew they'd been there. And you had this feeling
they never did find their way back.'' She gave a short, self-
conscious laugh, once again wondering what was making
her tell these personal things to *this* man—a stranger. And
why, even though she wondered, she couldn't seem to stop
herself. ''When I was in high school,'' she heard herself
say, ''and we were studying the Vietnam War, I used to
imagine—oh, it's stupid—''

''I seriously doubt that,'' Cory said, smiling in a way
that made her believe he meant it. ''What did you imagine?''

Sammi June considered, then threw it at him defiantly.
*You think I can't be stupid? Think again, mister! How's
this?* ''Okay. I used to tell myself my father was alive and
being held prisoner, like the ones in Vietnam. And that
someday he'd come home—'' Her voice deserted her, this
time her laughter sounded high and desperate.

''You see? It wasn't so stupid after all, was it?'' His
voice was so gentle. Sammi June looked at him through a
protective curtain of hair, precarious, teetering on the edge
of disaster.

''That's not the worst of it,'' she said, her voice growing
quiet and husky. ''Sometimes I'd even wish for it on the
Evening Star—you know… 'Starlight, star bright, first star
I've seen tonight…' like a little kid. And I must have
been…fourteen?''

''That old?'' said Cory, shaking his head. ''Shocking.''
Sammi June gave him a playful shove. He caught at her
arm, laughing and off balance, and then, looking beyond
her, dropped his voice to a conspiratory whisper. ''Oops—
I think we're about to be formally introduced.''

Following his gaze, Sammi June saw her mom and dad

coming toward them across the expanse of manicured lawn. She tried, but couldn't think of anything flippant to say. She was feeling so weird. All shaky and shivery in-side…heart beating too fast and cheeks too warm… annoyed with herself for sounding like an idiot—or worse, a *child*—in front of this man, this stranger. And even weirder was the fact that she, who was seldom afraid of anyone, was more than a little afraid of the man…a kind and compassionate man with a knack for drawing secrets out of people. A man with eyes that could see inside her soul.

Chapter 11

"I see you've met my daughter."

To Jessie's ears Tristan's tone seemed mild enough, but something about it...edgy undercurrents...sparked undefined warnings in her mind.

No time, though, for even a quick glance at his face; the young man with Sammi June was clasping Tristan's hand with the kind of silent fervor that among women would invoke warm hugs and squeals of joy.

"Good to see you again, Lieutenant." His smile was restrained, but the emotion in his voice was unmistakable, and his eyes glittered behind a screen of rimless glasses. He nodded at Tristan's dress uniform, and the smile grew into a grin. "You clean up pretty good."

"Yeah, Pearson, you don't look too bad yourself," Tristan said, returning the grin. There was a long pause, fraught with so many things unspoken, and then he said abruptly, "Uh...this is my wife, Jessie..." and the clasped hands broke apart.

As Cory Pearson turned to her, Jessie's first thought was,

He has nice eyes. He had a nice face, actually—not as handsome as Tris's, but attractive in its own way…long and lean, with a slightly crooked nose and sensitive mouth. Though, his eyes really were his best feature, she thought, with both compassion and intelligence lurking in their indigo depths behind a sparkle that hinted at both a sense of humor and an insatiable interest in everything and everyone around him. He had a nice handshake, too, she noted—firm and warm and enveloping.

Jessie murmured polite acknowledgments of the introduction, and she was thinking about what it must have been like for these two men from such different worlds, different generations, almost, discovering each other in an Iraqi prison. What had they talked about in those dangerous whispered conversations, she wondered, precious moments of communion stolen from under the watchful eyes of their guards. Had they shared memories and fears, given each other courage, helped keep hope and spirits alive? What kind of bonds must be forged from such experiences?

Nobody can understand. I can talk about it until the cows come home and it's not gonna make anybody know what it was like.

But *this* man would know, Jessie thought. Cory Pearson *would* understand. Because he'd been through it, too.

The thought blew into her mind like a brisk puff of wind, making her breath catch and her heart quicken. To cover that little spasm of hope, she turned to her daughter, who was standing off to one side, arms crossed and expression aloof, and managed to come up with something inane and falsely bright to say about how nice it was Sammi June and Mr. Pearson had already managed to meet each other. But all she was thinking about was getting Tristan and the reporter together, somehow. Tris desperately needed to talk to someone. And here was the one person in the world who would understand what he'd been through.

Once again, her Southern upbringing supplied her with

all the tools she needed to accomplish her purpose. Polite
phrases, tried and true, uttered by generations of Southern
women before her, dropped from her lips like magnolia
petals. "Well, now, I *know* you two gentlemen must have
so much to talk about…Sammi June, let's you and me leave
these menfolk alone so they can visit. Mr. Pearson, it's just
so *nice* to finally meet you. You be sure and come visit us
when you get a chance, now, y'hear? Sammi June, I want
you to come and meet the senator from Georgia. His wife
was askin' about you. She is just the *nicest* person…."
With a gay little wave and a shameless wink for the two
"menfolk," Jessie hooked her arm through her daughter's.

As she was turning them both away, she heard Cory
Pearson say in his quiet voice, "It was nice meeting you,
Mrs. Bauer. You, too, Samantha."

Samantha? Though her daughter mumbled an indifferent
reply, something…an awareness—mother's intuition—
found its way through the chaos of Jessie's concern for
Tris. Carefully picking her way across the lawn in the high-
heeled sandals with ankle straps Sammi June had insisted
she buy, she said casually, testing the waters, "Well, he
seems nice." Sammi June grunted. "Good-lookin', too.
Didn't you think so?"

Carefully not looking at her, Sammi June shrugged. "I
guess…" After a moment she sniffed and added, "Kind of
old, though."

Jessie threw her a look. "What makes you say that? He
didn't look old to me."

Sammi June threw her a look that said volumes, then
shrugged again. "He'd pretty much have to be. He's a
friend of Dad's, isn't he? I mean…he was in that
prison…." And even though her face was averted as she
intently watched her own high heels punch holes in the
grass, Jessie could see a sweet warm blush creep into her
daughter's cheeks.

Oh Lord, she thought. *Lord help us. First she tells me*

she wants to fly, and now this. It's too much. Lord, don't make me have to deal with this now.

She didn't tell her daughter that Cory Pearson was just about the same age her daddy had been that spring day when he'd met her eighteen-year-old momma on a Florida beach.

Jessie waited up for Tristan that night. And she didn't make the mistake of getting into bed to watch television this time, knowing if she did she'd probably fall asleep again. Instead, she took a long shower and shampooed her hair and did all the self-pampering, girlie things she used to do when she was a teenager getting ready for a date. She put on the diaphanous black nighty she'd bought in one of the hotel's boutiques, making herself blush and whisper, "Oh, my Lord...." Then, to cover it up and distract herself from the thoughts it provoked, she wrapped herself in the thick terry cloth bathrobe supplied by the hotel and gave herself a manicure. Then a pedicure. After that she paced, wishing she smoked so she'd have something to do while her heart thumped a monotonous tomtom beat and nervous shivers whispered beneath her skin.

This is good, she told herself. It's good he's with Cory Pearson. He needed this. This is good.

She'd been so glad when Tris had invited the reporter to join him and Jessie, Sammi June and Max for dinner after the White House reception. She'd been hoping he would. And she'd suggested they eat in one of the hotel's restaurants just so she'd be able to excuse herself afterward and give the two men a chance to talk together privately. She'd counted on Sammi June and Max having their own plans for the evening, but to her surprise both of them had elected to retire to their rooms early, after announcing their intention to visit the Air and Space Museum before catching their flight the next day.

Jessie had noticed that Sammi June seemed unnaturally

subdued during dinner, barely saying a word and only picking at her blackened Cajun-style flounder. Her mother hoped to goodness she was just tired or coming down with some virus or other, but she had a sinking feeling that what was wrong with Sammi June wasn't anything that could be so easily cured.

Undercurrents…

It was nearing midnight when Jessie heard the card-key click in the suite's outer door. Her knees immediately went weak. Too late now to jump into bed and pretend to be asleep. Nothing to do but put on her best face and go to meet her husband. My husband…this man I barely know!

She didn't know what to do with her hands. Or her galloping heartbeat. Once, she would have known what to expect when her husband walked through the door. If he was tired or had had a difficult day, he could be counted on to put his arms around her and hold her and exhale gustily into her hair…then fill his lungs with her scent as if she were a drug he'd been without for too long. If he was feeling good about himself and things in general, he might hug Sammi June instead or tease her and play with her while a wink and his secret smile for Jessie hinted at intimacies to come. And if he'd been gone a longer time, like on deployments, he'd be frankly and openly hungry for her, his appetites lusty and impatient as a teenage boy's.

But *this* Tristan…coming into the bedroom in a tentative, almost guilty way, barely meeting her eyes…the set of his shoulders and jaw defensive, as if not quite certain of his welcome…*this* man she didn't have the first idea what to do with.

"You're still up," he said, as he had the night before.

But this night she wasn't sleepy enough to walk unthinking into his arms. Instead she stood rooted in the middle of the room, wrapped in her bathrobe, twisting her fingers together. "Hi," she said breathlessly.

"Sorry to be so late." With barely a glance at her he

turned to the dresser and dropped his card-key on its top, then began to tug at his tie.

"That's okay…" He was unbuttoning his jacket. She drifted nervously closer and held the jacket for him while he slipped out of it. His body warmth and scent still clung to the jacket, and as she turned away to hang it in the closet she resisted the desire to bury her face in it and comfort herself in its familiar embrace. "Did you and your friend have a good visit?"

"It was good seeing Cory again. Seems to be doing okay…"

She could hear rustlings behind her as he took off his shirt. The back of her neck prickled with awareness, and the intensity of her wish that he would come closer…wrap his arms around her and bury his face in the curve of her neck.

"He sure seems nice. I'm glad I got to meet him." She turned and found him tugging his undershirt out of the waistband of his slacks. The two halves of his dress shirt hung loose at his sides. "Here, let me get that for you," she said huskily, and as she did she was moving close and easing the shirt over his shoulders and off. Then, daringly, she placed her palms on his chest and rose on tiptoes to kiss him. "Mmm," she murmured, licking her lips, "you taste like beer."

"Cory and I quaffed a couple." His tone was sardonic. She pulled back and saw his eyes resting on her, a mysterious light in their depths.

"Did you, now?"

"Mmm-hmm…but only a couple." His fingers had begun to toy with the collar of her robe, rubbing the texture as if he'd never felt its like before. She swayed toward him and was taken off guard when he backed away, towing her with him until he came against the bed. He sat on the edge of the mattress and drew her closer by the lapels of the robe, like a fish in a net. "Nice robe," he murmured. "Is it the hotel's?"

She nodded. "There's one for you, too." Her tongue felt sticky; it was hard to form words. "His and Hers. If you put yours on we'd be a matched set."

"I'd rather take yours off," he said, and his voice was low and guttural. Her breath caught and her hands flew guiltily to the belt of her robe. His eyes kindled. "What've you got on under it? Come on, let me see."

"Nothing. I mean—not *nothing*—" Breath whooshed through her lips as he tugged the belt free. The two halves of the robe unfurled like a banner.

There was a moment of utter silence. Then he said in a disbelieving voice, "That's not nothing."

"That's what I was trying to tell you," Jessie said with a nervous gulp. "I bought it this morning. I thought…I was hopin' it might turn you on."

He didn't say anything for way too long. Seemingly oblivious to her discomfort, he was intent on watching his hands guide the terry-cloth bathrobe over her shoulders. It fell in a snowy heap at her feet. His hands touched the nightgown's silky nothingness…it slithered coldly over her skin, and she began to shiver. His eyes trailed upward, searching the clouded outlines of her body. Then they snapped abruptly to her face. The fierceness in them made her gasp.

"Don't you know," he said harshly, "it's not your underwear that turns me on? *You* turn me on."

"Well—" she was trying for droll, but her voice was bumpy with shivers "—that's a relief."

"Take it off." Dazed and jerky, she hastened to obey, swaying a little, off balance with her arms lifted over her head. His hands on her waist held her steady. Totally naked, in an agony of self-consciousness, she endured the avid exploration of his eyes, and a silence that seemed to last forever. Then…

"God, Jess…it's been so long since I've seen…since I've seen you…like this." The raw emotion in his voice stunned her, speaking of so many long, empty years…of unfathomable longing and unspeakable suffering.

Only clenched teeth held back her instinctive cry of compassion. She reached for him, but he said thickly, "No…let me look at you…" and held her away at arm's length. Her hands had to be content to ride his as they traveled slowly, wonderingly over her body. "I remembered you…like this, but I didn't…" He shook his head like someone in a daze. His gaze clung, mesmerized, to the sight of his fingertips tracing the outline of her breasts. "Didn't really think you could be this beautiful. Thought…I had to be imagining you, that I'd been away from you so long, my mind had created some impossible ideal…"

Overwhelmed, she tried to laugh and failed miserably. "Oh, Tris…I'm not—"

"Shh…" His hands gently turned her. She stood with her head bowed, eyes closed, trembling…exposed…vulnerable…while his hands glided over her hips…buttocks… pelvic ridges, like a potter's hands shaping clay. When he kissed the nerve-rich spot above the base of her spine, she gasped, and her muscles contracted violently. Her knees buckled and she clutched at his forearms for support. Every part of her body had begun to swell and ache. In the protected, feminine places, she felt heat and throbbing pressure already building…building, pushing against the limits of her self-control. It had been a long time since anyone had touched her like this…. Had anyone *ever* touched her like this?

She felt his mouth, his breath, his beard-roughed skin caress her buttocks, the small of her back, while his hands slid around her hips and his fingers wove their way into the thicket of hair between her thighs. "I'm going to fall," she whispered, but didn't think he heard her. She began to whimper softly.

He turned her again, his mouth dragging kisses across her belly, then lower…and lower still. His mouth was hot…humid…and so was she, and his tongue slipped into her, found her throbbing place and began to move rhythmically with the beat. Her body jerked and she gripped his shoulders, breathing in ragged sobs while his hands, cupping her buttocks, held her firm against the relentless stroking of his mouth and tongue.

She must have cried out…she may have screamed. If so, she didn't hear it. Her mind had left her body, but her body no longer belonged to her…it was only a clenching, quaking, sobbing, trembling *mindless* bundle of sensation, and *he*…Tristan…controlled it all. He played her body like an instrument, spinning out the sensations, holding on to the throbbings, making the quaking go on and on, refusing to let it die. Until she thought she surely would.

When she came to herself again she was lying on the bed, cuddled in Tristan's arms with her face buried against his chest, and he was murmuring wordless reassurances into her sweat-damp hair. Her body ached, her breasts felt tight, and her feet tingled with pins and needles. Her cheeks burned. She couldn't bring herself to pull her face out of its warm, protective nest; she wanted to crawl into it and never come out. How, she wondered, would she ever look him in the eye?

But, the voice of reason inside her head asked, why should you feel embarrassed? *I don't know why, but I do.* But he's your husband! *Yes, and for some reason that only makes it worse.*

"Well," said Tristan, and his voice was a throaty growl, full of masculine smugness, "we know everything still works."

Jessie's self-consciousness vanished in a heartbeat. She rolled back onto the pillow of his arm, made little murmuring, settling sounds in her throat, then said in a parody of a Southern woman's honeyed primness, "No, suh, I do not believe that is true.'' Surprised, he raised his head to look at her, and she smiled demurely at him from under her lashes. ''I do believe there is one area that has not been thoroughly tested...''

''Is that a fact?'' His smile grew slowly, making the commas at the corners of his mouth emerge little by little, like shy children.

''Yes, suh, it surely is.'' Already thirsting for the taste of his mouth, she couldn't take her eyes from it, and when he lowered it at last to hers, she closed her eyes with a happy sigh and drank him in as if she would never have enough. The kiss was leisurely and deep, and she was quickly intoxicated.

''You sure you're ready to have me inside you?'' he murmured into her mouth.

Languid and dizzy she murmured back into his, ''Yes, please.''

He left her to finish his undressing and she lay naked under his avid eyes and stretched like a cat, too drunk with desire to be self-conscious. Back again, naked himself now, he knelt astride her legs, rising tall above her, his angular body mysterious to her in that gentle light. She gasped when he gripped her thighs and thrust them apart, but that was his only roughness. He lowered himself into the place he'd made and entered her with exquisite care, easing into her already swollen and lubricated body slowly, and as he filled her she arched into him and exhaled with a long, replete sigh.

''That about do it?'' he asked, his voice thick and broken, trying to tease, anyway.

''Oh, yes,'' she whispered.

''Better be...that's 'bout all I've got...''

Breathless, she couldn't answer, except to laugh. It felt good to laugh with him inside her, and to feel him laughing, too. She felt his arms quiver with the strain of holding his weight away from her and writhed upward to nudge him with her body. "You don't need to do that."

"Don't want…to crush you."

"Pshaw. I'm not exactly a fragile flower of Southern womanhood, and you're not about to crush anybody. Come here to me." She looped her arms around his neck and, laughing, he lowered his body onto hers, then quickly rolled them both so that she was on top of him instead. "Oh," she moaned, "now I'm gonna crush *you.*"

But when she would have risen to straddle him, he wouldn't let her. Holding her tightly around her hips, he brought his knees up between hers so that his thighs caressed her buttocks, and they were touching in every possible way. Then, as deeply seated inside her as he could be, he began to rock her, and all the while looked intently into her eyes. Without breath, he whispered, "Jessie…love…you feel so good."

Light-headed, sinking deeper and deeper into arousal, she wanted—needed—to close her eyes. But in a guttural rasping voice he cried out, "No…no. Look at me, Jessie…love…*look at me.*"

She moaned, but obeyed…and in all too short a time felt her body spiral once more out of control and sobs burst from her throat and tears jump from her eyes. "I can't…I…*can't,*" she wailed, and as her eyes refused to obey her a second longer and drifted closed at last, she felt his arms tighten and his body surge and shudder, then surge again.

Lying spent and sated on Tris's chest, Jessie tried to hold the world at bay. Like a child singing loudly with her eyes shut tight and her hands over her ears to keep from hearing what she doesn't want to hear, she closed her mind to all but loud and happy thoughts about staying right where she was forever. The world came in, anyway.

Tris was stirring purposefully beneath her. "Hate to do

this, love,'' he mumbled. ''Better let me up before I fall asleep right here.''

''Sounds good to me,'' she murmured, knowing even as she said it that it wouldn't make any difference.

He kissed her forehead and separated from her gently. He eased her to one side and himself to the other and sat up. ''Wish I could. But I think it's best if I sleep on the couch tonight.''

With her elbow planted and her head propped on her hand, Jessie watched the scars on his back stretch over the bumps of his spine as he leaned to reach for his pants. Her throat ached. Stubbornly she said, ''Why? You've been sleeping fine. Stay here. Hold me for a little while…''

''Sorry…'' He rose and turned, thin as a wraith, his smile dark and wry. ''Nothing I'd like to do more than stay and hold you. I'd like to spend the whole damn night holding you…sleeping with you in my arms. But…'' and his eyes were soft with regret as he leaned down to kiss her, ''I haven't had enough beer to calm my nightmares. So I'm gonna sleep out there…and you're gonna stay in here…and behave yourself…'' The kisses he inserted into each pause grew progressively deeper and more arousing. Jessie's heart had begun to thump and her head to spin by the time he drew back with a wicked chuckle. ''That oughta do you till morning, anyway.''

She didn't agree with him, but knew it was pointless to argue. Playing along, she slapped at him, pretending outrage, then snuggled back into the pillows with a Scarlett O'Hara pout. ''*Well.* I feel like Ah have been *serviced.*''

Grinning, Tris leaned down to drop a last kiss on her forehead. ''So you have been—and very well, too.''

''Nothin' wrong with your ego, that's for sure,'' Jessie said with a sniff, but she was secretly delighted with his arrogance.

He chuckled. ''G'night—sleep tight.'' In the doorway he paused. ''Oh—and remember, if you hear anything—''

"—don't touch you. I know." She blew him a kiss and snuggled back into the pillows with a quivering, throat-easing sigh. *It's going to be all right. He's going to be okay....* And for the first time, for that moment, she believed it.

Tristan walked with an unhurried stride, winding casually among families of tourists sunning themselves or picnicking on the mall, testing the spring in his knee and in the new grass, quietly appreciating the miracles of dandelions and laughing children and Jessie beside him and kites dancing in a pale-blue sky. *And freedom.* Yes, the biggest miracle of all, and he still wasn't sure it had sunk in completely. It would hit him every once in a while, though—come upon him unexpectedly, like now—and he'd feel kind of a kick in his chest, and there'd be a catch in his breathing, and the sting of tears would come into his eyes. *I'm free. And I'm home.*

Home. That was something else he had to keep telling himself. Because he still didn't believe that, either. Maybe because he didn't feel as if he was home. Maybe because he didn't know where home was, anymore.

One thing that had surprised him, though, was how he'd felt this morning, walking around Washington, D.C., with Jess. It had been her idea to spend some time seeing the sights before catching their flight to Atlanta, since it was something neither one of them had ever done before. Max and Sammi June had planned to visit the Smithsonian's Air and Space Museum, which had rather appealed to Tristan, too. But Jess had wanted to see the monuments, and he hadn't been in a frame of mind to disappoint her. Now he was glad he hadn't. It was a perfect day to be outdoors, not too warm, with a breeze that carried the scent of fresh-cut grass. The monuments were pristine white against that soft-blue sky, making him think of that line in "America the Beautiful" about alabaster cities, undimmed by human tears. But he'd expected beautiful. He'd even expected to be touched by it all…the history, the symbolism. What he hadn't expected was to feel proud. "My country 'tis of thee, sweet land of liberty…"

His eyes stung and, uneasy with that, he laughed out loud. Jessie gave him a questioning look, and he said, "Nothing—just glad to be here, is all," and reached for her hand. It gave him a little pang in his heart to realize she hadn't asked him to tell her why he'd laughed or how he felt. And that she'd probably stopped asking right after he'd snapped at her that day on the plane.

Ah hell, he thought, as familiar clouds drifted into his day. Just as well. That only meant he didn't have to try so hard to protect her from his thoughts…his feelings.

They paused to crane at the Washington Monument, hands lifted to shade their eyes from the morning sun but didn't join the line of tourists waiting to go inside. They were short of time, and Tristan's newly developed claustrophobia was a compelling enough reason all by itself to skip that experience.

"Feel like going all the way to the Lincoln?" Jess asked it lightly, and he knew she thought he'd be impatient with her "mothering."

So he squeezed her hand and forced a grin to let her know he didn't mind. "Sure, why not—we can always catch a cab to the hotel from there."

He didn't know exactly when it had come to him, the realization that it wasn't the Lincoln Memorial he wanted to see, but something else nearby. But he knew that this was a pilgrimage he'd have made on his hands and knees, if necessary. And maybe it was something in his face, his silence, or some kind of woman's intuition, but he didn't have to tell Jessie where he wanted to go. It seemed they both just aimed in that direction without either of them saying a word to the other.

They came to The Wall at its end, the tapering point of

the black granite slash that represented the conclusion of the war…that terrible war that had ended with a whimper rather than a bang. Holding hands, they walked slowly along the pathway that led deeper and deeper into the heart of the conflict…the worst of the killing. Beside them, The Wall rose ever higher, and at its apex, the names seemed to tumble out of the granite and overwhelm by their sheer numbers.

Finally Tristan's steps slowed. He paused, heart hammering, turned and faced the shiny black surface. The names…so many names…seemed to dance and shimmer before his eyes. He put out his hand and rested his palm against the cool, smooth stone. His fingers found and traced the tiny cross carved beside one of the names. He felt smothered. The breeze was gone, the bright-blue sky had darkened, and now the cold black wall seemed to close around him.

"The crosses mean MIA," he heard Jess say softly. "I read that, somewhere. When—if—an MIA is accounted for, the body identified, the cross is carved out to make a diamond, like the others."

Tristan nodded, not saying anything. Not trusting himself to say anything. What he wanted to do was bow his head and let the tears come. He wanted to cry for those lost ones as he could never cry for himself. The lost ones who'd never made it home.

But Jessie was there, and he couldn't let her know how much he hurt. So he nodded and said gruffly, "I know." He pressed his palm hard against the granite, as if he could imprint the name of that lost soul there. Then he turned to face the light…the sunshine…the grass and the sky…the towering spire of the Washington Monument.

At least, he thought, drawing the sweet-scented air deep into his lungs, I'm one of the lucky ones. *I made it back.*

Chapter 12

There had been Starrs in Oglethorpe County since before the War of Northern Aggression. Nobody in Jessie's family knew exactly how much before, since all the records prior to that had been burned up by General Sherman during his rampage through Georgia. All Jessie or any of her brothers and sisters had ever known was that after General Lee's surrender, one Joseph Jeremiah Starr had come limping back home to find the place burned to the ground, the livestock all run off or eaten, and the old folks dead and gone. Young Joseph being a resilient soul, once his wounds had healed and his dysentery cleared up he'd set about building himself another house, married a local widow woman—of which there'd been an abundant supply at the time—and started right in on establishing a new Starr dynasty.

Over the years, Starrs had continued to be born, live, build, procreate and sometimes die in Oglethorpe County. More had gone off to do most of those things somewhere else. A few found other wars to fight. Some of those hadn't made it back.

The house Joseph Jeremiah built burned down sometime in the 1890s and was replaced with a huge white Victorian complete with curlicues and cupolas; the Starr in residence at the time had made quite a lot of money in textiles, and his wife had her own ideas about what constituted high style. Forty years or so later that house, too, burned to the ground, taking its owners, then in their seventies, with it.

The one that replaced it was also white wood frame, but since it was the Depression, when money was scarce and labor cheap, this one had been built to be simple but solid, and was meant to last. It had two stories and an attic, high ceilings and a big cluttered kitchen that smelled of canned tomatoes in the summertime and wet shoes in winter, and a pantry upon whose doorjamb generations of Starr children, including Jessie and Sammi June, had had their growth recorded. It also had a big wraparound porch where Jessie and her sister-in-law, Mirabella, were sitting in creaky white rocking chairs, taking a moment's respite from the family gathering that was noisily in progress.

It was to this house that James Joseph Starr, just returned from the latest war—the Korean—and eager to begin carrying on the rest of the Starr-family traditions, had brought his bride, the former Betty Calhoun, a retired schoolteacher from Augusta. Having learned to drive big trucks in the Army, Joe Starr made good use of a G.I. loan to buy his own rig. With it he'd managed to provide reasonably well for the seven children Betty gave him, right up until his final heart attack—which fortunately did not happen while he was behind the wheel of his eighteen-wheeler. The three youngest of his children, including Jessie, had still been in school at the time, and Jessie's next older brother, Jimmy Joe, barely out of school himself, had stepped in to take over the trucking business. Jessie's momma, Betty, had gone back to teaching part-time, and the family had made it through the hard times, somehow.

And they'd all stayed close, except for Joy Lynn, who'd

gone off to New York City to live after her second divorce, and Roy, who was on a fishing boat somewhere down in Florida, doing who-knew-what. Jessie's oldest sister, Tracy, also a teacher, lived over in Augusta with her policeman husband, Al, and their three kids. The baby of the family, Calvin, or C.J., as he'd decided he wanted to be called, had gotten married last fall. He and his wife, Caitlyn, and the little girl they were adopting, were living temporarily a mile up the road while C.J. decided on where he wanted to hang out his shingle and start practicing law.

Troy, Jessie's oldest brother, had been a SEAL before he retired from the Navy and married Charly, a lawyer who'd grown up practically next door in Alabama before she ran away from home and wound up in California. Troy and Charly had met each other when Charly came back south to be maid of honor at her best friend Mirabella's wedding to Jimmy Joe. *Those* two had met when Jimmy Joe delivered Mirabella's baby in the sleeper cab of his rig during a Christmas Eve blizzard in the Texas Panhandle. Now, Charly and Troy lived in Atlanta, where Charly practiced law and Troy had his own P.I. firm. Jimmy Joe had built his daddy's trucking business into Blue Starr Transport, which ran both long- and short-haul drivers all over the country. He and Mirabella lived nearby in a modest brick house with a big yard for their three kids to play in. Their oldest son, J.J., from Jimmy Joe's first brief marriage when he was still a kid, had pretty much grown up in his gramma Betty's house with Sammi June and was a year behind her in school. He'd be graduating from high school in a couple of weeks.

Nobody, of course, could top Jessie when it came to sticking close to home. She and Sammi June had moved in with Jessie's mother when Tristan was deployed to the Gulf that last time, thinking it was going to be maybe for six months, no more. Instead it turned out to be almost nine years.

It had been a good arrangement, though, for all concerned, and Jessie knew how lucky she and Sammi June had been, to have had the kind of security and stability the old home place provided. Even after the news had come that Tris had been shot down, their lives had gone on pretty much as before, surrounded by family and familiar things, brothers and sisters and cousins and lots of laughter and love. They hadn't had much of a chance to be lonely. Well, hardly ever. There'd always been weddings and new babies, work and school, and family get-togethers at any excuse whatsoever, with barbecues and homemade peach ice cream and watermelon in the summertime and pumpkin pie in the winter and kids rambling off in the woods and the older ones playing touch football or baseball in the fallow field next door, and the menfolk with their heads stuck under the hood of somebody's car.

Like a lot of Starr family gatherings, this one hadn't really been planned. It had sort of grown out of everyone's natural desire to drop in and welcome Tristan back from the dead in classic Southern style, with gifts of—what else?—*food.*

It was Saturday; that morning Troy and Charly had driven over from Atlanta with a trunkful of sweet corn and watermelons, apologizing about the fact that they'd had to buy them at the supermarket, since nobody's gardens were producing so early in the season. Tracy and Al showed up around noon, bringing strawberries and homemade shortcake, and C.J. and Caitlyn hauled over a vat of potato salad big enough to feed the Seventh Fleet. Jimmy Joe had picked up baby back ribs at the supermarket and got the old, rusty half-barrel barbecue set up, while Mirabella, always the practical organizer, remembered to get paper plates, napkins, plastic cups and dinnerware, and all the other odds and ends vital for family picnics. To top it off, Mirabella's sister Summer and her husband, Riley, had showed up a little while ago, having driven all the way from Charleston with a huge cooler full of fresh shrimp—shucked—on ice. Now an enormous pot of water was simmering on the kitchen stove, ready to receive the shrimp, and the air outside was thick with charcoal smoke and the scent of lighter fluid.

Meanwhile, small children rolled and tumbled on the lawn, ignoring their mothers' warnings about chiggers, while the older ones were off in the woods somewhere, getting as filthy as they possibly could in the shortest possible time. The women visited and tended the food and the occasional child-related crisis, while the men…did what they usually did at such gatherings.

Except, at the moment it wasn't a car that had the undivided attention of every male member of the family, and a few of the others, besides. It was a motorcycle—a modest Honda, gleaming black and daffodil yellow—and its proud owner was Jessie's nephew and Mirabella's stepson, J.J., the soon-to-be high school graduate.

"We made the mistake of telling him he could have the transportation of his choice if he got straight As all senior year," Mirabella said mournfully. "I never thought he'd ask for a *motorcycle*." She'd left her rocking chair and was leaning against a porch post, gazing at the knot of interested males out in the lane, and the way she said the word it might as well have been *missile launcher*.

"Well," Jessie said, "at least it's not a Harley."

Mirabella shot her a look. "Oh, he wanted a Harley. Thank God, his dad drew the line at that. At least…well, I guess you could say they compromised. If J.J. proves he's responsible enough to handle this one safely, Jimmy Joe told him he could have a Harley for his college graduation present."

Jessie burst out with a cackle of laughter. Mirabella bristled and said, *"What?"*

"Nothing—except you reminded me so much of Momma just then." She paused, then added, "You do, you know—you're a lot like Momma—in more ways than one. I've always thought so.''

Mirabella considered, then smiled. ''I used to wonder what Jimmy Joe could possibly see in me. The first time he brought me here—remember?—and I saw you and Sammi June and J.J., all of you tall, blond and thin types— you could have been clones of my sisters—and my heart sank because here I am, you know, built just like a fire- plug—short, round, and redheaded. And then your mother walked out. And I remember thinking, Okay, *yes,* now I understand. I think it was actually at that moment I began to believe it could work between us.'' Her voice was the purr of a contented woman, and Jessie felt unexpected twinges of envy.

She studied her sister-in-law, realizing, not for the first time, that at nearly fifty, Mirabella was still an uncommonly beautiful woman. ''And…it doesn't bother you that your husband picked you because you remind him of his momma?''

Typically emphatic, Mirabella snorted. ''Why should it? It always seems to me, if a man has a reasonably healthy respect and admiration for his mother, it only makes good sense for him to use her as a role model when he goes to choose a mate for himself. Doesn't it? Ha—if only more men were that smart.''

Jessie smiled; Mirabella was famous for being forceful in her opinions. Then she shook her head and had to look away, because her smile was fading fast. She took a breath and let it out, and when it did nothing to ease the knot of fear and sadness that had come into her throat, said softly, ''Well, I sure don't think I'm anything like Tris's mother.''

''How do you know? I thought she died before you met him.''

''I've seen pictures—she was dark, like Tris—but that's not what I mean. From what he's told me about her, she must have been tough as nails. Typical German woman—

the boss of the *house,* if not the house*hold,* if you know what I mean.'' She sighed as she watched the knot of men-folk and adolescents of both genders gathered out in the lane. With arms crossed she absently rubbed her upper arms with her hands, though it wasn't chilly. ''With Tris and me it was different—maybe because I was young when he met me. Or…maybe I'm too easygoing, I don't know. Anyway, he was the boss, and that was that. About pretty much everything. I guess I just…wanted to please him. So I always—''

She broke off with a gasp as a metallic scream ripped the soft air. The black-and-yellow motorcycle had just shot out of the knot of spectators and was tearing off down the lane, a long, lean figure hunched low over the handlebars.

''Oh…God, that's Tris. What is he—'' She stopped herself with fingertips touched to her lips, and cleared her throat.

''He'll be fine,'' said Mirabella dismissively, following her gaze. Then her eyes came back to Jessie, and she made a sound that was half sympathy, half exasperation. ''Honey, don't *worry.* He's a big boy. I imagine he's got some catch-up living to do.''

''It's not that,'' Jessie muttered with a sniff, impatient and appalled at the tears that seemed to flow so easily these days. She scrubbed them away with her wrist and, because she knew Mirabella wasn't going to rest until she'd gotten to the bottom of the reason for them, she went on bluntly, almost angrily, ''Sometimes I think…maybe I was *too* damn agreeable. Back then. Too accommodating. I mean— if it's true men want a woman like their mommas, and I sure as hell wasn't…I can't help but think…you know…''

''Think what?'' Mirabella wasn't inclined to help her out.

''Maybe,'' Jessie mumbled, embarrassed to voice the thoughts that had been haunting her, ''he was bored with me.''

She expected another one of Mirabella's patented snorts, but instead her sister-in-law said, with unheralded gentleness, "Now, why would you think that?"

So Jessie snorted instead, and began pacing restlessly across the porch. "Because he sure didn't seem to mind being away from me. In fact, it always seemed to me like he was eager to be gone. I think he loved being out there, in the middle of the action. I don't think he was ever happy when he was home."

She stopped to dash away a tear and stare across the yard at nothing. "We fought about it," she said at last, softly. "Before he left for the Gulf, that last time. I'd stood up to him, for once. I told him he was being selfish and childish, going off to a war zone when he had a wife and child right here who needed him. He didn't have to go. But he'd missed the action during the Gulf War, because of that water-skiing accident, remember? And he figured patrolling the no-fly zone was going to be his last chance at flying combat missions. He was so damn stubborn about it—he just kept saying, 'It's something I have to do.' Like nothing in the world was as important to him, not me, not Sammi June—nothing. It made me so angry, 'Bella. I was actually…I'd started to think—" She put a hand over her eyes and drew a shaking breath. "Oh God. I was thinking what it would be like…*not* to be married to him anymore. Not to have to always be saying goodbye to him, then getting used to him coming back. I was actually thinking maybe, when he came back, I'd leave him. That's why I moved back here and got that job at the hospital."

"Oh, Jessie," Mirabella said softly. "I had no idea." After a moment she added in a thoughtful tone, "And yet, all those years, you never remarried."

Jessie angrily dashed away tears. "Well, it wasn't that I didn't *love* him. I was just so tired of being alone all the time…seeing Sammi June's heart get broken over and over again. And then he didn't come back, and—" she gave a high, hard laugh "—I'm thinking, Okay, God's punishing me."

"Oh, for heaven's sake," said Mirabella. "Like God's some sort of puppetmaster with a weird sense of humor? I never have been able to buy that." She shook her head, and her smile grew softer. "I think things have an odd way of working out, that's all." She paused, and then... "Jimmy Joe was angry with me when he first met me, did you know that? He thought I was being selfish because I'd had myself artificially inseminated when I was pushing forty and hadn't found Mr. Right. He thought I was just awful to bring a child into the world and knowingly deprive it of a father. But, you know what? And I told him this later—if I hadn't done that terrible thing, then I wouldn't have been out there on that interstate on Christmas Eve, having a baby in a blizzard, and I never would have met the one man in this world, I swear, with the temperament to put up with me."

"Oh, 'Bella." Jessie couldn't help but laugh. Then she was wistfully silent, thinking about it.

Mirabella airily waved her hand. "Look—maybe it's just a matter of neither one of you knowing what you had before. And now you do. Like...you get a second chance."

"Do we?" Aching inside, Jessie leaned against a porch post and watched as the motorcycle came zipping back down the road and turned into the lane, making a sound like an angry hornet hooked up to an amplifier. She watched Tristan deftly and gracefully dismount, pull off the helmet and hand it over to J.J. with a grin she could see all the way from here. She threw Mirabella a look. "Not a second chance—I mean, do we know what we have? Because whatever we may have had before, it's not gonna be the same thing now. He's for sure not the same way he was, and I'm not, either. What do we do if we can't—if he doesn't—"

She stopped, because thinking about it was like looking

into a terrifying abyss. After a couple of painful swallows, she gave an impatient, almost angry laugh. "Oh, hell, I'm just bein' a crybaby, never mind me. I don't s'pose we're the first married couple to have to readjust after bein' separated by a war. What do you think—a few million?"

"I don't know," said Mirabella with uncharacteristic gravity, "but I imagine quite a few of those marriages suffered as a result. But," she added in a more normal, positive tone, "you two loved each other once, enough that you didn't remarry—"

"Oh, for Pete's sake," Jessie interrupted, with an angry swat at the air, "it's not like I wouldn't have, if I'd met anybody I *wanted* to marry! I just didn't, that's all."

"Maybe," said Mirabella, "that's because you never found anybody who could measure up to Tristan." Jessie looked at her and didn't say anything. "So what was it about him, do you remember? What was it that made you fall in love with him, all those years ago?"

Jessie gave a gulp of guilty laughter. "Oh Lord—the sex. No—I swear, it was. Sex, hormones, chemistry…what can I say?"

Mirabella made an impatient face. "Yeah, sure, right. At first, maybe. Look—I know Tristan's got great eyes and a killer smile, but the sex-appeal thing doesn't last. I mean, what did you *love* about him?"

"Oh Lord." Jessie thought about it, hugging herself because, in spite of the warmth of the afternoon, she could feel herself shivering deep inside. "God…when I think about him back then, all I seem to be able to remember is the way he smiled…his eyes…he seemed so happy-go-lucky, so arrogant, so confident and cocky…." She laughed shakily. "Stubborn to the point of being bullheaded… opinionated…convictions as unshakable as his jaw."

Her sister-in-law shook her head and made a clicking sound with her tongue. "Hmm…not exactly an easy person to live with," she murmured, and Jessie caught a glimpse of the laughter in her eyes. Because, of course, Mirabella herself could have been that person Jessie'd just described.

"Well, no," she hastened to add, "but he was strong and brave and loyal, too. He wouldn't hesitate to risk his life for somebody, even a stranger. And he was about as softhearted as they come. I don't know if anybody knew it, but he was really sentimental. And gentle. And—" her voice choked and she finished in a whisper "—he really, really adored his little girl."

"And her mother, too, certainly."

"That I'm not so sure about," Jessie said with a bleak little smile.

"Oh, come on." But for once Mirabella wasn't going to have a chance to argue, because Tristan was coming toward them across the lawn. Max was with him, and the two men were talking and laughing and grinning like little boys who'd just done something incredibly foolhardy and gotten away without a scratch.

The sight should have warmed her heart…shouldn't it? Here it was, a beautiful day, much like when she'd stood on this very porch and watched those two officers in dress blues come across the lawn with the news that had blown her world apart. The climbing rosebush was in full bloom, the lawn was yellow-polka-dotted with dandelions, just as they'd been then. From the other side of the house she could hear somebody hollering that the ribs were 'bout done and for Momma to send somebody out with a platter. A screen door slammed, and laughter and conversation rippled and floated on the warm, humid air.

Home. This is my home…my family. And here in the midst of it all was Tristan…alive, laughing, grinning his old familiar Tristan grin. It was a miracle…beyond anything she could possibly have dreamed of. She should be overflowing with happiness. Giddy with it.

* * *

Later that evening Jessie stood before the antique oak chest of drawers that had belonged to Granny Calhoun, and gazed at the gold wedding band in the palm of her hand. Outside, the brief Southern dusk had deepened into its soft and velvety darkness, and somewhere out in the woods a whippoorwill had begun its frantic song. The food leftovers had been packed up and distributed, and one by one the families had drifted away—Troy and Charly were on their way back to Atlanta, and Tracy and Al to Augusta, and C.J. and Caitlyn to their little house down the road. Summer and Riley were staying overnight with Mirabella and Jimmy Joe; it was a long drive back to Charleston. Tris and Max and Sammi June were still out in the backyard, dismantling the tables and putting away the barbecue.

Jessie had finished helping with the last of the kitchen clean-up and had come upstairs to the room that had been hers alone for eight and a half years, and which, for the past two days, and for the first time in her life, she'd been sharing—sort of—with Tristan. *With my husband.* She'd been putting lotion on her hands when she remembered her wedding ring, still in its little velvet box where she'd put it years ago, in the old rosewood humidor that had served as her jewelry box ever since she was a teenager. In the hectic time since they'd been home, with all the demands of family and television interviews and tapings, neither she nor Tristan had thought of it.

Now she was remembering the terrible day she'd taken it off…the day of Tristan's memorial service. It had been hot, she remembered, and humid, with rain threatening and thunder grumbling in the distance. She remembered Sammi June's small, sticky hand in hers, and both of them jerking when the rifles fired their salute…and then the white-gloved hands holding out to her the folded three-corner flag. She barely remembered taking it and murmuring thank you. Later, she'd placed the flag in a drawer in this very dresser—the top one—and had taken off her wedding ring and put it in its box and put it in the drawer with the flag. Later that night, unable to sleep, she'd opened the drawer with trembling hands and taken the ring out of its box and put it back on her finger. Sometime after that, during a spring cleaning—she couldn't remember exactly when—she'd moved the flag to the cedar chest. The ring had stayed on her finger until she'd started working in the NICU. She'd started taking it off when she left for her shift, and then one day she came home and didn't put it back on. *Tristan's gone,* she remembered telling herself half defiantly, as if she were about to commit a sin. *He's not coming back. It's time to move on.*

Now, gazing at the ring, her eyes shimmered and filled with tears. *Tris is alive! I should be so happy,* she thought. *I am happy, dammit.*

So why do I feel this aching sadness that won't go away?

Behind her the door opened. She heard Tristan come quietly into the room and close the door. She didn't turn but watched his reflection come to join hers in the murky, oak-framed oval mirror above the dresser. He was smiling, and when he put his hands on her shoulders and bent his head to kiss the side of her neck, she smelled beer on his breath.

"Hmm," he murmured, nuzzling her with his chin, "wha'cha doin'? Ah—" Noticing the ring in her hand, he took it from her, and with both arms encircling her from behind, slipped it onto her finger. "There," he said thickly, "back where it belongs."

He nudged aside her hair and kissed the back of her neck, and she shivered. In response he chuckled and opened his mouth on her damp nape, at the same time wrapping her in his arms and covering her breasts with his hands. She felt a hot, drawing pressure on her neck, and nerves sang through her skin and hardened her nipples, and arousal pooled between her thighs.

"Are you making a hicky?" she mumbled, already half incoherent.

"Mmm...so what? Nobody'll see it. Unless you put your hair up...oops, damn. You made me lose my place. Oh well...guess I'll just have to start over..."

"Tris..." But his hands were under her shirt, cupping her breasts and plucking impatiently between them at the closing of her bra. She released it for him, then gasped when he brushed the bra aside and took each sensitized tip between a thumb and forefinger. The heat between her thighs coiled and writhed, and her legs turned to jelly. This time she whimpered it: *"Tris..."*

He lifted his head and watched her in the mirror while one hand found her zipper and ripped it down, then slipped inside her panties. His palm was warm, and his fingers splayed over her belly, gently kneading. The other arm, tight across her breasts, held her close against him while he continued to torment one taut nipple. "I enjoyed today," he said softly. "More than I thought I would." His eyes gleamed like dark pools in moonlight.

"Did you?" She could barely talk, now...barely stand.

"Umm-hmm...more than you'll ever know." The un-fathomable pools that were his eyes darkened...deepened. His lips tightened briefly and then quirked sideways, as if he'd felt a spasm of pain and was determined to hide it.

More than you'll ever know... How will I know if you won't tell me? she thought. But her mind and body were in different places. Her heart was bumping against his arm, and lower down, his fingers measured the frantic thrumming of her pulse.

She wanted to close her eyes but somehow knew he wouldn't want her to, so she fiercely ordered them to stay open and watched herself...watched him...as he slipped his fingers into her. Not gently—suddenly and deeply, and holding her tightly so that the thrust of his hand made her feel his hardness pressed against her buttocks. But she was ready for him, and the gasp that burst from her wasn't pain. Her body liquefied. Her palms and the soles of her feet felt scorched. In the murky glass of the old mirror, her eyes looked wild, and her cheeks glowed as if with a fever.

"*I can't—*"

"Yes—you can. *You can.*"

But her body was already spiraling out of her control— if it had ever been in it—and she was breaking up in a thousand tiny explosions, all cold fire and flooding warmth. She gave a soft, desperate cry and let the kindly darkness come, and as she closed her eyes she felt his mouth, hot and open on her neck, and his fingers inside her, playing her body's sensations like quivering guitar strings, making them last and last and last…

And then he was laying her down on the bed and taking off her clothes…guiding her thighs apart and entering her still-throbbing body. Gently now, he moved within her, braced above her on taut and trembling arms, eyes closed, neck muscles corded. Dazed, Jessie drew her hands down his back, stroking rigid muscles and sliding over the ropy ribbons of scar tissue, rocking with his thrusts, arching her body into his, remembering what it had been like, remembering this…*remembering.*

His climax was restrained, almost…polite, Jessie thought. Afterward, he kissed her, used his discarded T-shirt for a towel, then gathered her against him—her back to his front—and fell asleep, breathing softly…snoring gently into her hair.

It was early, nowhere near Jessie's customary bedtime, and she lay awake for a long time, afraid to move or get up and go to the bathroom or turn off the lights Tris had left burning.

It's going to be all right, she told herself, staring at the familiar room…the wallpaper, the furniture, the curtains she knew so well. *We've come so far already. Haven't we?*

It'll be better once we have a place of our own.

Chapter 13

Gradually the days returned to more normal rhythms. On Monday Max left to go back to his home in Florida, and Sammi June drove off to school in Athens in the little red Chevy pickup truck Jimmy Joe had fixed up for her to use. Her professors were being understanding about giving her make-up exams and extensions on overdue papers. The last of the media people had left; their interest in Tristan's story had waned rapidly when they discovered he wasn't going to share with their audiences any of the gory details about his POW experience.

On Monday Jessie called the hospital to see how things were going in the NICU and found out that two of her nurses were out with the flu and a third had fallen off of a stepladder and broken her wrist. So on Tuesday she went back to work.

Tristan started running every morning with C.J. and working out with weights in his garage afterward. He'd been putting on weight, and was beginning to look almost like his normal self again. In the afternoon and evening he studied flight manuals and answered some of the hundreds of letters that had been pouring in from around the country, and drank beer steadily until he fell asleep around dusk, which in mid-May was about eight o'clock. By the time Jessie went up to bed he was snorin' like a buzz saw, as Granny Calhoun would've put it. He got up early, though, sometimes as early as four o'clock, tiptoeing around in the dark so as not to wake up Jessie while he dressed in his sweats and went downstairs to wait for it to get light enough to go running.

One evening he'd dozed off in Granny Calhoun's old recliner chair, watching the evening news on the TV in the living room. Not knowing what else to do, Jessie left him alone until ten o'clock, when she was ready to go upstairs to bed. Then she leaned over him and murmured, "Tris? Honey, you need to come to bed now—you're gonna get a crick in your neck." And she put her hand on his shoulder.

He made a wild, grunting sound and shot up out of the chair so fast the top of his head hit her in the mouth, and at the same time he was flailing at the air with his arms. An instant later he was on his hands and knees on the rug, and his face...Jessie had never seen such a look on anyone's face before, and to see it on his—her husband's—was almost more than she could bear. Shattered, tasting blood, she dropped to her knees and reached toward him in desperate apology.

"Oh God—Oh God—I'm so sorry—I forgot. I forgot. I'm sorry...." Tears were streaming down her face. "Tris, it's okay, honey. It's okay..."

He was looking around, not at her, eyes darting here and there like those of a trapped animal. Then, slowly, the bright terror in his eyes faded to dull awareness. He darted one quick, embarrassed look over his shoulder and said in a choked voice, "Your mom—"

"It's okay, she's already gone to bed. Oh, Tris—"

He reached out to brush her lip with his thumb. "I told you not to touch me." His voice was as harsh as his touch was gentle.

She caught her lip with her teeth and sucked it in, hiding the blood from him. "I know…I know. It's just that…you look so…you've been seeming so…"

"Normal?" Wearing a travesty of a smile like a Mardi Gras mask, he got stiffly to his feet, then took her hand and helped her to hers. "I thought this *was* normal—for someone like me, anyway. At least, that's what they keep tellin' me."

Aching inside, she slipped an arm around his waist. "We just have to be patient, give it time…"

He dropped his arm across her shoulders and drew her close to his side. "Yeah," he said, as they started up the stairs together, "they keep telling me that, too."

Tristan slept in one of the spare bedrooms that night, regretting the pain he knew it was causing Jess, but knowing full well he wasn't going to be able to get back to sleep after all that. He could feel the nightmares lurking still…feel the walls closing in on him even before he closed his eyes. Damned beer must be losing its effect, he thought.

Either that or it's this house. It gives me claustrophobia. It's Jess's place, not mine. There's no room for me here.

It wasn't that it was uncomfortable, this house his wife had grown up in. Just the opposite, in fact. In some sort of complicated, perverse way, it was the very comfort of it, the homeyness of it, that made him feel so alienated. He couldn't seem to get his mind around so much softness and warmth, the clean smells and good tastes, the laughter and the love. The cold and hunger, pain and fear and darkness of prison wouldn't let go of him. In the daylight hours he could convince himself he'd left all that behind him forever, but in the dark of night he knew better. He still hadn't escaped from those prison walls, and he was beginning to wonder if he ever would.

The next morning he told Jessie he was going to start looking for a house for them to rent. "I know your momma's got plenty of room," he said reasonably, "but we need a place of our own." He didn't use the word *home*. He still felt a long way from being able to do that.

His biggest problem, he soon discovered, was going to be transportation. There seemed to be plenty of vehicles around, but no spares, and even if there had been, it went against his grain to borrow a car from one of his wife's relatives. The obvious solution was to buy himself a car—he was going to have to, eventually. And money wasn't going to be an issue—he'd been given the first installment of his back military pay before he'd left Washington, which had amounted to a pretty sizable sum. But it was only one more confusing thing about his return to "normal" life that he found the idea of buying a car both thrilling and terrifying.

He didn't know where to begin. There were too damn many choices, that was the problem. After having someone else direct every aspect of his existence for eight years, he wasn't used to making decisions. Used or new? Foreign or domestic? Should he go for power and performance or fuel economy? He sort of liked the idea of the SUVs, but they were really more car than he needed. Sports cars tempted him, naturally, but that seemed a little too much like he was trying to overcompensate. On the other hand, everyday run-of-the-mill cars…hell, how would he ever decide on one? There had to be hundreds of them, all more or less alike.

In the end he said "The hell with it," and went out for his morning run. He was pumping iron over at C.J.'s when J.J. came ripping up on his shiny new Honda motorcycle. Tris stopped what he was doing to watch J.J. put the kickstand down, take off his helmet and hang it on the handlebars, then dismount with a seventeen-year-old's flexible grace and come sauntering toward them, pulling off his gloves.

"Hey," J.J. said, grinning, the thrill of the ride still bright in his eyes.

Tris could feel that thrill himself, remembering his own brief spin on the bike. He felt it again now…a humming under his breastbone and a tingling in his thighs.

"Hey," C.J. grunted back to his nephew, between lifts.

Tris muttered something, he wasn't sure what. He was smiling and looking past J.J. at that black-and-yellow motorcycle.

"You did what?" Jessie couldn't believe what she was seeing with her own eyes. *A motorcycle?* But it was—a very big, very shiny, royal-blue motorcycle. And standing beside it was her husband, wearing a huge grin and a snug-fitting black leather jacket that seemed to have zippers everywhere.

"I bought it." He said it in a casual, offhand way, but the glow of pride in his eyes made her heart quiver. She tried to swallow the fear that had jumped into her throat and search for something positive to say.

"It's…" But it was no use. She shook her head helplessly.

"It's a BMW," Tris explained, as if she couldn't see that for herself. He was as enthusiastic as a boy. "It was between this and a Gold Wing—didn't want a Harley—I'm thinking, too much vibration—might be hard on my knee, you know? This hasn't got much vibration at all, just a nice, sweet hum…. Hop on. Let's go for a ride."

"Oh, God, no…Tris—" She couldn't stop an involuntary recoil. She was remembering the autobahn, Tristan behind the wheel of a Euro-model Ford, and the wild light in his eyes and the twisted bitterness of his smile. Remembering her terror, her anger, she felt her breath grow shallow.

"Here, I even got you a helmet. And look—there's a backrest—and you can have armrests, too, if you want. It's like sitting in an easy chair."

He was imagining her there already, thinking how it would be with her behind him, arms locked tight around his waist and breasts pillowed against his back, and all that power under him and the wind pummeling his face and tearing the breath from his lungs. Power, speed and sex—all the things he'd been denied—right here, in one sleek, sexy package.

"Come on, Jess...ride with me," he murmured, folding his arms around her and nuzzling her neck with his sweetest voice and most seductive smile. Making a conscious point of doing what once had come as naturally to him as breathing. He felt her body expand with her indrawn breath, and her heart flutter inside her hospital smock, printed with alphabet blocks and Teddy bears in primary colors. Her skin was warm and damp and smelled of lotion and powder and disinfectant. "Just a short one...I'll take it easy, honey, I promise."

"Oh..." Her laugh was weak and fragmented, and he could feel her body softening...trembling...responding to him the way she always had...always would. It was one of the things that had made her so irresistible to him, back then. He chuckled and rocked her in his arms, rubbing himself suggestively against her, shameless in pressing his advantage. "Come on, darlin'...don't you trust me?"

And even as he said it, even before she laughed again and finally gave in, he knew that she didn't. Once she would have—utterly, completely, implicitly. And now she didn't.

He kept his smile in place as he helped her climb into the BMW's rear seat, showed her how to adjust the foot- and armrests and strap on the helmet. Then he took her for a ride, down the lane and onto the paved road, past C.J.'s place and then left onto the dirt track that ran between

timber groves and came out on another paved road, this
one curving around past Jimmy Joe and Mirabella's house
and eventually back to where they'd started, taking it easy,
the way he'd promised. He kept the BMW's speed to a
sedate ramble that barely tapped its power potential, and
erotic fantasies were far from his mind.

She was smiling when she took off her helmet and shook
her hair loose on her shoulders, but more, he thought, from
relief than any real joy in the ride. Her eyes were bright
and her laughter breathless, and as he helped her dismount
and get her feet steady under her, he was careful not to let
her see how badly she'd disappointed him.

After a week or so, when Tristan hadn't managed to kill
himself or suffer any other major calamities with the motorcycle, Jessie began to relax, a little. It was, she told herself, only a bike, and a rather sedate one, as bikes went. A
BMW, for heaven's sake. After all, Tristan was a responsible adult, not some hotheaded, speed-crazy kid, and he
really did seem to be getting a lot of enjoyment out of it.
How could she begrudge him that?

Anyway, he'd been putting it to good use. For the past
week, he'd been out and about almost every day, looking
at properties for rent. So far, he told Jessie, he hadn't found
anyplace that felt like home to him. She'd suggested that
houses generally didn't come to feel like home until you'd
lived in them awhile, but Tris had insisted he'd know the
right place when he saw it.

The week before Memorial Day, Jessie came home from
the hospital to find him waiting for her in the kitchen. It
had been an unusually grueling day in the NICU. Rosie
Johnson, a twenty-four-week preemie who'd weighed less
than a pound at birth, after three months in the NICU, most
of that in the high-risk unit, had finally been moved into
an open crib, which was the last stage before release. Today
her ecstatic parents had given her her first bath. Another

long-termer, Kyle Rojas, had been rushed into surgery to repair a hernia, and for the Rockingham baby it had been one crisis after another. There'd been two new admits; one hadn't made it. Jessie had sat with the devastated parents while they'd held and rocked their impossibly tiny son, until they could bring themselves to say goodbye. It had been a gut-wrenching, roller coaster of a day.

Jessie was used to having some quiet time alone to decompress after such a day, maybe take a shower and wash the hospital smells out of her hair, or just sit on the porch with a glass of sweet tea and close her eyes and listen to the happy and unregulated sounds of birds and insects. She never liked to bring her job home with her, or burden anyone she loved with the emotional toll it sometimes took on her. Now, as she dropped her pocketbook on the table and saw Tristan's eyes glittering with poorly suppressed excitement, she could feel herself closing up, like a book interrupted at a particularly gripping spot and reluctantly put aside for later.

"Hey," she said as she went to kiss him. "You look like the cat that ate the canary." She didn't add that the last time he'd had that look, he'd just brought home a motorcycle.

"Mmm..." his lips curved and stretched, smiling against hers. "I bet I know what'd taste better."

"*Tris*—stop that! What if—"

"Your momma went to the grocery store. We've got all kinds of time. And right here's a perfectly good kitchen table..."

She squirmed out of his arms and gasped, "Tris!" But she was laughing, knowing he was teasing her. Knowing he could have worn down her resistance and her tiredness and taken her on that kitchen table if he'd tried, and in about half a minute, too, if he hadn't had something more important on his mind.

"Oh, right—so I guess this means the honeymoon's

over," he muttered in feigned disappointment as she turned away and opened the refrigerator. He waited until she was pouring herself a glass of sweet tea before he said, with a definite air of smugness, "I think I've got us a place."

"Really?" Her guilty longing to be quiet and alone fled. "Where? In Athens?"

He shook his head and picked up a letter that was lying on the table. "I've been working through those letters, you know, trying to get them answered, a few at a time. Don't know when this came—it's from Tom Satterfield—remember him?" Jessie shook her head, but he hadn't waited. "We knew them in...I think it was Bremerton—or maybe Norfolk—oh, hell, I don't know. They were younger, but we got together with them because his wife was from South Carolina, and we sort of had that in common. Later on, he and I served on the *Teddy Roosevelt* together. He was a hotshot, just coming up back then."

Jessie took the letter from him and sat down at the table to read it while he went on. "Anyway, he's a Lieutenant Commander, now, back in the Gulf, probably be there for another six months, at least. They've got this lake house—his wife isn't using it, she's staying in Norfolk because she doesn't want to take their kids out of school—and he says we're welcome to stay there until we figure out where we're gonna be. Maybe even buy the place, if we like it and decide we want to stay in the area. So...what do you think?"

"Lake?" Jessie frowned at the letter without seeing it. So many alarm bells were going off in her head, she felt as if she were flashing back to her day in the NICU. *Figure out where we're gonna be? But I want to be here! I don't want to go back to that life, always moving, moving, moving...* "What lake?"

"Uh, somewhere in South Carolina. Lake Russell, I think. That's over on the Savannah—"

"I know where it is. Tris, how far is that from here? It's

got to be at least forty miles.'' She was still staring at the letter; she didn't dare look at him.

"Yeah, probably. About that. That's closer to your mom than either Troy or Tracy—easy visitin' distance.''

She pushed the letter away. Her hands wanted to shake, so she pressed them flat on the tabletop as she looked up at Tris. A frown was hovering around his eyebrows, as if not sure whether it should stay or not. "What about work? Tris, I'd have to drive an hour to get to the hospital. Maybe more. Each way.''

The frown settled in to stay, and she saw his jaw tighten in a way she remembered all too well. He was about to dig his heels in. He'd got his mind set on this lake house, wherever it was, and nothing she said was going to change it. And wasn't this where she'd always given in and let him have his way? Wasn't this where she was supposed to swallow hard and go along with whatever he wanted, because she wanted to make him happy?

"Why do you need to work?''

Even though she'd been half expecting them, the words hit her like an electric shock. She felt herself go cold, and there was a singing in her ears that made all other sound seem as if it came from far, far away...

"I have eight years' back pay coming. Why don't you just quit your job? Then we can live anywhere we want to.''

Anywhere you *want to...that's really what you mean, isn't it?*

Her heart was racing and her breathing was quick and shallow—classic symptoms of panic, she realized, and yes, every impulse, every nerve in her body wanted to jump up and run away from there, away from danger, away from *him.* It took every ounce of control she had to make herself sit still. With her hands resting on the tabletop to help still their trembling, she forced herself to think calmly...

rationally. It was like counting to ten, she thought, without the numbers.

Danger? Yes…oh, yes. I'm in danger of losing something important to me…something I love. But is it him I'm afraid of, or myself?

I'm afraid I'll give in, she thought, cold now with an old familiar bleakness, trembling with an old familiar anger. *I thought I'd changed, but I haven't. Not all that much.*

"It's not about needing money," she said carefully. "Tris, I love my job. I don't want to quit. It's important, what I do." *It's important to me.*

She watched him, feeling wretched and ashamed, watched the frustration swelling inside his chest and stiffening his jaw. Saw his eyes glittering with the words he didn't want to say. *More important than I am?* Please don't let him ask, she prayed. And it occurred to her that she'd asked him that very question once, long ago. Her stomach writhed at the memory of it.

"I'm not asking you to quit," he said, gripping the back of a chair and leaning on it. "Can't you just…I don't know, take a leave of absence, or something? Just until I…" He stopped, and she could see a muscle working in his jaw.

He thinks I'm being selfish, she thought. Just as I thought he was then. *And he was. And, oh God, I am, too.* Here he'd suffered so terribly, and for so long, and how could she be worrying about a stupid job? What kind of person was she? What kind of wife? Didn't Tristan deserve every possible happiness? Shouldn't she be willing to make just about any sacrifice in order to help him find that happiness?

The answer was of course she should. She knew that. She knew she was being selfish and awful, and it didn't help.

It didn't stop her from saying, in a tight and trembling voice, "You know, Tris, you aren't the only one who's suffered." She looked at him, and her eyes burned, needing the relief of tears. "As horrible as it must have been for you, at least you knew you were *alive.* You knew *we*…were alive. Sammi June and I thought you were *dead.* We had to learn how to live without you. And we *did.* It wasn't easy, but we did it. And now…you're back in our lives. You had eight years of your life stolen from you, and that's horrible. It's not fair. But the thing is, you can't ask us—Sammi June and me—to give back those eight years. Even if we could. That wouldn't be fair, either.''

There was an aching, shivering silence. Then Tristan tightened his hands on the chair back. ''You're right—it wouldn't.'' He let go of it and walked out of the kitchen.

A moment later the screen door whacked shut, and Jessie jumped as though it had hit her. She closed her eyes, body tensed and waiting. It was only when she heard the *brum-brum* of the motorcycle's engine that the tears began.

It was late when Jessie heard the BMW's well-mannered thrum again. She was in bed but not asleep—Momma'd gone to bed hours ago—and the clock radio on the nightstand had just flipped from p.m. to a.m. She watched the pattern the single headlamp cast on her bedroom wall, and her heart thumped heavily in her chest.

I'll apologize, she thought. *I'll tell him—not that I'm gonna quit my job…not that. A leave of absence, though… We'll talk about it. If he's got his heart set on that lake house, we'll work something out.*

She lay like a board, listening for the quiet sounds of doors opening and closing…someone moving around in the kitchen…footsteps coming up the stairs. The footsteps passed her door and a moment later she heard the click of a door closing farther down the hallway. Tristan was sleeping in the spare room again.

Jessie put an arm across her eyes and let out a breath she didn't know she'd been holding. Her whole body seemed to be vibrating…aching…and she didn't know whether it was with disappointment or relief.

Tristan was still asleep when Jessie left for work the next morning, which surprised her a little; he'd been getting up faithfully at the crack of dawn to go running. It was probably just as well, she thought. They needed to have a good long talk, which there wasn't going to be time for before she had to leave. And with things the way they were between them, it was bound to be awkward and uncomfortable. She was sorry about that, she really was.

I'll apologize, and then we'll talk about it.

But even as she thought it, a bleak little kernel of hopelessness was forming in her belly. *Talk? But that's the whole trouble, isn't it? We don't seem to be doing very well in that department. Tristan won't talk at all—not about anything important. And I can't seem to get my own feelings across to him, even when I try. What hope is there for us?*

God, help me. I don't know what to do.

It was 11:36 that morning when Irene, the NICU receptionist, came to tell her she had a phone call. She knew that because she glanced up at the clock before she said, "Take a message for me, will you, hon'?" She was showing the Johnsons how to hook up Rosie's heart monitor and oxygen tubes, and Rosie wasn't at all happy about it.

"Uh…you might want to take it," Irene said. "It's Alysha, down in the E.R.?"

"Okay—be just a minute…" Jessie motioned to Ray, one of the staff nurses, to come and take over for her. A call from the E.R. wasn't unusual, and meant she'd most likely be getting a new patient soon—anything from an abandoned infant to an unexpected delivery in somebody's car or maybe the EMS wagon.

At her desk she stripped off her gloves and picked up the phone. "Hey, 'Leesha, whatcha got for me today?"

"Jessie?" The E.R. supervisor's voice sounded unusually restrained. "Honey, can you come down here, ASAP?"

"Uh...sure. What—" It took that long for something in the other nurse's tone to set off warning sirens in Jessie's head. Shocks, like electrical charges, zapped through her and sizzled inside her skin. She sucked in air. "Oh God. What's happened?"

"Honey, it's your husband. EMS just brought him in. There's been an accident."

Chapter 14

After being interrupted by Jessie's gasp, the E.R. nurse rushed on. "Don't be upset, now, okay? It looks like he's gonna be all right."

"What…what *happened?* Did— Is he—"

"MVA—motorcycle. Paramedics who brought him in said apparently somebody cut him off, he was going too fast to stop and went into a ditch. Or at least, the motorcycle did. Your husband went airborne." Jessie gasped; a giant hand was squeezing her heart. Then she heard Alysha's rich dark chuckle. "He was lucky—wasn't wearing a jacket or a helmet, but there don't appear to be any serious injuries—they're running a head CT right now, but he was seein' the right number of fingers. You might want to prepare yourself, though. Honey, the man is not a pretty sight. Seems he landed in a big ol' bank of blackberry bushes. Paramedics had a devil of a time getting him out. They look worse than he does. Anyway, honey, I thought you'd want to know."

"Yes…thank you—" Jessie's legs gave out and she sat

down abruptly—and thank God her chair was where it needed to be. "I'll be right down." But as she fumbled the receiver back into its cradle she felt hollow and sick and cold. There was a rushing noise in her ears, and she knew better than to try to go anywhere until the blood that had drained from her head found its way back again.

Oh God...Tris. What were you thinking? What are you doing? Or trying to do...

No! As soon as the thought formed in her mind, she rejected it. Rejected it with a vehemence born of panic. No—it couldn't be that. Tristan couldn't be suicidal. He couldn't be. He'd fought too hard to survive, to get back home. Now that he'd made it, he wouldn't throw it all away—he *wouldn't.*

And yet...she remembered the autobahn, and that strange, wild light in his eyes. She remembered, from too many other times, the bleakness there, as well. And the painful, bitter irony of his smile.

Unless... Understanding hit her with the smothering force of an avalanche. *Unless he doesn't believe he's made it back. And is afraid he never will. Oh God, Tris...*

Remorse and helplessness overwhelmed her, and she lowered her forehead into her hand and closed her eyes. *I don't know enough about this,* she thought, thumb and forefinger rubbing desperate circles over her temples that didn't ease the ache behind them. *Tris, I don't know what to do. I don't know how to help you. I wish I did...*

And then, as if those words did have the sort of magic fairy tales so often ascribe to them, it came to her that she *did* know how she might be able to help Tris. Maybe.

She sat up straight. Yes, she thought. *I'll do it. He's not gonna like it, but...too bad.* Taking her pocketbook from the bottom drawer of her desk, she set it on her lap and opened it. Took out her wallet, and from it extracted a business card. Gazing at it, she drew the phone toward her, lifted the receiver and punched in a number.

She didn't expect anyone to answer. She expected voice mail, or a recording instructing her to dial her party's extension, or press one for this or that option. Instead, after three rings, she heard a vaguely familiar voice say briskly, "Cory Pearson."

"It looks worse than it is," Tristan muttered, squirming under Jessie's unwavering gaze. She hadn't said a word to him, yet, just stood there in the doorway of his E.R. cubicle with her hands tucked in the pockets of her smock and looked at him. He'd expected her to be upset—angry, or crying, maybe—but as far as he could tell, she wasn't any of those things. He couldn't read her at all. Once he'd been able to, like a book. But now he couldn't. He'd have better luck trying to figure out what a stranger was thinking.

But then, he reminded himself, that's what she was now. A stranger.

She came toward him, her face calm…almost serene, and he found himself experiencing rather childish twinges of pique. He'd been in a motorcycle accident, for God's sake, she ought to be a *little* bit upset. Then he was instantly ashamed of himself. What she *ought* to do, he told himself, is kick your butt.

"You look like you tried to break up a cat-fight." She reached out to carefully finger the hair back from his forehead, uncovering one of his more spectacular contusions. She examined the neat and tidy little bandages that held it together, then let the hair fall back over it. Her touch felt cool…impersonal. Something inside him squalled in protest of that, like a child with a skinned knee. "So…what happened?"

"Ah, some idiot cut me off. Didn't have time to stop, so I opted to ditch…so to speak." His lips twitched themselves into a smile. Sort of. "Still have my flying reflexes, anyway."

Her eyes were quiet and dark. "What shape is the bike in?"

He made a face, as if he'd felt a twinge of pain—which he had. His brand-new bike. Jeez. "I don't know. Didn't look too bad, what I saw of it before they carted me off, anyway. *Damn,*" he added mournfully.

"You were lucky," she said in a shaking voice. He saw her throat move with her swallow, and remorse wrapped him in its clammy blanket.

"I've had a hell of a lot worse," he growled, and when her eyes flicked toward him, glossy with pain, he wanted to throttle himself. He must be more shaken-up than he realized, to have said something that dumb.

"Well," she said stiffly, "I guess I wouldn't know about that." Her mouth had a wounded look, and he felt dismal and misunderstood. She didn't have a clue what he was doing for her. What he was saving her from by not telling her how it had been for him. Probably, he thought, with a cold gray sense of futility, she never would.

"So," he said, "when are they gonna let me out of here?"

She took a lifting breath, like a mark of punctuation, accepting the change of subject with what he was certain was relief. Like turning our backs on the damned elephant in the room, he thought. *So be it.*

"You're gonna have to ask the doctor about that," she said, cool and impersonal again, looking past him with her hands in the pockets of her smock. "They've got you scheduled for X rays...some other tests...just to make sure you haven't got any internal injuries...." And he saw the way her throat kept rippling, and how tight her mouth looked, and he realized she wasn't as unmoved as she'd tried to appear.

His feelings for her welled up in him like a pot boiling over—nothing he could do to stop it. He called softly to her, and his voice made a gravelly sound. "Jessie—

honey.'' He held out a hand and she hung back from him
for a long, angry moment, as if touching him was about
the last thing she wanted to do. ''Come on, Jess—
please...'' his torn, wretched voice pleaded, and she gave
in with a breathy whimper of defeat. As she let him take
her hand he could see her fighting back tears. He reeled her
in so he could get his hand around the back of her neck,
then closed his eyes and with a gusty sigh, pulled her close
and tucked her face into the curve of his neck and shoulder.
''Honey, I'm all right...I'm *okay*.''

He could feel her nod. He could feel, too, the deep-down
tremors that rippled through her every now and then. He
rubbed the back of her neck gently, wishing he could im-
merse his hands in the warm, sweet-smelling softness of
her hair. But she had it twisted up and fastened to the back
of her head with some kind of clip, and he had to be content
with savoring the velvety textures of skin and fine down
on her nape, instead. ''I am, you know. I'm gonna be fine,''
he said.

''I know.'' She pulled away from him and straightened
up, delicately touching at her eyes with her fingertips like
someone trying not to smear mascara, though it was obvious even to him she wasn't wearing any. She took a re-
storative breath. ''I have to get back upstairs. When they're
done with you here, have somebody call me, okay? I can
take off early, whenever you're ready to go home.''

''Yeah, I will.'' She nodded, hesitated, then leaned down
to kiss him, a light, sweet brush of lips still damp and salty
from tears she hadn't let him see her shed. She straightened
again, and was on her way out of the cubicle when he
remembered something. ''Jess?'' She turned, eyebrows
lifted. ''Don't tell Sammi June.''

Her lips curved in a way that let him know she hadn't
forgiven him yet, by a long shot. ''Too late,'' she said, on
a little grace note of satisfaction, and left him.

Tristan groaned, then settled back to endure another long

day of waiting, of staring at a hospital ceiling and listening to the sounds of other people's crises. He didn't mind the pain he was in, so much; he'd learned to welcome pain for the message it carried, which was the assurance that he was still alive. In addition to that, he considered this particular pain justice, penance for the emotional pain he was causing Jess. He wished to God he could tell her he'd make it up to her, somehow, but the truth was, he didn't know how he ever could.

Sometime later, he didn't know how much, but probably midafternoon—he'd been to X ray and then dozed some while he waited for the lab work to come back—he heard a light tapping on the glass of his cubicle. He opened his eyes, then pushed himself hastily into a more upright position.

"God, you look awful," Cory Pearson said, pushing away from the door and coming toward him. "What did you do to yourself?"

"Ah…shoot. Looks a lot worse than it is." Well, hell, it was a good line the first time—might as well use it again. Tristan held out a hand for Cory to shake, then winced; some of the worst cuts were on his hands and arms—probably from trying to break his fall. "What're you doing here?"

Cory shrugged and looked guilty. "Ah, well. I was in Atlanta, actually. Taping a segment for CNN—follow-up stuff. You know—how does it feel, readjusting to life after being a POW? Since I was so close, I thought I'd—"

"She called you, didn't she?"

"Yeah." Cory's smile was only a little guilty. "The rest of it's true, though. About being in Atlanta—that's how I got here so quick. Your wife got me on my cell phone. And about the taping." He pulled a stool with rollers on its legs close to Tristan's bedside and sat on it. "Hell, you know, you're the one who should be doing this thing, not me. I was only there for four months. You're the one with the adjustments—make a helluva story.'' His eyes gleamed with a reporter's fervor.

Tristan snorted and looked away, shifting restlessly under the blood-spotted sheet. Cory watched him in silence for a few moments, then said, ''So.''

Tristan shot him a look, anger flaring. ''So what?''

''So, how're you doing?'' Tristan shrugged, and after a pause, Cory said quietly, ''If you don't mind my saying so—and even if you do—you don't look like you're doing all that well.''

''For...*Pete's* sake,'' Tristan exploded, ''I had a damn motorcycle accident. Some...jackass cut me off. It's got nothing to do with...anything.''

''Your wife apparently doesn't think so.'' Cory leaned back and laced his fingers together behind his head. ''She's worried about you, you know.''

''Well, she shouldn't be.''

''So...everything's working out great for you? Everything's just...hunky-dory, is that it?''

Tristan made an exasperated sound and jerked away from the reporter's gaze. No point in lying to this man. He could try, but they'd both know the truth. Four months or eight years, it didn't matter; this was somebody who'd been there. *He knew.*

He let out a breath, but there was still a heavy weight sitting in the middle of his chest. ''It will be. I just have to get back to doing what I do...you know? I'll be okay, once I get my flying status back. That's what I've been working on—getting in shape, getting my strength back. Studying...'' He stopped when Cory leaned forward abruptly.

For several seconds the reporter didn't say anything, just stared down at his hands, clasped between his knees. Then he lifted his head and as Tristan looked into those keen blue eyes, ageless and compassionate behind the rimless lenses of his glasses, he had the feeling of roles and ages flip-flopping.

"You keep talking about going back," Cory said, his tone gentle…diffident. "Did you ever think maybe…you ought to be thinking about moving forward?"

"I thought I was," Tristan growled.

Cory shook his head. "No, man. Flying Tomcats—that's your past." His grin was crooked. "Hell—nobody flies Tomcats forever." Tristan didn't say anything but jerked away from that relentless blue gaze with an impatient hiss. "Well, *do* they?" Cory persisted. "Tell me this—if you hadn't been shot down, if you hadn't lost those eight years, you think you'd still be flying Tomcats today?"

Tristan shifted uncomfortably and muttered, "Probably not."

"So, what *would* you be doing? Think you'd have stayed in the Navy?"

"Maybe—I don't know." He shifted again. *Damn,* but those cuts and scratches were starting to *sting.* Weren't the Chinese supposed to have invented something called the Death of a Thousand Cuts? Then he realized he was dangerously close to feeling sorry for himself, and closed his mind to the pain. "I do know I'd still be flying, though. Maybe something besides Tomcats, maybe commercially, but I'll fly as long as they'll let me. After that…maybe become a flight instructor…I haven't thought that far ahead yet." He scowled at his knees. "I'm still working on where I'm gonna live."

"What does your wife have to say about that? I'm assuming you two have talked about it."

"Tried to," Tristan growled. He felt a cold squeezing sensation in his chest. Cory, with a man's usual reticence about discussing personal matters, remained silent, and after a moment Tristan leaned back against the cranked-up bed and closed his eyes. "To tell you the truth, we hardly talk at all. Truth is, I don't know how to talk to her anymore.'' He opened his eyes and glared at the reporter, using anger to cover more humiliating emotions. ''She's a stranger to me, Pearson. She's made a life here without me.''

Cory shrugged. ''Did you expect her not to?''

''No.'' He shifted uneasily. ''No, of course not. I just don't know where I fit into it. It's like, the place where I used be isn't there anymore.''

Both men were silent, listening to the beeps and bells and voices and footsteps all around them. Then Cory drew a long breath and said, ''Well, I don't think there's any doubt she loves you.''

Tristan's laugh was low and painful. ''I'm not sure I'd agree with you, but even if it's true…you think that makes it easier? Because it doesn't. It only makes it worse.''

There was another silence, both companionable and difficult. Again it was Cory who broke it, leaning forward, hands clasped loosely between his knees. He began carefully, like someone entering a private space, not certain of his welcome. ''What I said a minute ago—about looking to the future rather than the past? That goes for relationships, too, you know. Maybe…it's not so much that there's no place for you in *her* life, as you're trying to make her fit into the place she used to have in yours. And that's not going to work, because she's not the same person she used to be.''

Tristan tried to smile. ''That she's not.''

''Then maybe what you need to do is work on getting to know the person she is now. I'm betting she's one helluva lady.''

Tristan's smile collapsed sideways. ''Easier said than done.''

''Well, I'm no psychologist,'' Cory said, with a touch of exasperation, ''but I'm always told talking's good. You said you two hardly talk at all.'' He paused, and getting no denial, added, "I'm betting you haven't told her anything, have you? About...what happened to you over there?"

Tristan shook his head. He could feel his jaw tightening. "And I'm not going to, either. I'm not gonna lay that on her."

"Well, you should." He held up a hand to shut off any arguments Tristan might have in mind, and to Tristan's own surprise, it worked. "And I'll tell you why. Best two reasons in the world—it's what you want, and it's what she wants."

"Oh, for—"

"Okay, forget you for a minute. Take Jessie. She's a nurse, right? By nature she's a mother, a nurturer, a healer. And here you are, one of the people she loves most in this world, wounded, hurt, in need of nurturing, and you—naturally, you're determined to be a hero—you won't let her. Look, she doesn't need you to be a hero. What she needs is for you to be honest with her. You think you have to protect her from the bad stuff? Forget that, man. She's tougher than you think she is. She's a woman, isn't she? Listen to me—you need to let her in. You need to tell her how bad it was. You need to cry, then let her comfort you. If you do that, maybe both of you'll be able to move on."

He paused, and Tristan, thinking he was finished, growled, "I hope you get paid by the word."

Cory laughed. "I wish. Look, sorry for butting in. I don't usually—unless it's family. Don't know why, but I...guess I, uh...I mean, you and I have a..." He stood up in a fidgety sort of way, clearly no more comfortable with expressing his emotions than Tristan would have been. And Tristan, who normally would have enjoyed seeing the reporter at an unprecedented loss for words, instead felt a wave of purely masculine sympathy.

Cory started to turn away, then swiveled back, fingers to his forehead. "Look," he said, frowning, "this isn't from me—something the shrinks said. About grief? What happened to us—to you—it's like a death in the family. We've lost something precious to us—time, months, years…a piece out of our lives. We need to grieve for that…bury it, then move on.''

"Yeah,'' said Tristan, with an impatient wave of his hand, ''they told me that, too.''

"But you haven't, have you?'' Cory said softly. "You've never allowed yourself to grieve. Or Jessie, either.''

Sammi June had been to the hospital any number of times. Normally she went in the front entrance, straight to the elevators and on up to the NICU. She'd never been in the E.R. before. She didn't even know where the bike rack was. Finally she chained hers to a handicapped parking post, and her hands shook so badly she almost couldn't get the lock snapped together.

She was out of breath, hot and sweaty, and as she approached the E.R.'s sliding door she could see from her reflection that her face was beet red, and her hair every which way. Not that she cared. She combed her hair roughly with her fingers and gave it a shake to settle it, then strode quickly to the E.R. reception desk and gasped out, ''Hi—I'm looking for my dad—Tristan Bauer?''

The receptionist, a heavy-set young black man, consulted a chart, then pointed. ''Third door.''

"Thanks.'' And she was already making for it, heart pounding as though she'd run all the way from her dorm instead of coasting downhill on her bicycle.

Her thoughts weren't anything she could have related or explained, just a jumble of guilt, fear, panic and remorse, centered on one identifiable concern: *Daddy!* The word screamed inside her head as she stormed through the E.R., becoming more terrified with every step, dreading what she might see beyond that door. The message her mom had left for her had said only that her dad had had an accident with his motorcycle and was in the E.R. *A motorcycle accident! Oh God.*

She burst into the cubicle expecting…God knows what, something like what she'd seen on TV—beeping monitors, clanging alarms, frantic doctors…blood. Instead there was her dad, half reclining on a cranked-up gurney, one arm behind his head, relaxed…smiling. And the only blood she could see were some smears and specks on the sheet draped across his waist, and a lot of little cuts and scratches all over his face and arms. Nevertheless, momentum carried her to the bedside with a breathless, "Dad, are you—" Relief came a heartbeat later. And it was then that she noticed there was someone else there, too. Someone she recognized, and maybe the last person she'd expected to see just then. Probably ever.

"Hey, baby girl," her dad said, stretching out his arm to her. Bemused, she let him take her hand. Shock had robbed her of her voice for the moment, and her heart had shifted into a new and unfamiliar rhythm. Thoughts tumbled into her mind like rocks in a landslide: *Dad's okay! Oh God,* he's *here—my hair's a disaster and I'm all sweaty…I look a mess, and why do I care?*

She didn't know where she got it, the composure that allowed her to say lightly, with a cool and unruffled toss of her head, "Hey, Dad."

"You've met Cory…"

Manners drilled into her since birth overcame a bewildering reluctance to look at the man standing relaxed, arms folded, near the foot of the gurney. She threw a brief smile and a breathless, "Oh, sure. How're you, Mr. Pearson?" in his direction and saw his eyebrows shoot up as she turned back to her dad.

"You didn't have to come," he said in a low, growly voice, shifting as if he felt uncomfortable on that gurney— which he probably did.

Sammi June said dryly, "I got a message saying you'd been in a motorcycle accident, Dad."

"Sorry." He made a face, a wry grimace. "That was your mother. As you can see, it's no big deal."

She tilted her head to one side and studied him, and all the time she was intensely aware of the third person in the room. She could feel his eyes touching her. Really *touching* her. "You look like you tried to break up a cat fight," she said. "What'd you do, land in a patch of kudzu?"

He made that face again. "Worse—blackberries."

"Ouch. You must not've been wearing a helmet. Shame on you." She touched a cut on his forehead, and at the same time had a self-conscious sense that she was playing a part—concerned daughter, poised and completely adult—for an audience of one.

She was mildly surprised when her dad seemed to accept her in the role. He made that wry face yet again and said, "Yeah…that was stupid." Then, with a softening smile, he was back in the daddy mode. "Honey, as you can see, I'm gonna live. You might as well go on back to school. Hey—you didn't skip any classes, I hope."

"Just finished my last final," she said, with a little toss of her head—and again, intensely aware of the second listener just outside the range of her peripheral vision. "I'm all packed, actually. I was getting ready to load up my stuff when I got Mom's message. So…guess I'll be home in a little while."

"Great," her dad said, and added, as if it had just occurred to him, "Hey, do you have any plans for this weekend? It's Memorial Day weekend, right? I've got the use of a lake house, ski boat included, over on Lake Russell. I was thinking we could all go. In fact—Cory, why don't you stay on, join us?"

It seemed to Sammi June that there was a long, shimmering silence between the question and its answer. *I won't look at him. I don't want him to think I care. And…why do I? He's Dad's friend, not mine.*

"Let's see…what's today, Thursday? I still have some loose ends to tie up in Atlanta, but I guess I can do that tomorrow morning, be back by early tomorrow evening. Will that be okay?"

"Sounds good," said her dad. "Then we can all head over to the lake together Saturday morning. How 'bout you, Sammi June?"

She shrugged and said, "Sure. I guess. Why not?"

Cory Pearson looked at his watch. "Well—I'd better be heading on back to Atlanta." He stepped forward and took her dad's hand in a two-handed, buddy-type handshake. "Take care of yourself, Lieutenant." From behind the lenses of his glasses, blue eyes touched hers briefly, and Sammi June felt a sensation something like a shiver. "So— I guess I'll be seeing both of you tomorrow." And then he was gone.

And now, alone with her dad and without the audience she'd been playing to, Sammi June found that she didn't know what to say. Her audience had left, but so had the distraction he'd provided, and without it she was once more forced to cope with the feelings she'd brought into the room with her. Feelings she didn't want to express because they made her feel much too vulnerable, too much like the child she was trying so hard not to be: *Daddy, don't you dare leave me again! Please…I don't know what to do with you in my life, but I don't know what I'd do without you, either.*

"Okay," she said, all brisk and light and perky, leaning to kiss his cheek, "if you're sure you're all right, I'm gonna be going, too. Gotta get packed. See you at home—later, okay?"

It was only when she got outside of the cubicle that she realized her heart was racing. As she strode through the E.R., she fluffed her hair with her fingers and gave herself little settling-down shakes, the way she did when she was taking her position on the soccer field, just before play began, to rid herself of nervous jitters and butterflies, and by the time she burst through the automatic sliding door and into the warm, muggy afternoon, she was feeling calmer. Until she saw that Cory Pearson was standing beside her bike, obviously waiting for her.

"Hey," she said, by way of a greeting, giving no sign of the sudden jolt she'd just felt under her ribs.

He smiled, squinting a little in the bright sunshine. "Thought this might be yours." He tilted his head toward the bike leaning drunkenly against the handicapped signpost. "Figured I'd better get directions to your place, if I'm going to be going there tomorrow."

"Sure," said Sammi June. "No problem." She bent over to unlock her bike, and was *way* too aware of the way her top separated from her jeans when she did that—only a couple inches of skin, probably, but she felt almost naked. She straightened, glad to have an excuse for her red face. "Got a piece of paper? You're gonna probably want to write this down—it's kind of in the middle of nowhere."

"In the car." She started walking, and he walked along beside her, the bicycle between them. He glanced at it, then at her and said, "Can I give you a lift back to your dorm?"

She gave a little snort of laughter. "That'd be great, actually. It's all uphill going back—and I mean a *long* way uphill." She paused, then said ruefully, "I didn't exactly stop to think things through when I left. I just sort of…jumped on my bike and took off."

"You were worried about your dad," Cory said with a shrug. "That's understandable."

"Yeah," said Sammi June, "I was." There was a quivery mass of emotion in her chest all of a sudden—the same one that had been there a moment ago when she'd faced her dad alone in the E.R., and that she hadn't wanted him to know about. Now, to her very great surprise, she heard herself saying to Cory, "It's really weird, you know? I mean, it's so strange and awkward, having him suddenly back in my life. I don't really know how to talk to him...how to act with him. And then, when I think about losing him all over again, I just about...I can't even..." She swallowed and jerked her face away from the eyes she could feel watching her, studying her—keen, blue eyes, and much too intent.

"Not strange at all," the owner of the eyes said gently, and she let go of an odd little gust of relieved laughter.

Chapter 15

They had stopped beside a nondescript tan-colored car. Cory took keys from his pocket and unlocked the trunk, then took hold of the bike by its handlebars. Sammi June took hold of the back wheel. They both lifted, then looked at each other.

"Think…mine's gonna have to go in first," Sammi June said.

"Okay," said Cory, "here we go. No, *here*…okay, this way—"

After a couple of false starts they managed to get most of the bike wedged into the trunk. They ended up standing side by side, so close to each other that Cory's shirtsleeve was brushing Sammi June's bare arm. Then, instead of moving apart and going their separate ways, they both went on standing there, not moving…neither of them saying anything. And somehow, although neither of them appeared to move a muscle, she could feel the space between them growing smaller, until it wasn't just his sleeve that was touching her arm, but the warm, firm muscle under it, as well. She felt her heart stumble, and heat envelope her. Her breath seemed to catch on something sharp inside her chest.

"I think that's got it," Cory finally said in an odd, strangled-sounding voice, and suddenly the warm place along the side of Sammi June's arm felt abandoned and cold.

"It's not very far—just up at the top of the hill." She went around to the passenger side of the car and got in, while he did the same on the driver's side. Their doors made twin slams, and then they were both busy settling in, buckling up.

Cory started the car and drove out of the hospital parking lot. He made a careful left and they headed up the long hill. Sammi June, her heart still thumping crazily, tried to think of something to say.

"So," Cory said after they'd gone a few blocks, looking over at her while they waited at a traffic light, "your dad calls you Sammi June?"

She made a disparaging sound. "Most people do."

He nodded thoughtfully. "I like it. It's cute."

She threw him a look. "Yeah, but I'm eighteen years old. 'Cute' isn't exactly the image I'm going for right now, okay?"

He laughed. The light changed, and he drove on. They covered a few more blocks. At the next stoplight he turned to her and said, "How do you feel about Sam?"

Behind the glasses, his eyes were that incredible, intense blue. As she gazed into them, Sammi June realized that what she felt was *afraid*. It reminded her of when she was a little girl and her parents had moved around so much. This was the way she'd felt standing in the doorway, about to go into a new classroom, a new school. On the brink of something scary and unknown. "I assume you mean, as a nickname?" she said, and then shrugged. "It's okay." A smile hovered. "I kind of like it, actually."

"Okay, then. I'll call you Sam." The light changed. The

eyes shifted away from her, and she could breathe again, but only in quivery, shallow breaths.

After that, neither of them spoke again until they reached the dorms. Then Sammi June told Cory where to turn and where to park in the visitors' section of the parking lot. Since it was moving day, they were lucky to find one, happening along just as someone else was pulling out.

Although she didn't really need him to, and certainly didn't expect him to, Cory turned off the motor and got out to help her wrestle her bike out of the trunk. When the bike was once more upright with both wheels on the ground, Sammi June flexed her fingers on the handlebars in a fidgety sort of way and thought about saying goodbye. The thought made her heart stumble and her breath grow shallow.

Before she could make the words come out of her mouth, Cory smiled at her and said, "How 'bout those directions, now?"

She flipped back her hair—casual, composed—and said, "Oh, sure. Got a pencil?"

He opened the back driver's side door, took out a laptop computer and set it on the hood of the car. "Oh, cool," said Sammi June, as he opened it and booted it up. She told him her parents' address, phone number and directions to their house, and watched over his shoulder while he entered the information into the laptop. She was thinking that she really liked the way he smelled, and was trying hard not to sniff audibly.

When he finished he closed the laptop and put it back in the car, then turned to her, smiling in an odd sort of way. Reluctantly, she wondered *Could it be…?* And her heart gave a sickening lurch, because she knew that now he was going to have to say goodbye, and probably tell her something like…he guessed he'd see her tomorrow. But all at once, tomorrow seemed an eternity away.

"I don't suppose," she heard herself say, in a disgustingly breathless, eager voice, "you'd like to help me load my stuff in my truck?"

His eyebrows went up and he said warily, "I don't know, how much stuff are we talking about?" But she could see that his eyes were laughing.

She gave him a sly, sideways look. "Oh...you know, the usual—clothes, books...computer."

"Uh-huh." He was gazing up at the dorm. "Which floor?"

"Fifth—but there's an elevator."

Muttering, "Why do I get the feeling I've been had?" he locked up the car and pocketed the keys while Sammi June stood by, holding her bike and grinning with an irrational joy.

They walked toward the dorm, one on either side of the bicycle, neither of them in any hurry. Halfway there, Cory looked over at her and asked somberly, "Is this a test?"

She repeated it, not understanding, and as she did, she felt her gaze collide with his and stick like glue. It seemed impossible to pull away from those terribly intent, all-too-perceptive eyes.

"To see if I'm young enough to keep up with you?" he said, and smiled.

Sammi June laughed, and in the warmth of that smile, felt all her fears of a short while ago fade away, like fog in the sunshine.

Jessie closed the lid of the old-fashioned hard-type suitcase, snapped the latches shut and straightened. What else? Had she forgotten anything? Tristan had assured her the lake house was completely furnished and fully equipped, but Jessie was taking no chances. She'd filled Momma's old suitcase with sheets, towels and cleaning supplies, just in case. Food, though, was another matter. She had no idea what to take, or how far from grocery stores and restaurants this lake house was. She was going to have to ask Tris, she realized with a sigh.

She stood gnawing on her lip and thinking dejectedly about that, and how awkward and uncomfortable things still were between them—Jessie tiptoeing around like a hunter trying not to wake up a sleeping rhinoceros, and Tristan being determinedly upbeat in an effort to convince her she had no cause to worry about him. Would things ever be right and easy for them again? There were barriers between them—huge barriers, impenetrable as the prison walls he'd supposedly left behind.

A tiny movement drew her eyes to the window, where two people were coming along the lane from the direction of the woods. Sammi June and Cory, back from an introductory tour of the place. As Jessie watched the two of them walking together, side by side, not touching, she felt an odd little ripple in her belly. Emotions stirred through her—not alarm or dread or dismay, exactly…and maybe there was even some happiness in the mix, and excitement, too—the kind of emotions that make a mother smile misty-eyed and at the same time tremble in fear. *My daughter's in love.* The body language was unmistakable. And unless she was very much mistaken, the feeling was mutual. *Like mother, like daughter,* she thought.

Tristan was on the front porch, enjoying the soft feel of humidity on his skin, thinking how much he'd missed this, the gentle easing of Southern springs into muggy summers…distant rumblings that weren't bombs or tanks but only friendly afternoon thundershowers…whippoorwills calling and bats swooping in the dusk. I'm a lucky man, he thought as he watched his daughter and the man responsible for his resurrection come toward him across the just-mowed lawn. *A lucky, lucky man. And Cory's right— I need to stop dwelling on the past and start thinking about the future. Particularly on how I'm gonna make a future with my wife and child.*

As always, when he thought about that, he felt doubts come to cloud his vision and darken his soul. *The future? But I can't even figure out where I fit into their lives here and now.*

But now he shook them off and called out, "Hey, 'bout time you guys decided to come home. Sammi June, I was just about to talk to your mother about food."

Behind him, the screen door banged, and Jessie said, "That's good, because I was about to ask you the same thing. What are we gonna take with us tomorrow?"

Tristan smiled at her and shrugged. "I don't know—the usual stuff, I guess. Hamburgers, hotdogs…chicken. We can stop at a grocery store on the way…pick up whatever we need. No, I was thinking more in terms of now. Tonight. What're we doing for dinner? Barbecuing? Sandwiches? Or—does your mother have something exotic planned?"

"Momma's got a church thing," Jessie said. "They're fixin' to spend tomorrow sprucing up the cemetery, like they do every Memorial Day weekend, so I guess this evening's the planning session. Anyway, they're havin' a potluck supper at the church, so we're on our own."

"Well," said Sammi June, "don't worry about us." Tristan turned his head to look at her. She and Cory were standing at the bottom of the steps, side by side, not looking at each other. And it occurred to Tristan all at once that, even in the dwindling light, her eyes seemed to be glowing. He felt an odd little vibration begin, just behind his breastbone.

"Cory and I are going out," Sammi June announced.

Tristan frowned. Behind him he heard Jess make a soft, wordless sound, like a cough. "What do you mean 'out'?"

"I mean, *out*—out." Now she did look at Pearson, and not only were her eyes glowing, so were her cheeks.

Tristan's heart gave a sickening lurch. In that moment

she reminded him so much of someone…someone he'd known a long time ago…. "Wait just a minute," he began.

"We're gonna go into town, have dinner…maybe see a movie. Come on, Dad, it's my first day of vacation—I'm not gonna spend it sitting at home. Anyway—" she grinned wickedly and gave a kind of wiggle that made Tristan's hair stand on end "—I want to show Cory the local night-life. If he thinks he can handle it."

Jess made a strangled sound that could have been laughter or dismay. Tristan opened his mouth, but couldn't think of a response, because in his mind he was trumpeting all sorts of dire paternal threats and proclamations, the kinds of things fathers of daughters have always thought, but these days, at least, are seldom foolish enough to say out loud: *Over my dead body! I'm gonna lock you in your room until you're forty and strangle with my bare hands any man who dares to touch you!*

"I don't think that's such a good idea," he mumbled at last, scowling, realizing he sounded more pouty than paternal. "You're gonna need to get up early tomorrow morning."

Sammi June's laugh was incredulous. "Dad, *hello.* I'm used to studying until four in the morning, then getting up three hours later to take a *test.* It's not like I'm a child, can't be up past my bedtime."

"That's not the point—"

Cory leaned his head close to Sammi June's and murmured something to her under his breath. In response to which her chin jutted out and tilted upward, and her mouth took on a stubborn look her father well remembered. "The point is, Dad, I'm eighteen years old. You don't get to tell me what to do, okay?" With that, she stomped up the steps, past him and into the house.

After a moment's hesitation Cory followed her, looking unhappy and apologetic. When he got to the top of the steps where Tristan was, he paused and said, "Look, man, I—"

Jess touched his arm and shook her head, and he bit back whatever it was he'd started to say and went into the house.

When the door had closed behind them both, Tristan rounded on his wife and growled, "What the hell'd you do that for? Maybe I could've talked some sense into *him*, at least."

"And then what? Make an enemy of your daughter?" Her tone was mild, but her voice sounded shaky, which set Tristan back momentarily.

He scowled at her for a moment, then huffed in a disbelieving tone, "What, over a damn *date?*"

She made an exasperated sound. "A date? For heaven's sake, Tris, that's not what this is about. Can't you see she's in *love* with him?"

"In—" He gulped the word as if he'd been punched in the stomach with it. "What are you talking about? That's just…ridiculous. She's…hell, she's not old enough to be in love."

"Now that," said Jessie, "is ridiculous. She's the same age I was when I fell for you."

"And," Tristan blustered on, not hearing her, "he's sure as hell too old for her!" He paced a few steps one way, then the other. Rubbed his forehead, ran into a blackberry scratch and winced. "Should be ashamed of himself," he muttered. "Damn well ought to know better."

"It's not Cory's fault." She was trying to keep her voice down so as not to be overheard, but even so he could tell it was shaking again. "And by the way, he's the same age you were when I met you."

"Yeah," he growled heedlessly, "and we both know how *that* ended up, don't we?"

She was silent for a moment, just looking at him. Her eyes, in the deepening dusk, nevertheless seemed to shimmer. Then, very quietly, she said, "Yes. And if I remember correctly, that was my doing, not yours. *You* were all set to walk away."

He opened his mouth to say something, but closed it again when he realized the shimmer in her eyes was tears. He looked back at her, and felt an ache in his heart that was part regret for her tears, part longing for that time of sunshine and happiness that was forever lost to him. "Why'd you do that?" he asked in a voice that felt as if it had rusted. "Call me back?"

"I knew what I wanted," she said softly. A tear spilled over and she brushed it away with a quick, angry motion. "And so does she."

His heart wasn't made of steel, and he'd never liked fighting with her. He would have gone to her then; he wanted to. He wanted to take her in his arms and hold her close to the aching places inside him and forget everything about the past except the fact that he loved her. But when he made a jerky move toward her, she held up a hand to stop him, like a traffic cop, and turned away, shoulders hunched and back stiffened against him. Pain stabbed through him, pain as bad as anything he'd endured at the hands of his Iraqi jailers. He'd learned ways to endure that kind of pain, but this was something beyond his experience. She'd never done such a thing to him before.

He turned blindly and went into the house. Farther down the hall, in the alcove behind the stairs where the telephone was, he could hear Sammi June and Cory talking, evidently checking on movie schedules. He tightened his jaw and went up the stairs, wondering why his knee was bothering him again all of a sudden, when it hadn't for days. The motorcycle accident, he wondered, or self-pity?

In the bathroom he washed his face, then stood for a few minutes studying his reflection in the mirror. He'd avoided looking too long and hard at himself since he'd been back. He didn't like to think he'd ever been a vain man, but it had still been a shock, seeing himself for the first time after so many years. He'd barely recognized himself. He'd grown old. His hair had gray in it now, and his face had lines and hollows—not to mention scars—that hadn't been there before. He could hardly blame Jess for looking at him as if he was a stranger, when he was a stranger to himself.

It hit him then, like a cold blast of wind. *Fear.* Fear that the dream he'd carried in his heart for so long, the dream that had kept him alive, kept him *sane,* might never come to be. All he'd thought about, all those years, was getting back home, home to his wife, his daughter, his *family.* And now—well, he was back, but he sure as hell wasn't home, and his wife and daughter didn't seem to have places for him in their lives anymore.

He'd known there was a possibility Jessie might have married somebody else, of course, but he hadn't believed it, not really. And when he'd found out she hadn't and in fact was still his wife, well…he'd taken it for granted things would eventually take up pretty much where they'd left off, after a reasonable adjustment period. It hadn't ever occurred to him he and Jess might not be able to make it work again…ever.

Look to the future, Cory had told him. But he had to face up to the fact that he and Jessie might not have a future—not together. *Face it.* Staring into his own bleak and shadowed eyes, Tristan felt cold to the very depths of his soul.

So far, the weekend was turning out better than Jessie had expected. Tristan's friend Tom Satterfield's lake house wasn't on one of the big Savannah River Corps of Engineers' lakes, but on a small tributary lake on the South Carolina side. The house, set on a wooded knoll, was small but comfortable, a mobile home that had been improved and added onto and now had a huge covered and partly enclosed deck that overlooked the water and zig-zagging wooden stairs running down to the boat dock.

A set of house keys had been left with the Satterfields' next-door neighbor, who had been instructed to turn them over to Tristan along with the keys to the ski boat parked in the carport. The neighbor even helped Tris and Cory launch the boat, explaining as he did so that the tank had been filled up with gas not long before Tom—the lieutenant commander—had shipped out. The neighbor knew all about Tris and shook his hand warmly and wished him welcome home with a catch in his voice.

As Tris had promised, the house was clean and equipped with everything they needed, but Jessie had made up the beds with the sheets she'd brought with her, anyway, to save having to launder the Satterfields' linens before they left. The house was only a little stuffy and muggy from being closed up for several months, but the air conditioner soon took care of that, and by the time Jessie had made the beds and stashed away the groceries, the men and Sammi June had the boat launched and were tooting and waving at her from the dock.

There'd been thunderstorms in the night. Now it was midafternoon of a clear, hot and hazy day. Sunlight sparkled on brownish-blue water, and the air was busy with the sounds of boat engines of every description. Pontoons churned sedately up and down, passengers waving at one another or at friends on the docks they passed; bass fishermen patiently rode the wake-choppy waters in coves and inlets; water-skiers swooped and soared, sending up joyful roostertails of spray. And darting in and out amongst them all, the inevitable wave-runners and jet skis sounded—and annoyed—like angry hornets.

Jessie, slathered with sunscreen and wearing shorts, her bathing suit top, a hot pink sun visor and dark glasses, was occupying one of the ski boat's rear-facing seats. Sammi June and Cory were in the water—she was teaching him to water-ski—and it was Jessie's job as observer to tell the driver, Tristan, when he no longer had a skier attached to the other end of the nylon rope. Understandably, this had happened with great frequency at first, although Cory remained game and was staying up for longer and longer periods while Sammi June rode shotgun on a knee board, like a proud parent running alongside her child's first two-wheeler.

The latest run, in fact, was going amazingly well. Cory looked relaxed; he even seemed to be smiling as, following Sammi June's lead, he successfully navigated the wake. With the skiers riding on smooth water outside the wake, Jessie took her eyes away from them for a moment to glance back at Tris. Her heart seemed to swell and tremble inside her chest as she watched him guide the boat with effortless, well-remembered skill...big, raw-boned hands steady on the wheel, the wind riffling through his hair.

How incredible this must be for him, she thought. And how hard. Incredible because it had been so long since he'd known such freedom...such joy. Hard because she knew he'd have much preferred to be out there in the water himself; on a single ski, Tris had been poetry in motion. But, while he'd come a long way in the past weeks and in spite of his determination to build back his strength to what it had been before his capture, he was still a long way from being ready for the rigors of the sport of waterskiing. And thank God, Jessie thought, he was smart enough to know that. Still...it must be hard for him, and she wondered if that was why he'd chosen to wear knee-length shorts, sandals and a print shirt borrowed from C.J. instead of bathing trunks.

Or maybe, she thought as she turned back to the skiers, it was that he felt uncomfortable about showing his scars....

A moment later the run was brought to a halt when a jet ski, manned by two young teenagers, cut too close to the skiers. Jessie sent up a yelp as first Cory, then Sammi June hit the water, but Tris had seen trouble coming and already had the boat throttled down. He was swearing under his breath as he brought the boat around in a wide circle, trailing the tow grips.

"Those kids don't have good sense," Jessie said.

"They're gonna kill somebody," Tris growled, skillfully maneuvering the towlines so the skiers could grab them easily.

"That was a great run," Jessie called, as Cory, grinning and exuberant, paddled his ski toward the tow rope. "Hey—you guys 'bout ready to take a break yet?"

Cory's mouth opened, and so did Sammi June's. But instead of words Jessie heard a shout and, a split second later, a terrible, grinding crunch. For a moment she stared at the skiers, unable to process what could have happened to her hearing. Then behind her she heard Tris swearing loudly, angrily, as he put the boat in gear and headed it out across the water.

"Take the wheel," he shouted at her, already half out of his seat. And she saw what he had seen.

At the mouth of a small cove inlet maybe fifty yards away, the jet ski that had brushed past them minutes before lay in the water at a crazy angle. Next to it, a bass boat was slowly sinking. One of the teenagers, a girl with long blond hair, was clinging to the jet ski, dazed and disoriented. Her friend, buoyed by his life vest, was floating nearby, facedown in the water. Of the occupants of the bass boat there was no sign.

All this Jessie absorbed in the space of a few seconds— or split seconds—how could she know, when time moved in stops and jerks? And even as she was moving to take over the boat's controls, knowing she had no choice but to do so, she was screaming, "Tris—no! Don't you dare— *Tris!*"

But he was taking off his sandals...and his shirt, and then he was perched on the side of the boat, like a runner in starting blocks. He wasn't wearing a life vest, and neither was Jessie. As she brought the boat as close to the wreck as she dared, he straightened up, measured the distance, then cut the water in a clean, shallow dive, leaving her anguished shout shivering in the air like the aftermath of a cymbal's crash.

"Tristan!" Frozen in terror and making furious, whimpering sounds, she railed at him. "Tristan, what are you *doing?* Damn you…oh, damn you—" Then, turning frantically, she began to scream for help, and she could see Cory churning toward them, swimming as if a whole school of sharks was in pursuit. Right behind him was Sammi June on the knee board, dipping both arms into the water in powerful strokes.

Still struggling to control her own panic, with help on the way Jessie turned back to the disaster in front of her. Relief burst from her in a gasp when she saw Tristan's head break the water, but that relief was short-lived. After looking around wildly for an instant, he gave a leap and back down he went.

Meanwhile, the teenage girl had recovered her wits enough to realize where she was and what had happened to her. Seeing her friend lying facedown in the water, she began screaming her head off. Jessie put the boat's engine in neutral, then gathered up the life preservers and threw them, one by one, toward the hysterical girl, at the same time yelling at her to grab hold of one and for God's sake, turn the boy over!

It was horrible—one of the worst things she'd ever experienced—watching that boy floating with his face in the water, and not being able to do anything about it. Every instinct she had told her to jump in the water and go to him. But she couldn't leave the boat—she *couldn't*. If she left the boat unattended and it drifted away, they could *all* drown.

Then, miracle of miracles, just when Jessie thought she wouldn't be able to stand by and do nothing one more second, the girl in the water stopped screaming. Face set in a mask of determined terror, she lunged for a floating life preserver…caught it and hung on. Paddling clumsily, sobbing, she made her way to her friend—brother?—and somehow, *somehow,* managed to get him turned over.

"Good girl! Now, hold on to him!" Jessie yelled, and slowly began to tow the life preserver back to the boat.

And all the while she was screaming inside her head, *Oh God, Tristan—where are you?*

Chapter 16

He'd been down a long time—*too long!* Or did it only seem so? Her heart was tearing in two. *Tristan, if you die I will never forgive you! How could you do this to us? How could you?*

Then...she saw him. His head had erupted from the murky water, his mouth open...gasping. His eyes found hers, wild and dark in his pale, gaunt face. She saw that he was struggling with a large object—the bass fisherman! Tristan had a grip on his collar and was trying to bring him to the surface, at the same time straining toward a life preserver that was just out of his reach. He reached again, struggling to keep the fisherman's head above the water. And then...he went down again. Not purposefully, this time, not diving, but sinking slowly, clinging to Jessie's eyes with that fierce black gaze, full of apology and regret.

Jessie sank to her knees, sobbing. The life preserver, with two teenagers in tow, one barely alive, had reached the boat. Leaning over as far as she could, she managed to get her arms under the unconscious boy's and, with a heave that left her gasping, hauled his limp weight over the side. At the same time, she heard a shout and glancing up, saw Cory with his arms around Tris. He was holding him above the water!

But before she even had time to register relief and joy because of that, horrifyingly, all three men disappeared beneath the roiling surface. And Jessie's mind filled with thoughts of terrible domino drownings, of tragedies beyond comprehension...

Then Sammi June was there with her knee board, and she was snagging life preservers right and left and yelling and pulling and pushing and dragging people toward the boat. By that time Jessie was on her knees on the floor of the boat, giving CPR to the teenage boy while tears streamed unheeded down her face.

It was evening of that beautiful, terrible day. The sheriff's deputies and fire trucks, the ambulances and paramedics with their lifesaving ventilators and defibrillators had long since gone back to their bases. The fisherman and the teenager had been air-lifted to the nearest hospital; according to the most recent phone call, it appeared both were going to make it.

Tristan had refused to go to the hospital in spite of Jessie's urgings. Instead he'd taken a hot shower and put on clean clothes, eaten a bacon and tomato sandwich and fallen asleep on the couch. Sammi June and Cory, after showering and changing, and tomato sandwiches, had taken the boat out to watch the sunset on the lake. It had been a beautiful, radiant sunset.

Jessie, after feeding everyone and cleaning up the mess and phoning the hospital one more time, was the last one into the shower. When she emerged, she put on sweet-smelling lotion and a flowered sundress with a softly flared skirt and went to see if Tristan was awake.

He wasn't on the couch. She went out to the deck, and

then she could see him, standing on the dock in the sunset's afterglow, looking out across the lake. She ran down the stairs, barefoot, and her heart was already racing faster than her footsteps.

"Hi," she said as she approached him, breathless as a girl. "What are you doing down here all by yourself?"

He turned slowly toward her but didn't answer the question. She wondered if he'd heard it. He seemed so distant. "Kids take the boat out?" he asked, and even his voice sounded faraway.

"Yeah." She tilted her head, smiling just a little, hoping he'd smile with her. "Have you forgiven him yet?"

"Forgiven?" He looked bewildered for a moment. Then suddenly the lost look on his face vanished, and he gave a rueful snort and rubbed the back of his neck. "Guess I'm gonna have to, aren't I? He saved my life. More than once."

"He's a good person," Jessie said, moving closer.

Tristan watched her warily, like a nervous animal eyeing an extended hand. "Yeah, he is. Sammi June could do a whole lot worse." His laugh was another soft snort. "Took me by surprise, is all."

"Me, too," said Jessie.

He inhaled cautiously, as if testing his ability to breathe. "I'm gonna have to figure out a new way to be with her. I know that... With you, too," he added after a moment, and looked away. When his eyes came back to her, they had that lost look again, but not the distance. This time the loneliness was right *there,* so close to her she felt the ache of it in her own heart. "I guess I always thought of you as somebody I needed to take care of, you know? Lead... teach...protect. I never knew how strong you are." He drew a quick, hurting breath and looked away once more. "The truth is, Jess, you don't really need me at all."

She wanted to cry out a denial. Instead she reached a hand toward him and said in a voice soft with anguish,

"Oh, Tris. I don't need you to take care of me...I just need you to *be*." His eyes jerked back to her, dark shadows in the dusk, and she cried out in a shaking voice, "Is that too much to ask?"

"Sometimes...lately...yeah." He looked at her, and the fear in her heart was like a vise, squeezing...squeezing. Then, so quietly she barely heard it, he said, "I almost died today, Jess."

"I know." The pain, the tension in her chest had become unbearable. She tried to lighten it. "And I'm not sure if I've forgiven you for that yet. If you'd died, I swear, I would've killed you."

Tristan's lips twitched, but the smile died before it reached his eyes. "I've been thinking...about what you said to me way back, before I left for the Gulf." Jessie caught her breath in a guilty little gulp. She'd been thinking about that, too. "You told me I was selfish," he went on, "to go off and leave you and Sammi June like that. At the time I didn't...but now I think you were right."

Jessie was shaking her head. "Uh-uh...no, I wasn't. Not unless being true to who you are is selfish." He gave his head a shake, not understanding. She reached out to him once more, touching his arm this time, and the tension in him made it feel more like steel than human flesh. The tension reached into her, and her voice quavered with it. "You told me then, it was something you had to do. I don't think I understood that then, but I do now. It *was* what you had to do, because that's just who you are. Like today. You *had* to jump into the water to try and rescue those people. I wanted to kill you for doin' it, but you couldn't *not* do it."

Tristan shook his head, and there was a stubbornness in his jaw she knew very well. "No. What I did—it was unfair to you and Sammi June. Look what—"

"It *was* unfair," Jessie interrupted, shaking in earnest now. "And, dammit, I'm not gonna let you take the blame for that. You know what? Life is unfair. Sometimes it just plain *sucks*. You went to the Gulf because you had to, and you jumped into that lake today because you had to, and both times I wanted to kill you because of it. But at the same time, I know it's just part of you. Part of what makes me love you.'' And she was crying now.

''Do you?'' he whispered, and finally asked it. ''Do you love me?'' The vulnerability in his eyes broke her heart.

She could barely get the words out. ''Yes, I do. I always have. And I always will.''

Tristan was gazing across the lake. And even through the haze in her own eyes she could see that there were tears on his cheeks. She caught her breath, bit back a cry, and he whispered, ''Jess—I don't think I'm going to be able to do this by myself.''

She brushed at her eyes, fierce and protective. ''Do what? You don't have to—''

''I can't...find my way home. I've tried, I thought I could, but...'' He shook his head and drew a breath, sounding overwhelmed by weariness. ''I'm sorry. I didn't want to burden you. But I can't do it alone. And I want to...so bad.'' His voice broke at last. ''I *need* you, Jess.''

Strength and courage surged up in her like a well of healing waters. Stepping close to him, she put her hands on his waist, looked up at him and said calmly, ''I was wondering when you were going to figure that out.''

He seemed dazed as he lifted his hands to her shoulders. The look on his face...the way his fingers walked across her shoulders, as if she were a miracle he expected to vanish in a puff of smoke...reminded her of the very first moments of his reunion with her, in the guest house in Landstuhl. But this time when he folded her into his arms, she could feel his body quaking, as if a terrible battle were being waged inside him.

And why on earth, she wondered, exasperated, is it so hard for men to cry? His voice, when he spoke, was like something tearing. "Oh God, Jess…they beat me so badly. There were times…I couldn't stop screaming. I tried to stay strong…I tried…"

She stood silent and strong, steady and brave…holding her husband tightly, rubbing his back and absorbing his pain while he talked. Around them the last of the sunset's color faded into darkness and the stars began to appear in the springtime sky.

Epilogue

"Look," said Sammi June, "it's the Wishing Star—see it?" She lifted an arm to point, and Cory gently brought it back into the circle his arms had made around her.

"Hmm," he said, bumping the top of her head with his chin, "that looks like Venus, to me."

She lay her head back against his shoulder, shimmering inside, while the boat drifted on the quiet lake. "I told you...I used to wish on it, when I was little," she murmured, and after a while added hesitantly, testing her new-found happiness, "and...when I wasn't so little. Sometimes I still do."

"Tell me how you do that," he said softly, melting her heart. As if it weren't already totally mush.

"Okay. First, you say the poem, 'Starlight, star bright, first star I've seen tonight, I wish I may, I wish I might, have the wish I wish tonight.' Then you close your eyes, and...you make a wish."

"Okay, let's do it."

She squirmed around to look at him. "Are you serious?"

"Sure, why not?"

She smiled and settled herself once more against his chest. She could feel his heart beating against her back as she drew a careful breath and whispered the poem and heard his deep voice echoing the childish words. She closed her eyes and after a moment felt his warm breath tickle her ear.

"Okay, what'd you wish for?"

"Uh-uh," she whispered, tilting her face to his, "you're not supposed to tell. Otherwise it won't come true." Then he chuckled and touched her smile with his, and she knew it didn't matter because what she'd wished for was already hers.

"What did you wish for when you were a little girl?" Cory asked, sometime later. "Did those wishes come true, too?"

"Oh, I always wished for the same thing." Across the star-spangled waters of the lake, in the last of the twilight, she could see her mom and dad standing together on the dock, the two of them making one silhouette. Her chest quivered, and suddenly she could only whisper. "I guess it's okay to tell you, though. Because I think it's coming true...."

Holding her tightly, maybe because he felt her tremble, he bent his head and murmured gently in her ear, "Tell me."

Sammi June drew a quivering breath, and as tears slipped down her cheeks she smiled. "I wished my dad would come home."

* * * * *

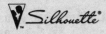

**The Wolfe twins' stories—
together in one fantastic volume!**

USA TODAY bestselling author

JOAN HOHL

Double WOLFE

The emotional story of Matilda Wolfe plus an original short
story about Matilda's twin sister, Lisa. The twins have
followed different paths…but each leads to true love!

Look for DOUBLE WOLFE in January 2004.

"A compelling storyteller who weaves her tales
with verve, passion and style."
—*New York Times* bestselling author Nora Roberts

If you enjoyed what you just read,
then we've got an offer you can't resist!

Take 2 bestselling
love stories FREE!
Plus get a FREE surprise gift!

e♦HARLEQUIN.com

The eHarlequin.com online community is *the* place to share opinions, thoughts and feelings!

- Joining the community is easy, fun and **FREE!**

- Connect with **other romance fans** on our message boards.

- Meet your **favorite authors** without leaving home!

- **Share opinions** on books, movies, celebrities…and *more!*

Here's what our members say:

"I love the friendly and helpful atmosphere filled with support and humor."
—Texanna (eHarlequin.com member)

"Is this the place for me, or what? There is nothing I love more than 'talking' books, especially with fellow readers who are reading the same ones I am."
—Jo Ann (eHarlequin.com member)

Join today by visiting
www.eHarlequin.com!

INTCOMM

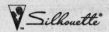
INTIMATE MOMENTS™

is thrilled to bring you the next book
in popular author

CANDACE IRVIN's

exciting new miniseries

Unparalleled courage, unbreakable love...

In January 2004, look for:

Irresistible Forces
(Silhouette Intimate Moments #1270)

It's been eleven years since U.S. Air Force captain
Samantha Hall last saw the man she loved...and lost.
Now, as Major Griff Towers rescues her and her colleagues
after their plane crashes in hostile territory, how can Sam
possibly ignore the feelings she still has for the sexy soldier?

And if you missed the first books in the series look for...

Crossing the Line
(Silhouette Intimate Moments #1179, October 2002)

A Dangerous Engagement
(Silhouette Intimate Moments #1252, October 2003)

Available wherever Silhouette books are sold!

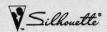

COMING NEXT MONTH

SIMCNM1203